THE TAKEN DUET

A DARK, SORDID MMF ROMANCE

DANI RENÉ

BLURB

Drake, Caia, and River are now bundled into a beautiful collection. The suspense, the dark and twisted storyline, and the super steamy scenes will keep you on the edge of your seat.

Caia

Taken from a life I loved, and thrown into hell.
This is where I found the Devil himself.

Drake

I knew Satan existed.
I was convinced I'd be like him one day.
Until my heart was stolen.

River

He was my only love.
Until she came along,
And then we were three.

NEWSLETTER SIGN UP

Before you dive headfirst into the darkness, sign up for my
newsletter so you don't miss out on sales, new releases,
recommendations, and much more!

FREE NOVEL! Download CRAVE!
https://dl.bookfunnel.com/ccq6xwf70g

*""It was raw, emotional, angsty - and yet- it was sweet and
heartfelt. This was an intoxicating read!"*
- **Jeannine Colette (Author of the Abandon Collection)**

STOLEN

THE TAKEN SERIES - BOOK ONE

PLAYLIST

The Unforgiven - Metallica
Behind Blue Eyes - Limp Bizkit
Nothing Else Matters - Metallica
Death Hymn - Lucas King
Dancing with Your Ghost - No Resolve
Sociopath - Lucas King
Blue Blood - Laurel
Deep End - Ruelle
Don't Let Me Go - Raign
My Eyes Adored You - Denmark + Winter
Do You Really Want To Hurt Me - Denmark + Winter
Angels - Within Temptation
Eyelids - Pvris

Find the full playlist here

DEDICATION

This is for those who like to dive into the darker, twisted worlds, this one is for you.

PROLOGUE
DRAKE

There are only so many dead bodies you have to bury before your life becomes nothing more than a long-winded repeat.

Over and over.

Again and again.

The blood is the same.

The graves are the same.

I smile when I do it now. When I dig a six-foot hole, I revel in the harsh stench of bodies — rotting and vile. It's a reminder I'm a Savage. I was born into this life, and I'll die in it.

The pieces of flesh and bone still chill me to my soul, but there isn't any salvation for me. My life has been tainted by the sins that come with the last name I've been born with.

I bear the sins of my father.

I carry the cross of his actions.

And one day, I'll be forced to run the organization he's built.

With each body I dig a grave for, and with every heart I've seen cease to beat, I know there's no escape. As much as I want to run, there are people here I can't leave.

Two boys.

My brother.

My best friend.

They'll forever have me here, living the life the man who's kept us prisoners for so long has forced us into.

A dark journey.

A sordid road.

And there is no escape.

Unless . . .

We're severed.

DRAKE

C losing my eyes, I breathe in the stench of the dungeon. No matter how many years I've been here, I'm still affected by the smell of the filth my father keeps them in. Each cell — cold and desolate — empty except for a bed and a bucket. When I first came down here, I was shocked, angry, confused, but it's become normal.

We all have our crosses to bear. Mine comes in the form of a family name I'd rather never have been born with. Every day, I wish I'd died with my mother when she birthed my brother and me.

My job is simple though. In this hell, I'm the one who gets them ready for the horror that lies ahead of them. I take those pretty, stolen toys who are thrown into the cells and I make sure they know there aren't any cuddles and sweet words. I'm the asshole parents warn you about.

Pulling on my suit jacket, I take a look in the mirror hanging against the gray wall in the dank office. This room is dimly lit for one reason — it's where the cameras are set up. Where we watch them. My dark hair is disheveled as usual, the blue in my eyes a stark contrast to my tanned skin. Most of my father's female clients want to fuck me. The men want to bend me over and make me grunt their names and beg them to hurt me, but that's never going to happen. I don't do shit with clients.

I do, however, get to touch the pretty toys we get in here. If they're listed as virgins, I don't go near them; but those who aren't, they're fair game. A good, hard fuck eases the tension for a little while.

No love.

No affection.

Just pleasure.

It's who I've become, and I'm proud of it. I've been told before I'm a bastard, and I wear that label with pride. It's easy to turn off the switch. There's nothing left inside me; there is only death in my eyes. I've perfected the icy glare that has every girl cowering when I stalk into her cell.

I'm broken.

I'm off limits.

I'm Drake Savage.

And like the name says, I am a savage. I'll fuck you up so bad nobody will recognize you — physically or emotionally. My favorite though is mentally. Fucking with someone's mind is my forte. It's the one thing I strive to do well. Needling my way in, into the depths where you hide your fears. That's where you'll find me. And that's where I'll lie until the moment you take your last breath.

The only people I allow close are my best friend, River, and my brother, Dante.

All cameras are on when I cast a quick glance at them. In an hour, Frederick will be here to watch them. His thankless job is to make sure the toys don't kill themselves by doing something stupid, like bashing their skulls against the wall or some shit.

I head out to the long hallway leading to the kitchen. It's empty. I know it will be because nobody is up this early. Our home has become a wasteland to love and affection. When I used to walk into the rooms, I'd find traces of our babysitter, but she walked out when we turned twelve. There's nothing even close to warmth in this place. The old woman couldn't deal with my father and ran. She never looked back, and I don't blame her.

Even though she offered some semblance of motherly love, it didn't help. I was still tortured by what I'd witnessed. I broke long before the day she said goodbye to us. My father and his organization have different ideas about what kids are for, and I was shoved into the life long before I even knew what any of it meant.

I always tried to protect my brother from it, but before long, he was taught we can never have a normal life. We'd always be the broken boys. The darkness in our souls will eventually completely take over, and we'd be just like him.

Just like the monster who made us.

Just like Malcolm Savage.

CHAPTER TWO
CAIA

I shift.

I can't move without my muscles protesting.

They're angry and rabid.

There's a burning sensation that seems to be coursing through my veins, in every part of me. I feel as if I'm on fire. But when I'm still, the scorching heat isn't there. So, I lie there, my eyes closed. Heavy from something I'd been given, I can only guess.

I can't recall what happened. My head is filled with a foggy reel of blurry images. I can't pick them apart, and I can't remember where I was or even who was there. I think it was a birthday party. The girls from school, those whom I called my friends, told me to go along for the ride. And I did. For the first time in my life, I broke my father's rules. They weren't really friends, but they were the popular girls, and I wanted to experience what it was like in their world.

Being the daughter of a well-known multi-billionaire, I've always been kept within the confines of my father's rules and regulations. His face is always plastered in the newspapers. His name is mentioned online more times than I can count.

I'm meant to keep myself on the straight and narrow. Nobody would know I've smoked a joint. And I enjoyed it. No one would ever guess I've kissed a boy. And tonight — at least, I think it's tonight — I was meant to have sex.

My first time.

There's an icy ache in my limbs causing tears to sting behind my lids. I don't know where I am, but when I finally crack my eyes open, I can't see anything in front of me, only darkness. There aren't even shadows to promise me a sliver of light in the space I'm in. Perhaps I'm locked in a box.

My fingertips trail along my arm, and I feel blood — at least, what I would guess is blood — dried and cracked on my skin. When I woke up moments ago, the cold was so harsh it caused my teeth to chatter loudly. I try to move again, to roll over, but it's pointless.

My body is rigid, almost paralyzed.

It's cold. Bitterly cold. It's as if I've been left in a freezer without any clothes or blankets to stifle the temperature. My arms prickle, as if a thousand pins are being shot into my flesh at resounding speed. I blink. The tears that burn my eyes dry before they reach my ears. I'm on my back, looking up into blackness so thick it threatens to choke me.

A click echoes in my ears like a foghorn warning a passing ship. A clank. The scrape of steel on the cement floor, or what I'm guessing is concrete.

"There she is." A deep rumble comes from somewhere in the darkness. I expect my visitor to say something more, but he doesn't. Silence falls around me again, enveloping me in its stifling madness. No words, not even a scuff of a shoe. Another switch clicks, and I'm bathed in a faded-yellow, luminescent glow.

"Wh-what am I do-doing here?" I croak, my throat protesting at the measly utterance. Five whole words voiced from my lips, and they sound like sandpaper grating against wood.

Raspy. Harsh.

I blink. Once. Twice. When my vision finally clears, I'm met with the steel-gray glare of a man I've never seen before. He's older, far older than I am at my eighteen years. He may even be as old as my father. His hair is silver, matching his cold eyes. There's a dusting of stubble on his face. It's dark, yet there's gray streaks through it as well, hinting that he must be in his early forties, perhaps even older.

He has a smirk on his face, evil, almost devilish. When he leans in closer, I try to make out who he is, but he's a stranger to me. The corner of his mouth kicks up; a sneer curls his vile mouth. He looks satisfied that he has a girl, a young girl, tied up in a dungeon.

What will he do to me?

I can't think about that right now. The only thing I need to focus on is the asshole before me.

"Your daddy sure does love you, poppet," he whispers across my skin, causing goosebumps to dot my bare flesh. The deep baritone of his voice vibrates through me, reminding me he's in charge. He doesn't need to tell me; it's clear in his expression.

I shiver, both from the cold and his ferocious stare. He looks angry, but there's another emotion brewing in his stormy eyes.

Lust.

"What?" I croak once more, only to earn myself a chuckle so deep and rumbling it sounds like thunder rolling in.

"He wanted me to pay him five million for you," the stranger informs me. "But I believe you're worth so much more than that." This time, he coos.

His hand reaches for me, his knuckles trailing a white-hot path down my icy cheek. The warmth of his skin against my almost-frozen flesh is a welcome comfort, and I find myself leaning into his touch.

"That's it, sweetheart," he whispers in a husky tone. "I'll be your daddy now."

"No, no," I whimper, pulling away from him, but he's too fast. Thick, calloused fingers grip my face harshly, turning my head to face him. His eyes glow with feral rage. His voice may have been the thunder, but his actions are the storm. He forces me to look at him, and I know there's no way I can fight the blizzard of this man. I'm ready for the lashing of lightning to burn me alive.

"Listen to me," he commands with fury burning through his words, igniting fear within my very core. "I don't care if you say no. In fact, I want you to say no. When you fight and wriggle against me, I'll fuck you harder. I'll make you fucking bleed all over me, all over my cock, and when I'm done, I'll ensure you clean me with your pretty pink tongue." His laugh is manic, vibrating off the walls as it tumbles from his slim, red lips.

"Sir." A voice at the door draws his attention. "We have contact," the man says. When my captor moves, I get a glimpse of the stranger at the exit to the hell I'm locked in. His eyes land on me for a split second before averting his gaze to his boss.

"And they know what we have?" my captor questions. The answer is a nod. "Good. Get her ready."

The stranger walks into the room. He has a confident stride, as if this is the most natural thing for him to do. His body is large, foreboding, with broad shoulders and a tapered waist. I take him in, wondering if I could fight my way free. If I can get my hands on a weapon, I'll be able to do something other than lie here like a fucking toy.

The dress shirt he's wearing is a dark color, but not black. Perhaps charcoal. His slacks match, but his boots are black leather with worn cracks. He doesn't speak, but I take my time watching him move around the room.

He fills a bucket from the sink in the corner, the sound of water causing my bladder to ache.

"I need . . ." When I utter the words, he spins on his heel to pin me with a glare. "I, uhm, need to pee," I tell him as embarrassment flushes through me, heating my cheeks, traveling down to my chest.

"Piss yourself on the mattress. The next girl won't be here till it's dry."

My mouth falls open, gaping at him in shock. Horrified at having to do what he said. I turn away, attempting to not listen to the trickle of the tap.

"Don't mind me, doll, I've seen much worse." This time he chuckles. "Working with him, I've cleaned piss, blood, and shit when he's finished with one of you, so you're definitely not special," he continues, not looking my way.

He picks up the bucket and strolls over to the icy metal bed I'm bound to. My wrists ache. Pins and needles pierce me as I tug and pull to get free, even though I know it's a pointless exercise. Standing above me, he takes the bucket and tips it over me and the mattress I'm lying on.

A squeal of surprise is wrenched from me, bouncing off the walls. I tug on my restraints only to have the twine bite into my torn skin, and I feel the trickle of water and blood as it oozes its way over my flesh.

The cold has nothing on what I feel now. My body is frozen. My limbs lose all feeling, and my teeth chatter loudly against each other.

My tormentor captures me in his arms, and I realize he's unbound me from the headboard. Even though I'm loose, I'm free, I'm still bound in another way. I'm so cold I can't move but then he's lifting me. My arms flail, one at my side and the other on my lap.

He turns us to leave the cell I've been in, but as he squeezes me through the doorway, my stomach lurches, and my bladder releases warm liquid over his stomach and arms.

"Are you fucking pissing on me?" he shouts, dropping me on the cold concrete floor. I land with a harsh thud on my hip, which causes me to cry out in agony. I grab at the side of my body, attempting to ease the pain shooting through me, to no avail.

His hands swipe at his shirt and slacks, but they're drenched in my urine.

"You little bitch!" His foot makes contact with my stomach with a resounding thud. My lungs lose all air. My hands fly to my abdomen in an attempt to protect myself, but I know it's futile.

"Stop playing with the toys," the captor's voice comes from behind me. My vision is blurry, but I can make out the man who has just knocked the breath from my lungs.

He leans in, his face close to mine in a sneer so cold it turns my blood to ice. "I'll make you pay, little toy. That silky hair is like the wings of a bird, and I'll pull and tug until you have nothing left. And then, you'll fly no more," he grits out angrily.

Before he turns to leave, he spits on my face, saliva splattering on my cheek.

"Enough!" my captor orders him. "She's worth more alive and looked after."

Then I'm being tugged to my feet, dragged and thrown into a room which resembles a horror movie bathroom. Blood pools on the floor, the walls have the word help painted in the crimson liquid, and my stomach turns when I think about what happened.

"Clean yourself. Clothes will be set out for you when you're done."

The older man turns, leaving me in the room with no privacy as the door is no longer on its hinges.

I open the tap, cupping my hands and splashing the frigid water on my face. The toilet sitting to my right is stained with black marks, which makes my stomach roll.

I shove my panties down, hovering over the seat. Once I'm done, I wipe myself with the hard paper used for cleaning kitchen counters. The scrape of it against my sensitive flesh only makes the torture worse. My skin is normally sensitive to abrasions, and I can only imagine it's bright red from the burn over my core.

As I head out of the bathroom, I look around, praying I find a doorway, an exit, but as I feel along the dark wall, I find nothing.

I'm a prisoner, and there's nothing I can do about it. Sighing, I give up after my third attempt at trailing my fingers over cold, smooth concrete.

Making my way back toward the room, I find a white,

cotton dress on the bed, noting the mattress is no longer on the metal frame. He must've moved it since he decided to soak me, along with the thin mattress, in water. I pick up the dress; the feel of the fabric is soft between my fingers. It's pretty, but far too big for me. I slip it on, thankful for the chance to cover my modesty. Not that it will help. I'm sure the men have already seen me naked while I was passed out.

I sit on the bed frame and wait. My tormentor, whom I earlier relieved myself on, arrives once more with a look that tells me not to try anything. He stalks closer, and I notice he's dressed immaculately. The suit he's wearing hugs every muscle of his lean frame. He's tall, probably over six feet. There's dips and valleys in the shirt, and I realize he must be extremely toned to look that good in a suit. My eyes drop to the front of his pants, finding a hard bulge against his zipper. It's so close it catches my eye.

"You look pretty all cleaned up," he smirks, causing my gaze to lift back to his.

His mouth tilts into a smile, which causes me to catch my breath. He's handsome. Devilishly so. His square jaw is smooth. The dimples dipping on either cheek are deep, making him look far younger than I think he is. He turns to the sink in the room again, ignoring me as he fills the bucket, and I wonder if he's going to drench me again.

"Why do you do this?" I question, suddenly anxious to see if he has any human emotions left from working down here. I don't know where my confidence comes from, but I want to stifle it back down when he turns to regard me with a penetrating blue glare. The color of his irises is almost see-through, reminding me of sunshine streaming through a window on a bright morning. Sadness washes over me when I realize I may not see the sunshine again. There's tension in the air, reminding me of when my father would tell me I shouldn't do things or he'd admonish me for wanting to go out with a boy.

"If you ask questions, you'll not make it through the night," he warns, his gaze piercing me. It's so harsh I'm bruised by the mere look he offers.

His words are a cold reminder he's not my friend and I shouldn't think he's here to save me. He isn't. He's as much of a monster as the man who wants to hurt me.

He leaves the bucket on the floor of my room and pulls me up by my arm. Then, he shoves me in front of him and warns, "Behave, and you'll get out alive."

I don't ask what he means. I don't even look away from the path in front of me. Instead, I focus on each step I take. We silently make our way down a long, dark hallway.

At one point, he maneuvers his way in front of me to open a door. My eyes adjust to the darkness, but my tormentor is hidden in the shadows. His dark suit makes it difficult for me to see him, and when he comes to a stop, I slam into his solid back.

Muscles tighten and tense when I place my hands on his shoulders. Every inch of him taut with . . . *Frustration? Anger?*

"Get your hands off me," he barks angrily, causing me to stumble backward.

"I . . . I'm sorry," I mumble, dropping my gaze to the floor, but he can't see me because the space we're standing in is pitch black. It's then a beep echoes around us, dinging loudly as a hiss of a door that's been locked for some reason slides open.

Light streams from the entry, and music comes from the

other side. There's laughter traveling from where the muted yellow light is beckoning — men's chuckling, which sets me on edge.

My tormentor hands me an object in the darkness, then leans in closer. "This is the only option you have. Use it, don't use it. That's all up to you," he informs me.

When I turn to look at him, he's gone.

Straightening my shoulders, I step through the doorway and gasp.

CHAPTER THREE
DRAKE

Shoving my bedroom door open, I enter, sighing when I see River on my bed. He's lounging against the headboard, his body naked except for the small pair of blue boxer-briefs hugging his hips and thighs. My bedroom is stark, just like me. The dark space, with the white and silver paintings along the walls are almost clinical. I don't like color. I don't enjoy being outside. The sun is far too cheerful for me to endure. Thankfully with my natural tanned skin I don't look like the walking dead.

His green gaze lifts to my blue one. Silence is heavy in the air as I shrug off my jacket. The clink of my gold, engraved cufflinks are the only sound when I drop them on my chest of drawers. Next are my slacks, then my shirt. When I'm in much the same attire as he is, I join him on the mattress.

"How is she?" he asks, knowing I've been in that hell all day. I want to tell him about her, about the feisty little girl.

"Malcolm isn't going to be happy about her," I inform him. "She's far too fiery, and she's not going to break easily." My assumptions on Caia are strong. I've never seen such fight in a girl before.

"Perhaps she'll be easier to break," he suggests, pulling me closer, and I place my head on his chest. His heartbeat slowly thrums in my ear. It's the only time I allow myself to not think about the dark. River is as broken as I am, and he understands there are times I just want silence.

"Dante is out with a girl," he informs me, and I hear the agony in his tone. River and my brother have history. I have a feeling my best friend is in love with my brother, but he's never said anything to me. Perhaps it's because I fuck River as well.

"Good for him," I respond, placing my hand on his soft cock, hoping to wake it up and have him forget Dante for a moment.

"You can't do that, you know," River smirks. I hear it in his words.

I don't look up at him, but question, "What?"

"Fuck me to make me think about you instead." Pulling my hand from his bulge, I sigh and push off the bed. Padding barefoot into the adjoining bathroom, I turn the shower on and shove my boxers down.

Under the spray, I close my eyes and imagine Caia. Her slim body, those big eyes filled with fight and innocence. I want to steal it. To fucking take everything from her so my father can't.

My cock jolts when I remind myself of her slight frame in my arms. She was so delicate, so fucking soft. Fisting my dick, I stroke it slowly, taunting myself with images of her, of what I could do to her.

I've fucked so many women in my short life, but there's something about tearing apart her body that does things to me. A fire burns in my veins when I squeeze my shaft, almost to the point of pain.

Realization dawns that I want to take her sweetness, and it stills me for a moment, but only one moment, because soon I'm pumping my release down the drain imagining her virtue slick on my cock.

I will have her.

I'll break her, make her mine, before she's taken and defiled worse than I ever can do to her.

THE DARKNESS SURROUNDS ME.

It always has. By the time I was thirteen, I had seen far too many horrors. But it's all him. He took and took, and when there wasn't anything left, he preyed on others. Then again, he's always done that. I recall the first time I learned what he was.

A monster.

It was that day my life changed. I'd never be the same again, and now that I'm twenty-five, I feel as if I'm an old, ragged man. Even though I'm only starting my life. Not the life I wanted, but the one I was thrust into at an early age.

There's a stench in the basement when I enter. Five rooms sit to my left, and another five to my right. That's ten captives he holds each year. One month, four weeks, he takes one of those lucky ten and ensures they shatter. The process is simple. They come in, they get tortured and used, and then on their final day, a group of men and women walk in, watch the show, and choose which they'd prefer.

He's broken them in for years. It's the way he gets off. I've seen the vilest of acts being done to girls over the years.

He's had boys here too. However, they don't earn him enough, so he focuses on girls. They can offer him what boys can't.

And as many years as I've been here, I'm still trying to find a way out. A way where I can run with my brother and my best friend and never look back. Slowly, with each night that falls, I know that day will never come. But I hold onto that faraway emotion we're taught as kids.

Hope.

The problem is, in this place, that's a fruitless wish. There's no such thing as hope in here. Life will end here the same way it started. In agony. It's the cries and screams that haunt the walls of the mansion. Even though the captives are kept in the basement, being on the upper levels, even in my bedroom, I hear them. As if they echo to me, to taint me for what I've helped be done to them.

I recall the day I walked into the basement when he was in one of his *sessions*.

The door is ajar. There's a dim light telling me to run, to hide, but I don't. I'm intrigued. I'm ten years old, and all I want is to learn to be a good boy. He tells me I need to be, but I never understand what he means.

I reach the last, cold, concrete step and peek through the space in the door. A gold light comes from within. A scream so loud, so filled with pain I can't help stumbling back. It's a girl. I can tell that already.

I lean forward once more, and the door slides open another inch. The image before me causes me to retch. The sound echoes along with her screams, and he snaps his vicious glare at me.

"Bring him in." The familiar, deep voice I've known all my

short life vibrates through the walls of the basement. Cold concrete greets my ass when I fall back.

Two strong meaty hands grip my bony shoulders, lifting me with no effort. My skinny legs flail wildly in the air as a man who's the size of an ogre carries me inside the room where he's standing.

"What the fuck is he doing in here?" the man questions.

I recoil when a hand reaches for my face. Gripping my neck, he lifts me onto a steel gurney and presses me flat on my back. The smell of blood is thick in the air, and I retch once more.

My body folds in the middle, my small arms hold onto my stomach, but he growls, ordering the ogre to bind my arms and legs to the four corners. Once I'm unable to move, he chuckles when I beg for mercy. But I know for a fact he won't show it.

The little girl on the gurney beside me is not moving. Her long blonde hair is matted with dark red liquid. It looks like she's sleeping —her eyes closed, her face at peace—and I notice her chest isn't moving. She's no longer breathing.

"What did you do?" My question is hoarse. My throat burns at the realization running through my mind. I shake my head when he looks at me and nods.

"She served her purpose." His words are cold, then I notice him pulling up his zipper on the dark slacks he always wears to work.

I don't understand. My brows crease in confusion. He hurt her. I know that.

"Perhaps we can have him trained?" the man asks the ogre. They both look at me as if I'm an experiment. I'm not sure what they mean, but my chest tightens, and my breathing gets more difficult.

"I think he'll be a good investment," the ogre agrees after a

long while of studying me. He smirks, his mouth curling evilly as he watches me.

"Tie him in the training chair." The old man grins happily. He cups my cheek in his hand and leans in. His breath stinks of alcohol and blood which makes me choke on the spit dripping down my throat from his open mouth.

"What if he doesn't—?"

"I said tie him to the fucking chair," the man bites out angrily at the ogre. "He'll learn to appreciate my business. He is my son after all."

SHAKING MY HEAD TO CLEAR IT OF THE GLOOMY TIME IN MY LIFE, I move into the empty cell and start my clean up. I couldn't sleep after I'd left her in that room, so here I am at one in the morning working when I should be asleep.

The wet mattress has already been pulled out of the room, and the bucket needs to be removed and cleaned. Grabbing the mop, I start on the floor now dried where she's pissed herself while I was holding her. I shouldn't have gotten angry, but it was her weakness I hated.

When he told me there would be more coming, he mentioned bringing a new, special girl in. I knew what he'd want from me. I've become wary of the girls who arrive, because I know the moment I see them in their beauty, it will be the last time they'll ever look that way again. But after my jerk-off session last night, I closed my eyes, with River curled around me in bed, and saw her eyes. I recognized the plea in them. She needs a knight to save her, and as much as I never believed I could be anyone's savior, this girl makes me feel something I never did before — I want to be the one who saves her from the Devil himself even though it may kill me.

I want to sever the link to him and have her be mine.

But as much as I want that, I know I can't ever have her because he owns them all. Each one brought into hell, he takes them and makes sure they never see the light of day again.

But it's not the fact that he takes from them, it's the way he does it. A scrape of a boot sounds from behind me, and I find my brother at the door. He eyes me warily. We've both been working here for the man we call father for so long it's become second nature to clean up the mess left by each toy.

"She going to last?" he questions naturally, as if we're talking about the fucking weather. He looks like he's been well fucked, and I wonder who the girl was.

"I hope so." I've never uttered those words. Never once cared if the girls come back from their sessions or not, but with the pretty toy I've just led to the den, I wonder if I'll ever see those soulful eyes again.

"There's no hope in here, Drake," my brother grunts in frustration. He's younger than me by two minutes. But I was dragged into the darkness much earlier than he was.

"I know," I finally respond, causing him to glance at me. The blue eyes that match mine stare at me for a moment. My father told us we were a gift to him from our mother. That she had told him how special we were as she birthed us. In her screams, she told him we'd carry on the Savage legacy. I think he's full of shit.

My mother may be a stranger to me — I've only ever seen a handful of photos of her — but there's something in her gaze whenever she looked at the camera. A faraway look that reminds me of the girls in here.

Her ancestry took us back to Europe. Both our mother's and father's bloodlines originated there. But now we live in what is known as the "land of the free", which to me is a lie, because it seems to stifle everything good in our lives.

"Is she pretty?" he questions as he unscrews the bottle of bleach. The harsh scent still bothers my senses as he douses the floor in the clear liquid.

Is she?

Yes.

"It doesn't matter," I tell him, not answering his question because I know there isn't any reason for me to want her. As much as I could attempt saving her, it would be pointless.

"Then perhaps you should go in there and ask Dad if he'll allow you to play the final round." I glance at my brother then. It's the first time we've really gotten to talk about something like this. An option of perhaps winning and keeping one of the girls.

But even so, if I do get her, she'll hate me for what I allow to happen to her. I've left her in there with the Devil himself. I know what she's going through right now. In my mind, I recall the *training chair*. My father's idea of teaching impressionable youths on the basics of human nature. That's a fucking joke. More like the intricacies of being an animal.

"That will never happen," I tell him.

"You never know," Dante murmurs as he carries the bucket from the cell and disappears, leaving me to wonder if I'll ever have a chance against our father.

CHAPTER FOUR
CAIA

My tormentor left me in the softly lit room four hours ago with an object. It's small, and when I lift it to the light, I note it's a pocket knife. But the blade is serrated, and even though I've never been a fearful person, this makes me shudder. If I need this, then whatever I'm about to experience may kill me.

Nobody has come to me, but I'm locked in a small room where I can't see much. All I can hear is the melody from the other side. I've screamed, yelled for someone, but it's fallen on deaf ears. I have lost all sense of time, when suddenly the music and voices fade, hands grab me from behind and shove me into a dark closet.

The person wrenches the knife from my hand, and in that moment, all hope leaves me. I'm blindfolded, and there are plugs in my ears to keep out the noise.

My body aches when I'm shoved forward and then forced to sit on a small wooden chair. My wrists and ankles are bound to the legs of the chair in seconds.

The person moves fast to ensure I can't fight, and then I'm left alone.

Seconds pass, then minutes.

"Please let me go. If you tell me why I'm here, I can get my father to talk to you. Do you want money? He has money." Nobody responds to my plea. Tears sting my eyes as my mind plays scenarios like a horror movie before me.

I'm hunched over. The tension in my shoulders is unbearable. I've tried tugging at the bindings, but they're knotted too tight. With each tug, the twine cuts into the harsh wounds from being bound to the bed earlier, and I know I'm not making it better by trying to pull myself free.

Suddenly, the plugs are pulled from my ears, and I can hear the music again. Classical and operatic. It's not loud, merely a whisper, but almost torturous in volume.

"She's pretty," a deep rumble comes from somewhere. The blindfold hinders my sight, and I don't know how many people are in the room, but if I had to guess, I'd say two. The man who hurt me earlier and another. The stranger's voice is deeper, more ragged than my captor.

"Get her ready," a voice comes, the one of the men who's keeping me in here. "She's to be trained as soon as possible. I want her ready for next month's auction."

There are hands pulling at my arms and legs, untying me hastily from my bound position. Tugging my wrists together, he twines the rope tightly. Then suddenly I'm thrust into the air. A hard shoulder pressing into my stomach as he grips my ass and another arm snaking around my thighs.

He walks through the space I'm not allowed to see. When he finally sets me on my feet, I'm placed against a wall, or something cold and hard. Concrete. Perhaps the same type as the walls of the cell I woke up in.

My hands and legs are bound against the icy wall, and I'm once again locked in place with nowhere to go. A chuckle comes from my left, and his hot breath on my cheek causes me to shudder.

"Don't worry, pet, you'll soon enjoy this," he grits out in a devilish tone. His calloused finger paints something on my lips. As soon as my tongue darts out, the metallic flavor causes me to retch. "You look so pretty painted with crimson." His voice is cold as ice, and it chills me.

The blindfold is ripped from my face, and the harsh light is blinding for a moment. Blinking to clear the sting, I find myself in a small dark room and realize the blinding light is coming from the television set before me.

"What are you doing?" I croak, but he ignores me as he moves to the corner and pulls out a small trolley he wheels over to me. Placing it between my legs, I notice it has one of those magic wand vibrators attached to it. "Please, you don't have to do this." I know my words fall on deaf ears, but I try anyway.

He locks it in place and moves to the television shining a bright-white screen. When he clicks a remote, an image appears. It's a video paused on the title I'm sure is something gory from the word on screen.

Severed.

"Enjoy your movie night, princess." The man who reminds me of an evil ogre smirks viciously as he walks out, shutting the door with a resounding click. My gaze darts back to the screen, and before I can think about what's about to happen, the wand placed on my core starts a gentle vibration.

Another older man appears from behind me. He's dressed like a doctor, with blue plastic gloves and a stethoscope around his neck.

"We're going to test your restraint, little one," he smirks. "They asked for a strong one, a fighter."

I frown at this information, wondering who he's talking about, or even what he's talking about. "Please, why are you doing this?"

He doesn't respond, merely gestures to the screen with his chin, silently ordering me to turn my attention back to the television.

The name disappears, and a scene appears with a man who looks to be in his early forties, graying hair with a scraggly beard that reminds me of barbed wire. The lens follows him to a bed where a girl who can't be much older than my eighteen years is bound helpless.

I can't look away, and I can't close my eyes. I'm bound so well with my head fastened to hooks on the wall that don't allow me to move an inch. There's something on my eye lids that allow me to blink, but I can't keep them closed.

She's begging, crying, and pleading with him to let her go. The vibration between my legs intensifies, and I'm lost in pleasurable confusion. My body is reacting to the stimulation, but my mind recoils at the scene on the television.

I'm assaulted by the scene before me of the old man thrusting himself inside the girl. There are feral grunts, screams of pain, and when the lens zooms in, blood is dripping from where they're connected.

My body gives in to the pleasure. My stomach convulses from the scene before me. I can't stop my orgasm, and I can't stop the puke that's dripping from my chin. My mind feels almost fragmented, shattered and torn at the emotions racing through me.

The man, who's dressed in an immaculate suit, continues to violate her, to torture her with his cock, his grip around her neck tightens as her choking intensifies, while he spits on her. It's horrific to watch, and I'm afraid to see what's to follow. His large hand grips her tiny breast, tugging on the flesh harshly, as if he's trying to rip it off. Her cries echo in my ears, and his grunts fill the room.

It's sick.

It's vile.

And I can't move away, turn away from the scene. The large, silent man dressed in a white lab coat stalks closer, his hand holding an object dripping blood, and when I finally take a good look, I notice it's a human heart. At least, that's what I've seen pictures of in biology class. My body is rigid with fear, my blood turning icy cold. *What are they doing with that?* My thoughts are erratic, fliting between fear and revulsion.

"She had so many pretty parts," he sneers, pushing his hand holding the organ against my mouth as I try to fight him off. The screams still echo around me as he feeds me. With his other hand, I feel the pressure between my legs as he forces two thick fingers inside me. "You'll be broken soon, just like her."

I can't close my mouth as he shoves it into me, and I'm painted in the crimson liquid while the video plays, and my body leaps over an edge I've been fighting, but the assault on my clit is too much.

I'm drenched in red. My mouth and my shoulders are slick as he grips me, ensuring I'm soaked in the metallic liquid.

"So pretty, little girl," he sneers.

My body locks and convulses as pleasure shoots through me. It's not from the scene. It's from the forced orgasm I've been subjected to. But the vibration only intensifies. I cry out, begging for mercy, even though I know they'll never offer it. I feel another release on the edge, it's right there, and the filthy words from the TV vibrate though me, and I cry out in pleasure, in pain, in disgust.

Another notch on the vibrator is turned up, and I'm wet. My clit is throbbing now, and I can't stop the moan that slips from my lips. A third orgasm is close, I'm watching a girl get violated, and all I can do is find release, pleasure watching pain.

The piece of filth steps back, admiring me shaking and shuddering wildly. My captor turns around and calls out to someone I can't see.

"Get Dante in here. She needs to be cleaned up."

"Why?" I whimper, attempting to spit the blood from my mouth.

He spins on his heel, glaring at me. "Because, little girl," he says in a low, menacing tone. "You're going to bring me a lot of money. Every part of you." His blue eyes glow with evil intent.

My body is rising to the edge. I'm standing on the precipice as the old man on screen pulls a blade from under the pillow and severs her head as the wand is turned to full pelt and I come harder than I've ever known a woman could.

My body is wracked with a sob, convulsions, and an orgasm that turns me inside out. My toes curl. I watch the head of a beautiful girl fall off the bed, and the man finds his own release in her now dead body.

When the door flies open, I'm crying. The white-coated man steps back after turning off the vibrator that's assaulted me for as long as the video had been repulsing me. He smirks at the newest member to the room.

"Get her cleaned up," he orders, then leaves us, his footfalls disappearing into the darkness.

The screen is black, but the dim light streaming in from the room beyond offers me a glimmer to see who's walked in. My tormentor. The dark-haired man with the blue eyes that remind me of an ocean. *Dante.*

"You're quite surprising," he tells me. "He'll make sure you break." It's a veiled threat, and I wonder if he's telling me that in warning, or if he's disgusted at what I've just been through.

"Help me."

He stills in his need to unchain me. "I'm not the good one, pet. Perhaps you're mistaking me for my brother. There's no escape from the dungeon. You either conform, or you die." *Brother?*

He continues to move swiftly, and then I'm in his arms, and I realize it's not my captor from earlier. He smells different. Not as spicy. He has a unique scent which I commit to memory. If there's two of them, perhaps I can figure out how to get them to help me.

When we enter the adjoining space, there's a bed he places me on. I'm shoved onto my stomach and once more bound to the metal poles on either end.

I'm open to him as he washes me, his fingers probing me painfully. I can't stifle the whimper and attempt to close my legs, but he only chuckles at the movement.

Once he's completed his task, he leans in close to my

ear. "If you can survive this," he starts, "then perhaps there's hope for us all."

With that, I'm left alone to wonder what he means.

All I do know is that it can't be good.

CHAPTER FIVE
DRAKE

I haven't seen her in hours. My mind is filled with images of what I imagine is going on inside that room. The cameras before me are empty. None of the girls who are in their cells have moved.

But Caia hasn't been returned to hers. I'm angry that she's captured my fucking attention so much, but I haven't been able to focus on anything else. Even River has been in here a few times to check if I'm still breathing. I don't think I am.

Shoving the chair along the concrete floor, I cringe at the noise it makes. The moment I rise, I see her cell door open and her body flung onto the mattress like a rag doll. Rage implodes through me, simmering in my veins like a goddamn poison.

What have you done to me?

I wait for the asshole to leave her cell before my feet hastily carry me to her door. As soon as it creaks, she opens her eyes wide and watches me. Her long, dark hair hangs matted to her head. I notice the blood that's been knotted in her locks, and my fingers itch to wash it out, to clean her, but I know if I go near her now, she'll scream. She'll lose her shit.

"Are you okay?" The question comes unbidden from my lips, causing me to cringe. Of course she's not okay.

"Does it look like I'm okay?" she bites back, causing me to chuckle. Jesus, she's beautiful when she's angry. Her pale flesh is marred with red welts, and I know she's been through phase one.

"Don't mistake my question for caring, little bird," I growl, stalking closer to her, causing her to cower in the corner. Her small frame shifting, offering me a glimpse of her white panties. She must've been changed before they brought her back in here, because those weren't what she was wearing earlier.

"Fuck you," she mumbles, her wide eyes pinned on me as I lean over the bed. Reaching for her, I grip her hair. Fisting it harshly, I pull her closer toward me. A tremble trickles through her; goosebumps rise on her porcelain skin. She's perfection. Pure perfection.

"I'd be happy to oblige you, little raven," I smirk down at her.

Her lips purse into a tight line, and from the way her body is shaking, I'm certain she's a virgin. With a fierce tug, I pull her to the edge of the bed, her face against my groin.

"Feel that?" I whisper, a low hiss of a question that earns me a whimper, which only causes my dick to jolt against her cheek. "That's all yours if you want it," I tell her.

"Never."

I smile. I shouldn't be proud of her, I shouldn't even be hard for her, but something inside me has awakened, a beast that's hungry and wants a piece of the sweet fruit on the bed before me.

I lower my gaze to hers, finding her looking up at me. Her face has paled even more, making her eyes contrast against her flesh. Her lips are a soft, rosy color, and I wonder what they taste like. More so, I wonder how my cock would look sliding between them. Deep into her throat until she can't breathe. Until she's clawing at me, attempting to push me out.

"Your feisty little mouth is going to get you into trouble," I inform her, still holding onto her. Strangely, she allows me to keep hold of her hair. I wonder why she's not fighting.

"Just let me go," she says then. "I just want to leave, to go home." Her plea, along with that beautiful pout, is enough to have me shoving my zipper down. I reach for my cock and pull it from its confines.

"If you keep begging, I'm going to have to shut you up," I tell her, slapping her cheek with the thick angry shaft.

"You're disgusting," she bites out, and I'm done. Pushing her to the bed, I grip her throat and press my fingers on either side, cutting off her air. Her tiny body flails wildly on the filthy mattress.

As soon as her lips open to attempt to pull in air, I shove my dick deep inside her pretty throat. It tightens, pulses, grips the bulbous head, and I'm lost in pleasure. Holding my dick in her body, I close my eyes, feeling her teeth scrape the base as she attempts to bite me.

Too bad the little princess will find out that I love the pain. It makes me even harder, throbbing inside her as I slowly pull out and slam back in. This time, the heat of her puke rises. Before she throws up, I pull out completely as she scrambles for the bucket.

Righting myself, I zip my slacks and watch her empty her stomach in the plastic bucket that's going to waft a stale stench all night. Her watery eyes meet my hard ones.

"You're worse than them," she tells me, stilling me for a moment before I reach for the bucket and head for the door. I don't respond, taking the filthy object to the cleaning room and grabbing a clean one.

Back in her cell, I set it down and turn for the door once more.

"You're broken, aren't you?"

Her question halts me at the door, my hand wrapped around the steel handle. Lowering my head, I cast a glance over my shoulder at her kneeling on the floor. She's shattered, her body still shivering as she regards me.

"I'm not broken, little bird," I tell her. "You'd have to be whole before you can break." I leave her alone to mull over my words before I go to my room for the night. I shouldn't have done what I did, but I couldn't help it.

In the shower, I recall how she felt. Just those few seconds of ecstasy and I've got my cock in my fist once more. As much as I fucked up, I don't regret a moment of it. If I could do it again, I would.

CHAPTER SIX
CAIA

He's violent and dangerous. My throat burns from his abuse, but my mind wonders how he's become so cold. When he looked at me, there was a flicker of affection, of something he refused to admit. His anger was palpable, a force that made him act out in a rage, but then guilt marred his handsome face.

He is handsome.

Far too beautiful to be in this place.

I've known what it's like to be hidden away. My father was overly protective of me, ensuring I'd never gone out partying like the other girls my age. I was like the princess locked away from the world, until the night I was stolen.

I stupidly went out of my way to defy my father for the first time in my life, and it's landed me in here. I lie back on the bed. In an attempt to close my eyes, I'm assaulted by the eyes of my captor. The man who looks so haunted it made me question him. I expected him to stalk toward me and slap me, or worse, but he merely glanced my way with such sadness it tugged my heart.

Stupid girl.

There's no way he can be good. He works for the devil, but he looks like an angel. My thoughts are at war. I can't shake the questions racing through my mind. I want to ask him everything. I want to delve into his mind and find out what he's hiding. But something tells me climbing those high walls he's built will be pointless.

He could be my way out of here. I should've asked him about his brother. Or even perhaps why they do this, what the point is of hurting people. No, not people, girls.

My chest aches, but the pain between my legs is like nothing compared to anything I've ever felt. Rolling over, I curl into a ball and hug my thighs to my chest. It's the only way I have some relief, but even then, there's no escape from the nightmares I know will follow. My eyes flutter, and I sadly allow sleep to steal me.

***

THE CREAK OF THE DOOR, THE ECHO OF METAL UPON THE concrete wakes me. My body is still curled into a ball. When I move, every muscle tightens.

"Wake up."

The voice isn't that of my captor, and my heart sinks. It's not even his brother. When I finally manage to turn around, I find green eyes peering at me. It's my captor's friend. I'm not sure what his name is, but they both came to me on my first day here.

"You're going with me today." He smiles. It's a friendly gesture, but a cold pit of dread sits in my stomach at his words.

"Where . . . where am I going?"

"Today you're going to see what Drake can do," he informs me. That must be my captor. It would make sense if he and Dante are brothers, twins. Dante warned me last night he was the bad one, the violent one. I can only pray Drake is not as volatile.

"And Drake is Dante's brother?" He nods. "So, where is Drake taking me today?"

He stares at me for a moment, as if he's trying to figure out if he should tell me what's going to happen or not. I can't deny the fear trickling through my veins. Those green eyes hold far too many secrets as they linger on me.

"Drake is the second in command. Dante, third." He sighs, pulling a long white dress from the bag he'd been holding when he entered.

"And you?"

"I'm the foot soldier, sweet thing," he smirks. I notice then how handsome he is. When he's serious, those tattoos snaking up his neck from the white collar of his shirt make him look scary. But it's his dimpled smile that makes him seem less intimidating.

"You're only their lackey? Seems a bit strange. You and Drake looked like friends," I observe, causing him to stop at the foot end of the bed. He doesn't respond, merely throws the dress on the mattress.

"Get up, you'll need a shower before you go out there. I'll bring you something to wear as well." His gaze takes me in, sizing me up in the dirty clothes I'm wearing. "Tonight, you need to look perfect."

I silently take the material and slide it over my half-naked frame. The slight warmth it offers is welcome, but I know it won't last long. Comfort in this place is short-lived.

"I'll bring you food, and then I'll take you to him."

The man turns to leave, but I call to him, "What's your name, foot soldier?"

He drags his gaze over to me slowly, pinning me with a curious stare, and I'm certain he won't offer me his name. But then he smiles. "My name is River."

"I like that." I grin in return, and for the first time since I've been in here, I find light within the darkness.

"Don't mistake my smile for friendship, sweet thing," he says, twisting the handle on the door. "I'm not one of the nice men. Actually, this place doesn't have anyone nice you can befriend. It's best you don't become attached," he sighs. "Especially to Drake."

He leaves me wondering what he meant. How can I become attached to a man I don't know? A man who's most likely going to hurt me? Make me cry? Is that how he likes it? How he gets off?

I sit in silence and wait for my food to arrive, but even though River has given me a few answers, it's only unlocked so many more questions than I had before.

CHAPTER SEVEN
DRAKE

The room I'm in is lit with candlelight. I'm always reminded of the first time I was brought here. The nightmares that followed have never left me. Even though it's been years, I still see the images in my mind. They're ingrained behind my lids, and I know I'll forever be scarred.

But today, I have a job to do. The beast that resides within me is hungry. It's been a while since my father has allowed me to sate it. I'm looking forward to this pretty toy to feast on.

Closing my eyes, I take a deep breath. The gentle scent of lavender and eucalyptus hangs in the air. It's meant to be calming, but nothing about what I'm about to do will calm the beautiful Caia.

The tumbler sitting on the glass table is half filled with amber liquid that glimmers in the flames. I needed time to prepare, and now that she's on her way with River, I feel as if it's my first time.

I turn on the stereo. "Silence" by Beethoven greets me through the speakers, and I close my eyes to the melody of the piano. So ironic that soon there'll be no silence in this room.

The beast inside me roars to life when the door clicks open and I inhale her. The scent of this girl lingers as she enters and exits a space. There are many vices in my life that I allow to rule over me, but this need for her, it's something I can't contain for too much longer.

I turn to her. She's dressed in the white dress I asked River to give her. Purity. So fucking innocent. Too bad I want to tear her apart with my teeth. I hunger to drench that material in crimson.

I lift the tumbler to my lips, tipping my head toward my best friend who looks at me with sadness, knowing what I have to do. He leaves. We're alone then, Caia and me. She glances my way, unsure, nervous, yet there's a flicker of indignation in her pretty eyes.

She offers a smile, which shoves me off kilter for a second before I right my stance and set the glass on the counter behind me.

"Sit." I gesture at the chair positioned perfectly where I need it. Silently, she obeys me, and I can't help smiling. *Such a good girl.*

Her hands are splayed on her thighs, her legs pinched together, and her long, dark hair hangs down her back in a sleek braid. River always ensures the toys are perfectly made up for me.

There isn't an ounce of make-up on her face, and I'm happy for that. I hate those fucking dolls that look fake when they're crying as I use them. Father was adamant that she's to remain a virgin. He told me to see if I can shatter her defiance, and I know that anything I do to her in here will not do that. She's far too strong. But I'll gladly give it a good try.

Her gaze finds mine. There's a plea in those wide eyes. *No, darling, tonight, you'll not shock me like you did last night.*

"Why am I here?" she finally questions. I find that most times, if you leave them in silence for long enough, they'll break.

"You're here to learn, little bird," I tell her. Unbuttoning my suit coat, I shrug it off. Feeling her gaze roam over me, I turn and set the jacket on the chair. When I face her, she's staring at me, her lips slightly parted.

"And is my learning meant to make this ordeal easier?"

I consider her question for a moment. *Would it?* Perhaps. Stalking toward the bar, I grab the Scotch along with a small glass, which I fill to the brim. I set the drink before her on the table and straighten.

"Drink that," I command, watching her eyes narrow with suspicion. *Fuck.* This girl is utterly intoxicating, more so than the alcohol I've consumed.

"I'm eighteen."

"I don't give a fuck. I said drink it," I bite out, my teeth clenched so tight it feels as if I'm about to crack them.

The song changes, and we're met with the melodic sounds of Lucas King, classic, dark, and haunting. Caia lifts the glass, sniffing the contents before scrunching up her nose in disgust.

"I don't have all day."

She glares at me but swallows the shot in one grimacing gulp. When she sets the glass down, she sits back once more, waiting on me to make my move.

"Rise. Take off your dress." My gaze roams her as she discards the material that was covering her body from my view. A shiver trails over her, and I know she's feeling the heat of my stare violating her.

"Drake," she utters my name, causing my body to heat at the word alone. Just hearing her say it in her sweet voice has my slacks tightening. "Please, this isn't you. I know it isn't."

They all plead for their lives. Each one of them wants to go free, wants to be saved by the knight in shining armor.

Sadly, I'm not him.

I'm the beast that will devour them piece by piece.

I stalk around the chair where she's sitting. Her gaze following me, but by the time I'm behind her, I feel the absence of her stare.

Leaning in, I place my lips at her ear and whisper, "There's nothing, and I mean nothing, that will prepare you for what you'll experience in here."

She pulls in a sharp gasp, and I wonder if it's from my words or my warm breath on her sensitive flesh.

"There is no escape. There is no getting out," I tell her. It's the truth. There is no way I can lie to her, because for some unknown fucking reason, this girl has gotten under my skin.

"Do you truly believe that?" she asks without looking over her shoulder at me but twisting her hands in her lap.

"I do, little raven."

She's silent for a moment before she responds, "You hurt me last night." Her confession burns through me. Every inch of my skin is aflame with rage, but I tamper it down. I'm angry at myself for losing control, but I feel no guilt when the memory of how her mouth felt on my dick assaults me.

I know I'm not allowed to do anything to the girls

unless father instructs us, but Caia has a hold on me. A dangerous fucking grip.

"What exactly did I do that you didn't want?" My question is raspy at best, and I hope she doesn't hear the need in my voice. The desire that she innocently elicits from me.

"You shoved your cock into my throat. You were violent."

Hearing her utter those filthy words only serves to make me harder. The image of seeing her choke on my dick makes me throb in my boxers.

"Did it make you wet, little bird?" I question. "Because if it did, I'd certainly enjoy doing that to you again."

"I puked, and no, I did not enjoy it." Her biting remark makes me chuckle. "Are you going to hurt me now?"

"You're not here for me to hurt," I tell her. "The pretty ones are to be savored." I pull out the sleek blade and bring it around so she can see it. "This here is what we're going to play with."

"Please, Drake," she begs again, her voice timid, lower than it was moments ago when she was sassing me.

"I like this part, Caia," I tell her. "When you're scared, your pupils dilate, and those pretty lips part as your breaths come hard and fast."

I smile as she shivers, the cold metal trailing over her bared tits. The sharpness evident in the way it scrapes against her flesh. When I reach her belly button, the tip presses inside. But I'm careful. I know how to use this to either harm or to toy with someone.

"If you move, it will cut you," I warn her. "Be a good girl and stay very still for me." My movements are slow, meticulous, as I reach her panties and slice them from her hips. On either side they fall away. "Open your legs."

She does, and her cunt is bared to me. Beautiful and smooth.

"Oh, darling," I murmur. "How I'd love to eat you right now. Would you like that?" I don't wait for her to respond. "I'd dip my tongue into your tight hole and lick your juices."

She gasps when I nick her with the blade. Watching the sweet crimson drip from the mound of her breast. In a slow trail, it finds her nipple, stopping on the peak, and I lean forward, my tongue lapping at the metallic liquid.

Our gazes lock, the fear in hers sates my beast. It feeds him like never before. It's addicting, not because I enjoy this, but because it's her. She's everything. Her beauty is my tranquility.

The piano plays in the background as I continue trailing my mouth over her flesh. She shivers when I dip my tongue into her belly button. But she watches every moment of my travels. When I finally get to her cunt, I shove her legs open, pressing the knife against the smooth lips, and I wonder just how pretty it would look if my cock was sliding into her in that moment.

I shouldn't be doing this. I shouldn't make her feel good. But her flavor on my tongue is the only thing I can think about. I near her pussy, inhaling her scent, and I know I'm never going to be able to hurt her.

Fuck.

"Tell me your name," I question her. Not moving my face, keeping it near her entrance.

"Caia Amoretto," she confesses in a fearful whisper.

The realization dawns on me when I look up at her from my position between her thighs. She's the one stolen for my father's ultimate job. The music reaches a crescendo, and I breathe her in once more.

I never saw myself as a savior.

I never saw myself as a knight.

But with her beauty, with her name, with everything she is, I'm going to steal her from my father.

I rise, lean in, find her lips, and meld them with mine. She whimpers when my tongue darts into her warmth, licking and tasting the sweet flavor mixed with the spice of the alcohol she consumed, and I'm addicted.

"Caia," I whisper along her lips. "You've been stolen for a reason."

"Please help me."

Her gaze pierces mine as mine searches hers. I'm eager to have my body against hers, to feel her pulse and tighten, to have her soul entwine with mine, but it's far too dangerous to show I care.

I grip her throat, lifting her from the chair as she flails in my arms. Shock on her features make me smile. As much as I want her, I'm also a sadistic bastard. I shove her against the wall, pressing my body tightly against hers.

"I'm going to fuck you. I'm going to take your virginity and own it. And when I do, you'll be mine."

"Then do it." Her challenge burns through me. "I don't want them to have it. Please?"

"Hearing you beg me to do it makes me even harder for you. It makes me want to rip into you and make you cry," I utter, and while the words leave my lips, I'm shoving my slacks down, my cock in my fist, and I'm driving into her tight cunt, causing her to cry out from the pain of her hymen tearing as I rip into her.

My hips don't slow. I don't offer her a kiss or kind

words. I take it. I fucking own her body, and she lets me. Her nails rake down my neck as she holds on, but she doesn't beg me to stop.

All she does is hold me hostage with her gaze.

And as good as she feels, I know I've truly fucked up now.

CHAPTER EIGHT
CAIA

Once he's found release, he sets me down slowly. He's almost gentle in the way he touches me. Nothing like moments before when he took my virginity.

"That should never have happened," he tells me without meeting my gaze. Those blue orbs are dark as he stares into the distance. Lost in his own world.

"Then it didn't." My words cause him to snap those eyes to mine. "It's done. You've taken it; they can't own it."

"And I can't own you." His counter response does something to my heart. The ache in my chest isn't something I'd like to admit to because I shouldn't feel anything for him. But I do.

"You can leave."

"I can't," he says, pulling at the shirt he was wearing. I watch his fingers button the material, closing off his toned torso to my hungry view.

"Then you'll stay in this hell with the devil beckoning you to do vile things?" My question stills him from pouring two drinks, his hand gripping the crystal decanter, and I'm certain if he doesn't ease up, it will shatter.

"There are things at play here that you know nothing about, little raven." He smirks, filling each shot glass with amber liquid. "Drink this." He hands one to me with a smile that makes my heart stutter.

I take the offered glass and gulp the liquid down in one burning swallow. Tonight shouldn't have happened, but in a way, I'm glad it did. He's taken the one thing they wanted from me, and now, he owns it. And deep down, I know he owns me too.

"I have many secrets, Caia," Drake says sadly as he settles in the wingback chair. "But there are many others who know about them. If I leave, I break promises to people I love."

"Love?"

He chuckles at my raised brow and sips on the alcohol. I set my glass down, then turn to him once more, wanting his blue-eyed gaze on me. It's as if when he takes it away, I am cold, empty.

"I never thought a monster could love," I tell him, goading him to say something, or to do something. I don't know why, but I need it. In this moment, I crave his touch.

"No, you're right." He rises, stalking toward me, causing me to falter and step backward. He's beautiful in his darkness. It shrouds him as if it's attempting to consume him. When he reaches me, my back hits the wall. The same wall he'd just pinned me against. "You see, little bird" — he leans in, our bodies inches from each other — "my life is not filled with sunshine. Hell, it doesn't even have a glimmer of light." Hs words feather over my skin, making me shiver. "But I've accepted it. Just as you've accepted your fate."

"How do you know I have?" Lifting my eyes to his, I find questions dancing in the waves of blue.

"Because you asked me to take what you held onto for so long." It's as if I should've known this would be his answer. "No matter what happens here," he breathes, allowing the heat of his breath to tickle the sensitive skin on my neck. "You'll always be mine."

DRAKE

She's been here for two weeks. She's survived every fucking method of torture, and she's still fighting. I know he's angry, raging that this little girl isn't shattering for him. And soon, she will. He'll pull out all the stops.

My gaze trails over her. There's blood everywhere. She's sleeping, passed out from the pain. I sit at her bedside, my fingertips tracing the scars on her back, on her ass, and down to her feet. The skin the same color as porcelain is bright red with welts. Crimson still drips from the open wounds, and I wonder just how well she did in there.

The fact that she's not dead tells me she's a fighter.

I knew she would be. There was a blaze in her beautiful dark eyes that told me she's going to take everything thrown at her and mold it into something that will eventually allow her to fight her way out of here. The only problem is she'll never get out.

We'll all die in this place.

My gaze is locked on her body, the way it lifts and drops as she breathes evenly. Her long hair is matted with something. I'm not sure if it's blood or semen, but it's sticky, making her dark locks knot.

I shiver when she does. Her small feet are curled under her ass, the bones of her spine are protruding against her luminescent flesh. It's a haunting image to see a woman, well, a girl, lie there near death, and even more disturbing to still want her. Still desire her.

The silence hanging in the air is heavy with the chill the concrete walls offer. There are no luxuries in any of the rooms. Each cell — a gray square space that only has one bucket for bodily functions and a steel bed with a worn-out mattress to offer some form of comfort for the girls.

It's been a long while since he brought a boy back. I recall the last boy who came here; he was bought by a man who was in his early fifties.

They're all rich. Each of them with more money than God. And darkness within their souls no amount of prayer can expunge.

"Do you watch?" A voice comes from the bed, startling me. I shift onto my knees, leaning on the edge of the mattress with my gaze glued to the girl.

She shifts, wincing when her body falls onto her back. I want to touch her, to feel her milky skin, but I don't dare. I know if I do, I may not be able to stop. The thought makes me hard. My jeans are uncomfortable now.

Thinking about her pink flesh, open and wet, I cough, hiding the groan that rumbles in my chest.

"You're hurt," I tell her, stating the obvious. I admonish myself silently. I feel almost immature beside her. I don't know how to be around a woman. Especially one who makes me feel things without being in the *dungeon* where my father forced the most horrific things on me. The psychological games he plays are for his *clients* to benefit from. The depraved acts the men and women who come in here to experience are far worse than anyone can imagine.

With each session he administers on the girls, he ensures they're no longer able to fight back. That they're just broken toys. And he made sure I'm as cold as he is, but what he doesn't know is I still have my heart. He may have darkened my soul, but I'm a lot stronger than he gives me credit for. *And he just doesn't need to find out what I did to Caia.*

The mansion he's owned all his life, inherited from my grandad, is beautiful, decked in expensive furniture, but what people don't know is the darkness lurking beneath. The rooms where the girls are held, and the dungeon where the sessions happen, have been hidden from plain sight. When the clients arrive, they enter through a secret door and exit from it as well.

I look at the girl once more. She offers me a small smile. It's an honest, sweet gesture which angers me. There's something about her that makes me weak, makes me want to kiss and hold her.

I rise to my full height, stalking toward the corner, then back again. I do so a few times, pacing. There's an ache in my chest, and I hit it with my fist. As hard as I can, I continue the attack, but it does nothing to help my desires.

"What are you doing?" she questions from behind me. I can't look at her. I'm so fucked up, the moment I turn I'll hurt her. I'll fucking break her just to hear her cry. And it's not because I like hurting her, but it's the only way I know how. My mind has been fragmented so many times the only way I know how to get off is by pain, inflicting it, watching someone do it. I hear the springs of the bed creak, and I'm certain she's going to come to me.

"Don't come near me." My command is harsh, as cold as the room we're in. I'm dressed in warm clothes, jeans, socks, and boots, with a heavy woolen hoodie. But the girl, the pretty dolly, is only dressed in panties. They're also bloody. I'd looked at them earlier. I'd traced my finger over them while I'd jerked my dick. I'd stroked myself in my fist while I touched her bloody cunt.

"Why are you being like this? After what we did?" she questions, but she doesn't come near me. Her obedience is perfect, just what he'd like. The man who's now her owner until someone comes along and pays good money for her.

"Don't act like we're a couple, little bird. You're a good fuck. Don't go falling in love with me."

"I don't fall in love with monsters," she says softly. "I have no choice but to be here, it seems. All I wanted was to talk to someone. After what happened between us, I thought—"

"You thought wrong, so stop talking and just let me finish up in here. Tomorrow, you're going to be taken back to him. There's no longer anything I can do."

I still, turning to face her. The movement is slow, almost wary because I don't know if she's actually there. If she's real. But I did fuck her. I felt her break around my cock, and I savored it. I reveled in taking her violently, and she in turn moaned my name even though she didn't come.

"My father is the owner of a tech company in Miami," she starts talking again, but I ignore her. "But, I mean, he's not a good person." She sighs, the sound sad, but there's also frustration clear in her tone. "Is this because of him? What am I doing here? Please, talk to me." She looks at me as she questions me as if I should feel something for her.

I don't.

My nonresponse is met with a gentle gaze. We're not friends. We never will be. She won't live long enough to be anything to me, but the way she regards me, it's as if I've known her my whole life.

A knock on the door has her shooting to the bed, the squeaky springs under the threadbare mattress echo in the room, and I cringe. I don't know who's at the door, but all I can hope for is that it's not my father.

When I pull it open, I find my best friend standing on the other side.

"Hey," he says, his lopsided grin greeting me, and I exhale, allowing the tension in my shoulders to ease slightly.

"Does he know you're here?" River shakes his head and glances over my shoulder. I know he can see her, and I wonder if he's jealous that I'm here and not in bed. "Did you want to head out?"

I shake my head no. I should want to go, but the thought of leaving Caia alone here only sets my nerves on edge.

"Hi." Her voice is sweet behind me as she greets River.

He pushes by me, entering the small space, and I grip the handle of the door in fear, hoping my father doesn't decide to walk down to the girls' cells to check up on them this morning. I glance at the time on my wristwatch and note it's almost five in the morning. He'll be here soon.

"We can't stay long."

River nods in understanding. We both watch Caia for a moment as if she's the show and we're paid attendees.

"Will I see you tomorrow?" Her question jars me. None of the other girls who have been in here have ever asked me that.

"Maybe." I tug open the door, leaving enough space for River to exit, and I follow him out. I don't look at her again when I click the door shut behind me.

"You like her," he observes.

I shrug, not looking at him as I respond, "She'll be dead tomorrow."

CHAPTER TEN
CAIA

Alone.

I've been alone for a long while. I can't tell if it's night or day. The space I'm in offers some artificial light, but I can't see outside. The thick concrete walls have kept me prisoner. My back aches. It stings as I move, and I try my best to recall what happened when I was bound to the metal bed.

"YOU'RE SUCH A PRETTY LITTLE TOY," A GRUFF VOICE FROM BEHIND me speaks. A small trolley is rolled closer. On it is a computer, which is currently black. The screen is dead, and I wish I was.

I'm still sick from the images I saw earlier. From the girl being beheaded. There was a sick satisfaction on the man's face as he did it, as if he found pleasure in doing what he did.

I don't speak now. I know it's pointless. A cold device is pressed against me, and I feel my body opening, the object slipping inside my core.

"She's a virgin," the man says. I can't tell the difference

between the two anymore. There's no distinct change in tone, and I wonder if I'm losing my mind. A small sharp prick against my shoulder shoots something warm and languid through me. My muscles are limp, and I find I can no longer move my limbs.

"There, there," a voice coos. Then a large, hairy hand reaches for the computer, and the screen lights up with images. Scrolling from one to the next of similar scenes to earlier, it plays on a loop, and I can't move my eyes. They're watering from tears, but I can't close them.

That's when a vibrating object is placed at my entrance. Against the spot of my body that sends pleasurable tingles through me.

"You'll learn to play the game, little one," the man tells me with confidence. A click sounds behind me, but I can't move. Frozen. Captive. A prisoner. I'm stolen.

When the screen changes, a video appears full screen, and the tears I'd been blinking away burn a path down my cheeks onto the cold metal gurney.

Once more, a man walks on screen. As he undresses, something is pushed inside me, tearing through me so harshly I cry out, the sound ricocheting off the walls.

The sound is turned up on the computer, and I'm met with the old man grunting inside the throat of a girl who looks so familiar. A girl whom I've known my whole life. And I recall the moment the man moves to offer us a view of her pretty green eyes —the image of my sister.

There's blood dripping from her nose, but she's lying upside down, and I watch in horror as she's violated once more by the man who turns to the camera and chuckles as his cock is lodged in her throat.

My heart catapults wildly when his face comes on screen,

and the vibrator against my clit is turned up harshly, causing pleasure and pain to skitter through me like a ten-pound weight.

An orgasm rocks me when I look into the eyes of my father, and all I can do is succumb to the force of agony that I'm thoroughly fucking broken. I've been torn from a normal life.

I'm severed.

THE DOOR CREAKS OPEN, AND I'M MET WITH THE DEEP BLUE EYES of the man who has been my captor for the past few days . . . weeks? His dark hair is a stark contrast to the asphalt color walls. He doesn't say anything, merely shuts the door and heads to the bucket in the corner. It's empty. I haven't eaten anything in the past few days. I don't recall drinking anything either. My body is weak, and I know there's no way I can fight my way out of here.

"You'll get lunch shortly," he bites out coldly. There's something strange about him, something I can't place my finger on. When he turns to regard me once more, he sees my face is glistening in the low light of the oil lamp he's carrying. "Are you crying?"

I don't want to tell him I am. I don't want to admit to feeling broken, shattered. I don't want to tell him what I saw. But something tells me he knows. Surely, he does.

"I asked you a question."

"Yes, of course I'm crying. I'm locked in hell with the devil and his foot soldiers, and I am wounded beyond repair."

He stalks toward me, and I'm certain he's going to hurt me, but he stops just short of my bed. He leans in close, his face right in mine. I meet those eyes that remind me of freedom, of the clear blue sky and the cool ocean waters.

"If you cry, he'll only make it worse."

"What do you care?" I bite out in frustration.

"Did you come when you watched the video?" he smirks. A cold, cruel grin curls his lips. "Did your little cunt get all wet and achy?" He leans in closer, his mouth almost on mine. "And when you came, did you cry out for God?"

"Fuck you!" I spit, the clear saliva hitting his face just below one of his beautiful eyes. The man is sinful, like the devil in disguise.

"Your next training session is today. After lunch, you'll learn just how much worse it can get." With that, he spins on his heel, and I want to crawl to him and beg him to free me. My mind is awash with confusion, everything is blurry and cloudy. The door opens. Another young man walks inside carrying a tray. He sets it on the bed beside me and they leave me alone.

I don't know what to do, but the food on the tray is my only sustenance, and I wolf it down in the hopes it will strengthen me. I need to fight. I have to get out of here.

The bread is soft and warm, the butter melting on it making my mouth water. I stuff it in my mouth, not bothering to chew. I need to eat, and the ravenous feeling overwhelms me. Tears trickle from my eyes once more as I revel in the flavors on my tongue.

I drink the water from the mug on the tray. It satiates my thirst like I've been given life once more. Moments later the tray is empty. I lift it in order to place it on the floor, but as soon as I attempt to stand, my legs give out and I fall to my knees, the metal clanking loudly. My ears feel as if they're about to shatter, and that's when my eyes flutter closed once more.

CHAPTER ELEVEN
DRAKE

"You're ready, son." My father glares at me. Malcolm has been a man of many faces. Most think he's an upstanding citizen, but those who know who he truly is, down to his rotten soul, they're the ones who respect him more than anything. They fear him. They fucking love him.

And you know why?

Because he offers them what they want. Fantasies that would make the most fucked-up asshole cringe.

Depraved.

Vile.

Filthy.

"You want me to do it?"

He snaps his gaze to me, those blue orbs that match mine and Dante's pierce me, and I feel it down to my fucking soul. At twenty-five, I should be out chasing girls and partying up a storm. Instead, he's imprisoned me as much as he has the rest of those who work here.

"If you're a pussy and can't do it, you can watch," he grunts, waving his hand at Ivor who's been in this dungeon for more than eight years. The large man who resembles an ogre is fast on his feet, and he's got me in a grip so tight it steals my breath.

"I can, just let me go, Dad," I try to reason with him, but he's already got the opera playing through the speakers. "Ivor, just let me go. I can do the training." All my pleading falls on deaf ears. As much as I've been working for my father, he's still in charge. I'm pushed onto a steel contraption similar to the seating at a sports stadium at the far wall, which offers me a clear view of the table he's about to mutilate Caia on.

A flannel gag is shoved into my mouth, and I spit it out immediately. Ivor knows better than to attempt this shit with me. He may be my father's right-hand man, but I'm the son of Malcolm Savage, and one day I'll make sure he pays for the shit he's done.

The door flies open, and one of my father's men stalks in with her passed out, and I realize the lunch she'd eaten must've ensured it. She's placed on the table; a cold, metal surgeon's table, and my body turns rigid.

Another person is brought inside, and I meet his gaze. My best friend. The only person who's stood by me besides my brother. I hope Dante doesn't come downstairs. He doesn't need to watch this. Even though we're the same age bar a couple of minutes in between, I feel overly protective of my brother.

"You shouldn't be here," I hiss at River who finds his place beside me.

"I'm not letting you go through this alone." His words are a salve. But I know they'll never heal the brokenness inside me.

"Ah, young River. You're here to enjoy the show?" My

father glares at him, and I know he doesn't like my best friend. We've never learned who River's family is, and over the years, he's become like part of the family. Only, I know my feelings for my best friend run far deeper.

I know it's about to go downhill when two men stalk into the space, bodyguards, and they're followed by three men and two women. All dressed immaculately, they seat themselves not far from the table.

We're not to move. My father's rules have always been very specific. Even though I can physically walk out of here at any moment, I know I can't because he'll do something he's threatened me with all my life. He'll kill River and Dante. Two people who mean more to me than anything. So, I sit.

Watching the scene play out before me. One I've watched so many times. The girl is lifted onto an apparatus that has her bound to an X-shaped wooden cross. She's naked, and her supple body causes my cock to throb.

That's why we're all broken here. Our minds have been fractured, and in the gaps where sanity should lie, we've been drenched in the depravity. Her eyes flutter open, and they land on mine as if they're opposite poles of a magnet.

CHAPTER TWELVE
CAIA

The gathering watches me cry. The heat of the blood dripping from between my legs scorches me. I can't move, my legs are useless, my brain screaming at them to do something, but they can't.

"Please," I whimper. It's almost inaudible, but he hears me. I know he does. All I receive in response is a chuckle. I'm shut down, completely numb, I feel nothing. I pray for my end. I pray for the pain. Perhaps it will wake me from this nightmare. Maybe, just maybe, I can be saved, and this is all just in my mind. But how would my imagination think up the depraved acts that have been happening?

"What do you think, ladies?" he questions the onlookers. The two women dressed in beautiful evening gowns have the material bunched up to their hips with their legs spread wide and two boys who look to be my age between their thighs. The men seated beside the women have their gazes locked on me. Their hands move over their thick erections as they grunt and smirk, looking at me with the hunger of wolves. They're predators, nothing but animals.

"Why don't we test her ability for pain? If I'm going to spend ten million on a toy, I'd want to make sure she can handle a bit of rough." One man offers me a wink that recoils my stomach. The incisions on my stomach already burn with the puke dripping from my chin, but when one of the women finds her release, she grips the boy's head, and just like in the movie they forced me to watch, she pulls a sleek blade from the holster on her thigh and slices through his neck as if it's a hot knife cutting through butter.

Revulsion shoots through me when I'm impaled with the thick handle of a blade used only moments ago to trail blood-red lines over my white flesh. My eyes flutter. I'm weary. This is far too much for me to handle. I can no longer hold on. He told me I was stupid to fight back, to resist, and now I believe him.

I glance at the man who looked at me with more affection than I've ever experienced. His lips move, his mouth tells me something, but I can't hear. I can't read his lips.

He shakes his head sadly as he watches the scene unfold. He told me I was going to be in trouble. If I cried, only worse would happen, and he's right. Well, he was right because I'm losing consciousness.

The men were here to get off from the pain they inflicted.

Another girl is brought in. She is younger, smaller, but the two large men don't care. Once more, I'm hooked up to a vibrator that offers pleasure, pressed tightly against my mound as I watch the gruesome scene before me.

The girl is pretty; she giggles as if she's high. Perhaps

she is and doesn't even realize she's about to be killed. I open my mouth, but I'm quickly stopped by the large ogre-looking man. There's a harsh material shoved into my mouth, and I'm choking on the fine filaments of hair and the taste of metallic residue. I'm certain it's blood, but what makes me retch is the fact that I know it's not mine.

"Shhh, little one. Tonight you'll see what it is we really do here," the ogre tells me proudly. The girl is bound to the table before me, her legs are spread wide, and I watch as one of the women walks up to her. It's the same one who just killed a boy.

She leans in, inspecting the girl as if she were a painting at the Louvre. Her fingers trail down the smooth porcelain flesh of the young girl. When she reaches between her legs, she nods, prodding the girl's opening.

A giggle falls from the girl's lips, and I know for a fact they've given her something. There's no way she can be happy with her body on display like that. Her eyes are wide, glassy. She's drugged so much that she can't focus on me. Her eyes flit left and right, her body also limp on the silver gurney. Another giggle falls from her lips, but she doesn't speak, as if she can't. When the woman grips her chin and tugs it open, I recoil at the sight of her missing tongue. The burning acid that trails up my throat makes my eyes water in my attempt to swallow it down.

"Is she to your specifications?" The old man grins like the fucking Cheshire cat.

"She is. I'll need this done tonight," the woman responds. I don't know what is happening, but the girl is bound to the table, and as the older man places a silver scalpel to her stomach, he presses down, and crimson floods the table immediately.

"How far along is she?" the second woman questions as she rises, pulling the boy that was between her thighs along behind her like a dog on a leash.

"Two months. It's just the perfect amount of time," the man in the white coat informs her.

"Good. Then we'll take whatever you can salvage." I'm tortured with the device between my legs as the man in the white coat begins his incisions to the girl's body below her belly button. I stare in horror as he slices through her flesh easily.

She's numb, because there are no screams, no cries or whimpers from her. She doesn't feel anything. Her body is limp as he lifts a layer of her stomach and shoves his hand into her.

That's when she starts gurgling. It's a vicious sound, her body convulsing, and one of the men who was merely observing rises, shoves down his zipper, and pushes his cock into her mouth. Her throat bulges obscenely as the scene is set before them, as if they're watching a porn video.

My own body responds to the vibrator on my clit, but my stomach heaves. My head is once again cloudy, foggy as confusion sets in. My scream is muffled by the cloth, my body tightens and pulses as an orgasm wracks through me as I witness the man in the white coat pull the womb from the young girl, and I realize they were talking about her being pregnant.

How far along is she?

Two months.

The perfect amount of time.

CHAPTER THIRTEEN
DRAKE

Today is the end. I can feel it in my bones.

"I thought you said she'd be dead," River whispers from beside me. I'm so numb I don't even notice the scene before me. I sit like the mechanical robot he's turned me into. My heart thuds as I watch her. I want to cry, to go to her, but I can never fight all of them off, even with River and Dante's help.

"I did say that. I lied."

I feel his gaze on me. It's burning through my flesh, turning my body tense and rigid. He's the only person I've ever allowed to come near me. To touch me. After what I'd been through, I no longer enjoy the gentle caress of another, and I don't offer it either.

"I need to do something."

That doesn't mean I haven't fucked my dick into some of the corpses. Those who are cold and rigid. I can't handle warmth anymore. It's not who I am. I'm a monster, and as the girl's womb is ripped from her body, I feel nothing.

I sit.

I watch.

I feel a pulse in my dick. I'm hard. Turned on by the depravity. Because he made me that way. He's forced me, just like he's forcing her, Caia, to feel desire at the sick deeds. Only she doesn't know why.

I do.

I know all his moves. And soon, I'll make sure that he takes his last breath. I won't do it quickly.

No.

I'll revel in the slow torture of his filthy flesh. Those pieces of him he finds pleasure in, I'll ensure they're burned while still attached.

How beautiful it will be.

The bright orange flame dancing along the wrinkled old skin of his cock. I'm lost in my violent thoughts, so I don't notice when he has Ivor drag Caia over to the table that the dead girl has just vacated.

"Do it." River's voice cuts through the clouds in my head. I'm not even sure how he managed to fuck with my head so much, but he has. He's broken me. "Drake, if you don't do something now, you'll lose the girl."

It's only when her muffled screams seem to jolt me into action that I realize I'm moving. My feet are racing to her, watching as he brings his scalpel down onto her smooth stained and bruised flesh. There's a man fucking her throat, violating the tight hole that I want.

I realize then that I want her.

I need her.

"No!"

My father's gaze snaps to mine with a fury I've never seen before.

He smirks, pressing the cool metal against her pretty

face. Her beautiful cheek is soon oozing crimson liquid, the color of Merlot I have at the dinner table.

"I knew you were a fucking pussy," my father grunts. There's a cock of a weapon, the click of a barrel, and I lose all sense of what I'm doing. It feels as if my body is slowing down when I reach her.

I grasp her hand, pulling her from the metal table and onto the floor. Her throat is turning blue, the convulsions wracking through her are violent, and the pungent stench of puke falls onto my chest as she expels the drugs they've clearly injected into her.

It's then that I see it.

Behind her.

The man who was using her throat like a cunt pulls the weapon, and its only seconds before I register the shot. It sears through her, into me, and I cry out in agony when I realize I've just lost the first thing I ever wanted to care for.

The only thing I wanted to nurture.

And her limp body is now on top of me.

SEVERED
THE TAKEN SERIES

PLAYLIST

Beautiful Girl - Broken Iris
Love Triangle - RaeLynn
The Blackest Day - Lana Del Rey
Lovesick - Banks
When It's All Over - Raign
Don't Let Me Go - Raign
Ungodly Hour - The Fray
Heal - Tom Odell
You're the One That I Want - Lo-Fang
Zombie - Bad Wolves
Sacrifice - Lucas King
Ghost - Bad Flower

Click here for the full list

DEDICATION

Thank you to my ladies who loved Drake so much and asked for more. I hope you love him and all his darkness as much as I do.

PROLOGUE

The sins of the father fall to the son.

Violence has been in my blood since I was born.

Love has never been something I wanted, needed, or thought of. I smile when I think about the one girl who almost managed to weasel her way into my heart, but she was stolen from me. Our link was severed, and I became the monster my father wanted me to be.

I buried my feelings for her along with the memory of her body bleeding out on top of me. The images haunted me each night. They replayed in my mind, but after my search for her came to a dead end, I locked away that damned muscle called my heart. Securing it in a cage, I ensured I'd never allow anyone to ever free it again.

I'm a Savage.

I'm the heir to a throne that was never my choice. It was forced upon me, and even though I shouldn't want it, I have no choice. The moment my father took his last breath, I knew I was never going to be free.

Dante, my brother, wants me to stop the Savage Organization. He's begged and pleaded, but what he doesn't understand is there's always more to a story than meets the eye.

I'm doing this for him. For me. For our family. If only he can give me time, I'll show him that the secrets that lie locked within the walls of the mansion hold so much more.

River, my best friend and part-time lover, is the only one who knows why I stay, why I continued the legacy left by my father, Malcolm Savage. And he's the only one who help me.

Sometimes, we must do things we don't want to.

We do things that will ensure our morals are challenged.

And, at other times, we do things to keep those we love safe.

CHAPTER ONE

DRAKE

G ames.

Sick, twisted games.

I spent my childhood learning how to play them.

He taught me. Turned me into a monster. He played them with me. I witnessed horrors that will forever be stained in my mind. Those vile images I've tried so hard to tamper, they rage within me, like a fire taking out a forest. Each night, I close my eyes, and those eyes haunt me. As much as I've tried, I can never stop them.

Guilt sits within my gut. It burns its way through my blood. I can never be free from the nightmares, and perhaps I don't want to be. It's those memories that allow me to do what I do. To finally attempt to rid my hands of the blood my father spilled.

The dark web my father had built for his organization still runs today. With new clients messaging me daily, I know time is running out. Before long they'll realize I'm leading them on. I don't have much longer to keep them at bay. The monsters are beating down the door, and soon, I'm going to have to let them in.

Bit by bit, as the days passed and the older I got, the more I lost myself. I knew if I didn't get away soon, there'd be nothing left of the boy I used to be. For years, my father got away with what he did. My only escape was my bedroom, where I would lose myself in River, in his touch, his body. And if he wasn't around, I'd sit silently in the shadows and watch Dante like a fucking stalker. He would have one of his latest conquests around, and I'd dive into the darkness with them. A voyeur to pleasure. It was the only way I could feel again.

I'm broken. I'm a fucked-up monster. And there's no longer anything that can change me. Four years ago, I thought there was a chance. I believed I could be someone different, because of *her*. A girl with the most beautiful soul I'd ever seen. She weakened me, and I almost let myself go. I wanted to steal her away, keep her for myself. But in the end, it was *she* who was stolen from *me*.

Her blood still stains my hands. The metallic taste of her life essence still coats my tongue. She bled out, her slight frame draped over me. One moment she was there. The next, she was gone.

The video I've been watching is on a loop. The body of the girl onscreen is bruised as one of the guards gets her ready for tonight's show. I'm lost in the darkness as my hand finds my hardened cock. I blame my father for this. He broke my mind, leaving only shattered fragments of my innocence.

I am no longer my own person. He owned me in ways I forced to the back of my mind. With each vile act I endured, he made sure that my only escape was to die. But I couldn't give up my life. I had to be there for Dante and River.

Instead of running, I planned. Each day and night that passed, I made sure I had everything I needed to take him down. His friends, partners, all of them would suffer. I would make sure of it.

Everything he did to me, all those things he made me witness, I'll perhaps never forget, but I can clear my conscience by killing the assholes who supported him. My father died from the wounds I inflicted only six months ago. We've kept the news from everyone because my plan can finally start.

Revenge.

Such a beautiful word.

Blood will be spilled. I will bathe in it. Drench myself in the metallic liquid because that's what they deserve. I played hide and seek from a young age. I hid as best I could from the men and women who frequented our estate. And now that my father has met his maker, I'll ensure those filthy pieces of trash answer to me.

And only me.

I'll run a rampage through his organization so violent, so bloody that no one can save them. And when I walk away with their blood staining my hands, I'll have my vengeance.

It took years to learn, to observe their movements. Each small nuance is ingrained in my mind. It makes me more dangerous than they can ever be. It makes me the killer they never saw coming.

"Are you listening to me?"

The voice drags me from the horrors replaying in my mind on a loop. I glance at the blue eyes that match mine and nod. My brother, Dante Savage, is all grown up now. I haven't been listening to a word he said. But I nod in any case.

"Drake, we can do this together," he tells me, placing a hand on my shoulder. Dante wants something I can never have. He's told me before how he wants to find a girl and settle down. Strangely, I can see him doing that, but the problem is, those dark desires that seem to ignite when he's fucking someone have always scared them away. I want to laugh when I think about my volatile brother, but then I realize, in all my years trying to protect him, I didn't do a very good job because he's just as fucked up as I am.

"You need to stay here, make sure they don't come looking for Malcolm," I inform him once more as I watch the screen. I know Dante can see my hard-on. There's nothing hidden between us. We've both witnessed each other in our worst states. We've shared women. We've shared River. Our sexuality is nothing like anyone else's. Our minds don't work right. And after the childhood we've had, nobody can blame us.

"Do you still look for her?"

I know he's talking about Caia. The girl I wanted. The one who attempted to make me feel. Perhaps I did. But then she was stolen, severed from my life before I had a chance to really know her. Even though we've searched for her high and low, I now believe she's never coming back.

Our lives are filled with darkness. Hers was only light. If only I wasn't late in stopping my father that night, I would never have lost her. I could've fucking saved her. And every time I think about it, I hate myself more. She didn't deserve what happened.

"No. She's dead." My cold words cause him to flinch;

only slightly, but I see it. As much as Dante plays the hard-ass, I know deep down he's not like me. Nowhere near.

"And what if one day you walk into a house and find her there? Are you going to finish the job father failed to do?" he questions me. "Or will you admit you fell for her?"

"I fucking told you time and again," I bite out, turning to pin him with an angry glare. "She's dead."

"If you say so," he utters. "I don't believe she is, because father would've had a file on her burial spot, like he does with everyone else he's killed." *Could she be alive?* I almost believe him. Only for a moment I allow my mind to wonder how it would feel to find her, to feel her touch, her lips. I let myself feel happiness, normality. But in the same second it appears, it's gone.

Since the moment I walked into the cell and laid my eyes on Caia, I felt my world tilt off its axis. Not one other girl who had been brought here made me want to protect and hurt her in equal measure. She fed the hunger my father ingrained in me. He's turned me into this. A sick monster who yearns to see the vile acts being portrayed before me.

Dante keeps me sated in his own way. He allows me to watch, to be a voyeur, and through him and River, I find release when I need it.

I still want to hurt though. There's nothing like seeing shimmering tears on pretty porcelain flesh. To see pouty lips wrapped tightly around my cock until tears drench rosy cheeks. I still get hard when I think of depraved acts. There is no help for me anymore. Nothing can remove what's embedded in my mind.

If anyone else witnessed what I have, they could never be sane.

"Let's get this meeting underway. I have somewhere to be tonight," I tell my brother. I need to feed this desire, and there's only one way to do it. To visit the cells. I need it like a shot of heroin to the vein.

And as we walk out the door, I feel almost normal once more.

Almost.

But I know I'll never be again.

CHAPTER TWO
DRAKE

I'm still frustrated from our meeting only an hour ago with one of the biggest clients my father had. The man that's next on my list. I've planned how I want him to die, and watching him play "happy family" with his wife tonight makes me want to rip his perfect life apart. Knowing tomorrow night, when River and I head out there again with my team I'll get to watch his blood drip from the wounds I inflict, makes me hard.

The room I enter is bathed in darkness. I can barely see the small form of the pretty toy huddled in the corner. As soon as Malcolm died, I changed how things run in this house.

"Get up," I bite out, my voice booming through the dark space. The girl's small body shoots up from the mattress. She's dressed in a thin, white cotton nightdress, and I know she's not wearing anything underneath.

"Please, don't hurt me, he . . . he's already . . ." I know what she wants to tell me, but I'm not here to fuck her. I'm here to watch. I can't do shit to any of them, and it pisses me off. As much as I want to be the monster, I can't even do that right.

"I said get the fuck up." My words are a low growl vibrating through my chest as I stalk toward her. Those dark eyes widen, and for a moment I'm taken back in time. To her. To Caia.

She attempts to crawl away, but I'm far too quick for her, and my fingers wrap around her thin arm. Tugging her to the edge of the bed, I lean in and flick the switch against the wall.

The yellow light illuminates her face, and I stare at her for far too long. Her eyes fill with tears when she sees me. Her lips are full, pouty, and as much as I want to feed her my dick, I know it's not going to bring me the satisfaction I want.

"Open your legs." My order is clear when I release her and step back. I pull the chair closer to the bed and settle on the seat. She's still frozen in place, and I know she's in shock that I'm not hurting her.

"I . . . I—"

"I said open your fucking legs," I grit out through clenched teeth. When she finally obeys, I smile, noticing her smooth-shaven little cunt. She trembles before me, and it only makes me harder. "Spread them wider," I order, and she silently submits to me. I wonder then if she's only doing it because I'm not hurting her or trying to shove my cock in her tiny hole. "You're a good girl." I smile. "Now finger yourself."

Her pouty lips part on a soft gasp that makes me throb behind my zipper. Tentatively, she moves her hand between her legs, but she doesn't do anything further. I wonder if she's ever done it. Surely, she's not *that* innocent.

"You've never touched yourself?"

She shakes her head, her cheeks darkening as she watches me. Her sweet innocence is similar to that of Caia's. She may be scared, but she's not a doormat. I love fire in a girl, her fight, and that stubbornness that only makes me harder every time I taunt her.

"Do it," I insist, nudging my chin toward her. "Put your index finger inside. Feel your warmth." My eyes are glued to the juncture between her thighs. Her toes curl into the mattress when her digit disappears inside her tight core.

A soft whimper falls from her lips, and my cock jolts with the need to take her, but I don't. I never can. She continues to finger herself while I palm my dick, watching the way her eyelashes flutter on the apples of her cheeks.

"Stop." My command has her gaze snapping to mine, her hand frozen between her legs. "I'm not a nice man."

She nods. "I know."

"How do you know that, pet?"

She's silent for a long while, her eyes never straying from mine. Her lips part, and I expect an answer, but all she does is inhale a deep breath, then let it out before shutting her mouth.

"Take your fingers and lick your juices off," I tell her.

Quietly, she complies, and the sight has me groaning. She moves to close her legs, but I shake my head.

"Do you want to go home?" My question has her pretty brown eyes lighting up. She nods, a small smile playing on her full lips. "Do you want to go see your mommy and daddy?"

"Fuck you," she bites back when I taunt her. "I hate you."

Rising, I button my suit jacket, take a step, and lean over

her. Fisting her strands, I tug her closer, pulling her against me. She attempts to get free, but I'm far too strong.

"I like when you fight. It makes my dick hard," I smirk. She stills, her gaze burning into me, and all I see is Caia. Leaning in, I run my lips along her wet cheek, my tongue darting out to lick her tears. The salty liquid igniting a primal need deep within me, and I know if I don't walk out of this room now, I'll fuck her. I'll hurt her. I've always taken women who remind me of the one woman who made me love. As much as I want to offer love, I can't.

Cold settles in my veins, reminding me that I'm not *him*. I'm not the monster I grew up with. I can be better. I can be more than the asshole who fucked up so many lives.

Shoving her away from me onto the mattress, I turn and stalk toward the door. In the hallway, I lean against the wall and breathe through the desire to maim. Sighing, I make my way up to my bedroom. My mind is still on the girl when I find River asleep on the bed. His form is relaxed, and the comfort of his soft breaths calms me somewhat. There are times I wonder how you can stay so loyal to a person when they can never offer you what you need.

Tomorrow, I'll start my reign of destruction, and soon enough, I'll free Dante and River from this life. And hopefully, I'll save myself in the process.

I settle beside him in the silence. I want to reach for him, to feel him in my arms, but I don't. I shove my feelings deep down so nobody can find them. Not even me.

When I first realized how I felt about River, I was scared. There wasn't anything I could do anyway. No relationship would've been enough to apologize for the life he'd been forced into. So, I pushed him away.

There was only one thing I could give him. One way of saying sorry for all the years of pain. Staring up at the ceiling, I recall the moment we freed ourselves from Malcolm's grip.

The room where my father has been lying in bed for the past few months stinks of death. Over the past six months, I've been slipping poison in his food. I've spent my life learning how to kill him. I wanted to make sure he suffered with every breath he took, and now as I stare at the withering body of the man who was once formidable, I realize my work is done.

"You were always stronger than your brother," he croaks when I near him. His hands are wrinkled, the skin pallid. His hair has grayed and has mostly fallen out. The balding old man is no longer scary. He's scared.

"I was stronger than you."

"You are certainly more intelligent than I gave you credit for, Drake." He attempts to laugh, but the wheeze on his chest makes it sound like he's about to die any second. "This life was something I didn't want."

"You could've fooled me."

"Drake, there is always more to what you see on the surface," he informs me, lifting a shaky hand toward me.

I don't move, and he lowers his reach. "I don't need a lecture from you today, Malcolm," I tell him. "It's time you left us forever."

"You can never take back what you do today, son."

"I don't ever want to take this back. I never want to forget when I see the light flicker from your eyes. I'll remember it for the rest of my life." Finally closing the distance between me and the bed, I look at Malcolm Savage. Seeing him alive for the last time

is something I've waited for since the moment I learned who my father was.

The door behind me creaks open, and their footsteps near me. The two men who will stand beside me as we do this. Dante leans in, his face close to our father's. I'm not sure what he's about to do, then he lifts his hand, twisting the kitchen knife my father enjoyed using when he tortured someone.

"Goodbye, Daddy Dearest." His grin is manic when he pushes the tip of the knife into Malcolm's left eye, causing blood to spurt from the wound. He twists it around as the old man cries out in agony.

Next, River reaches for his other eye, holding it open so he can't blink. "This is for me, for the two men I love, and for all those who came before and after us." He tilts the small, amber glass bottle and drips out three clear drops of acid, which only makes my father's groans of agony echo around us.

His mutilated face makes me smile. If only Caia were still here, still alive to witness the scene before me. I would've bent her over this bed and fucked her into oblivion while my father died.

Dante and River step back as I take the rope and tie it around his neck, ensuring the knot is tight, I tug on the leash-like twine and drag his body off the bed. Only when I reach the door do I feel it. The sag. No more fight, no more life.

Malcolm Savage is dead.

CHAPTER THREE
DRAKE

I hid in the shadows of the corner watching them sleep.

The man who worked for my father for over ten years lies peaceful beside his vicious wife. Both of them sick, vile monsters who will soon pay for their sins. I like being the reaper. The man who takes lives as I see fit.

Don't get me wrong. I don't kill innocent people. No. I extinguish the lives of those who have done wrong. With the list of contacts I've made, there is no escape from me and my team. Alongside my best friend, River, each one that has been jotted down will be paid a visit. The numerous, well-known names who prey on the weak, the young, and the desperate.

"Ready."

River's voice in the earpiece clipped to my head cuts through my thoughts. Two men enter, and I watch from the corner as they bind the two struggling bodies to their four-poster bed.

"Who are you?" The man's tone is heavy with sleep, but low and gravelly, reminding me of the first time I saw him.

He and his wife have a penchant for young boys. Something my father offered them freely in the bowels of the Savage Mansion.

"Please, don't hurt us." The wife's voice comes out raspy, fear dripping from every word. My team flicks on the lights, and I finally step forward. I don't cover my face. I don't wear a mask, because my childhood was spent covering up my real emotions. Their eyes widen in shock when they see me.

"Drake? What are you doing here, boy?" The words uttered in confusion. *Boy.* If only they knew I'm no longer a young, scared child. This time, I'm the one who will ensure they feel the dread I did for so long. Each time they visited my father's mansion. Every time the asshole choked me with his filthy, old cock.

Lifting my hand, I pull the syringe from my pocket.

"Mr. Walsh, it's so good to see you." The venom in my voice is enough to chill the whole fucking room. And it does. The two men who are here to aid me hold down the man, his body wriggling as he tries to get away, but he can't.

I smile down at his terrified face and press the needle into the soft skin below his eye socket. The clear, acidic poison dripping from the metal tip wrenches a scream from his throat so loud and piercing, his wife flinches from the sound alone.

"Please, Drake. Your father—" Her voice grates on my nerves.

"My father is dead," I bite out with satisfaction. I'll never tire from saying that. "Make her watch," I instruct one of the men, who turns Mrs. Walsh's head toward her husband, whose face is liquefying. Her screams are beautiful. Music to my ears.

"Please, please, no, no," she pleads.

"I used to say that to you, to him," I tell her, gesturing with my chin toward the asshole who's gulping the last few breaths of his life. His body convulsing as his flesh bubbles. My body tingles with excitement. Tonight, I'll head out and find a beautiful woman to fuck. I'll slide into a tight hole, warm and wet, and I'll spill my seed inside her thinking about how beautiful the scene before me is.

"Listen to me. We can fix this, Drake. You and Dante—"

"Shut the fuck up!" My voice booms through the room, bouncing off the walls, causing the old bitch to cringe, cowering against the headboard. "Can you imagine how it feels to be a young boy, scared shitless when two people visit his home?" I rage, losing the control I'd held onto until she mentioned my brother's name.

I'm at her side in seconds, my hand gripping her frail throat. I never pictured myself killing a woman, but right now, I don't care.

"Drake," my name on River's tongue comes from behind me, stalling me for a moment. "You don't have to do that. We have the team here."

He doesn't come near me. He knows when I'm like this I need to come down by myself. I'll never hurt him, but when I snap, all I see is red.

"She's not worth it," he tells me.

Shaking my head, I blink, and I realize I'm crying. The agony gripping my chest is painful, breath-stealing.

"You have a choice right now, Drake." He's right. I do have a choice. A split-second decision causes me to reach for my knife and plunge it into her throat, trailing it along the wrinkled skin. Blood spurts from her body as the light in her eyes flickers and dies. "Jesus."

I turn to my best friend. My partner. And the boy who suffered alongside me all those years. When Dante left for London, I told River to go with him. They were friends, and I knew if anyone would look after my brother, it would be the man I gave everything to.

Turning, I use the bedsheets to wipe the blade before heading out the door. The soft footfalls of River sound behind me, but he doesn't say anything. My body is still vibrating from the rage, exhilaration, and utter astonishment of making the kill. Some people tire of doing the same thing each time. I, on the other hand, love it.

With each kill, every life I take, I revel in it. Maybe that's what makes me crazy, fucked-up, and that's okay. I've learned to live with it. I'll never admit or deny it. I've come to terms with it.

"I need to get some pussy tonight, some chick to use for the evening. You joining me?" I question my best friend as we descend the stairs. River's gaze burns into me, and I know he's not happy with the way I handled that. We were meant to keep her alive, but anger got the better of me.

"Yeah, you know I will."

His response is clear. The unhappiness of what I did is heavy in his tone. This was my mistake, but it's over, and I learned a long while ago, once something's been done, there's no going back.

The night is cold, the moon hanging in the inky sky reminding me of the light River brings to me and my life. He's the only one I've let inside. He's seen me at my weakest.

"Do you still look for her each time we go out?" The

question comes from River, causing me to snap my gaze to his. "Caia Amoretto is dead."

"Don't you think I know that?"

"Then what's up your ass, man?" He sounds tentative because he knows he's walking on thin ice tonight. My mood is sour enough right now. This morning, Walsh's supplier dropped another shipment at the compound, and this is the only reason I decided to pay them a visit. This has got to fucking stop. And it's up to me to finally end it.

But that's not the only reason I'm pissed, and he knows it. The reminder that I've still not found Caia, or even learned if she's dead or not, plagues my mind constantly. However, there's one tiny thing that's been bothering me for some time, and I haven't told River or Dante about it. I know I should, but if it's not true, I may just upset them even more.

Something niggles at my mind, the night our father was murdered by the three of us, I learned a secret I've kept from them both. And I know soon I'll have to come clean.

"There's nothing wrong. Let's just get out of here." Sighing, I swing the car door open, slipping into the driver's seat without answering, because I don't know what else to say right now.

"Drake," River starts, and I have a feeling I know what he's going to say. But I stay silent and wait for it. "If we're going to do this, you need to keep your mind on the list."

I made a list when my father died. Names of men who need to suffer for what they've done. Each name will be crossed off as we take them down. I don't care if they've got families, businesses, I'll fucking rule over them. I'll be the one in charge.

"I know what I have to do," I respond without looking

at my best friend. I can feel his eyes on me, boring into me, attempting to find out everything I'm hiding from him, and he knows I'm keeping secrets. If there's one thing I know about River, it's that he can see right through me. He knows exactly when I'm lying.

Shaking the thought from my mind, I weave through the darkened streets, back to the Savage compound where I have at least fifteen girls that were meant to appease my father's clients.

I should free them.

I know I should do the right thing.

But if I do, I'll lose the key to unlock the secret my father kept from me and my brother. I cast a quick glance at River who's seated beside me and wonder if this is the moment I should confess. If I should tell him I know where his family is. Well, not his whole family, just his mother.

I know if I do, he'll never forgive me. If what I found in my father's safe is the truth, I don't know if my best friend will ever find it in his heart to love someone with the Savage name again. Not after the lies he's been fed all his life by Malcolm Savage.

I pull up to the ornate wrought-iron gates. I haven't thought about what I've just done. Killed someone. I know my team will do a clean-up of the house, and I'll be having a drink by the time the police find the bodies washed up on the shore. But somewhere deep-down, guilt still festers. Even though they deserved it, I now have more blood on my hands. Soon, I'll be stained with the metallic liquid, and I'll never be able to cleanse myself of it again.

"You know, we could just go to the house and get some rest," River suggests. "And you—"

"Would you cut the shit, River?" I snap, frustrated at his

insistence. "Look, I don't need anything else right now. We'll call over a pretty blonde from the place we always get them from, pay the fee for the night, and send her packing when we're done." I groan as I park the car. "Tonight, while she's sucking your cock clean after you've fucked me, I'll ram her tight little cunt. Is that so difficult for you to understand?"

His chuckle lightens the tension between us, and I exit the car without waiting for his response. I went overboard tonight. I love control. Usually, I'm calm, but those two monsters needed to pay for what they did to River, Dante, and me. I feel like it's an evening for a celebration. My best friend joins me as we head into the mansion.

"I'm sorry," I find myself uttering before I have time to rethink it. River's been there for me through everything. He's stayed by my side even though he's seen what my family has done. I know it's because he's got nowhere else to go, but when my father died, I gave him an out. I told him to leave. He refused, telling me he was staying beside me until this is done.

He's supported me when I asked him for things no friend should do for another. And even through our difficult path, we've still found friendship, and he's given me a love I can't return. Even though he knows I can't, it doesn't stop him from telling me how he feels.

THE DUNGEON IS LIT IN THE FAMILIAR YELLOW GLOW. MY BODY aches. I've been bound to the bench. I'm bent at the waist. My hands are fastened with thick twine holding me in place. I can't think because they've drugged me or something. I'm not sure, but I know this isn't over.

"Drake." I hear my name, but I don't open my eyes. I'm hallucinating, and if I do glance up and he's not there, I'll feel the agony of my heart breaking once more. I can't allow him to see me like this. "Drake. Open your eyes," River's voice comes again.

When my lids finally crack, I find green eyes piercing me with concern written on his beautiful face.

He reaches for me, cupping my cheek in his smooth hand. His touch is tender, affectionate, and I allow myself a moment to lean into it. I shouldn't do this. But I can't stop the need to feel something other than the pain burning through my lower half.

"What did they do?"

"Help me," I rasp, tugging on the rope that's secured to the legs of the bench.

He nods. His fingers move swiftly, and it doesn't take him long to free me. River helps me dress in a pair of sweatpants and a T-shirt. His arms wrap around me, offering me the love I can never return.

We've known each other for seven years. We're both reaching the age where most kids are graduating from high school, but we're held in here like prisoners. He leads me up to my bedroom. Once I'm lying on the soft mattress, he curls up beside me and questions once more.

"What happened?"

"They made me watch the videos again." I shudder as I quietly recall the moment the television screen lit up with images I can never expunge from my mind.

"And the blood?"

Another shudder of revulsion races through me when I open my mouth to speak. But the words I want to say don't come. I can't tell my best friend what happened. Even if he knows, he's been through it as well, I'm ashamed of myself for surviving and for the pleasure I found as they forced me to endure it.

"Drake, it's not your fault," River insists as he reaches for me once more, but this time I don't allow him to touch me. I don't let him get too close because he's already far too attached to me.

He needs to be free. He needs to have a normal life. And that doesn't include me.

Somehow, I need to free him, and that means I have to stop this . . . thing . . . between us. He needs to hate me. I'll make sure he does. It's easy because I'm not worthy of the love he so clearly holds for me.

"Get out of my room," I bite out, shoving myself off the bed.

He doesn't say anything. There's no response as I stalk into my bathroom and push the sweatpants down my thighs. As soon as the material falls to the floor, I see it. The blood he asked about.

Swallowing past the lump in my throat, I focus on the shower as I step into it. Opening the tap, I let the water prick my skin violently as it heats up.

My eyes are closed when I hear the door slide open.

"You can push all you want, Drake," River tells me with sadness lacing his tone. "But one day, you'll have to learn to accept that I'll never leave you."

And then I'm alone.

Like I should be.

That's when I allow the tears to fall.

GROWING UP THE WAY I DID, I WAS FUCKED-UP BEYOND MY YEARS by the time I was sixteen. My attachment to both men and women drove me to make stupid choices, and in those moments, I ensured my best friend would never leave me.

He fell in love with me long before I even knew what that word meant. At times, I still don't. I'm nearing thirty, and I have no idea what love is. And I know it's not something I'll ever want. Even if it hits me right in the face.

I push River away.

I push everyone away.

I don't deserve any affection, but there are times I crave a touch. I glance at River who's watching me intently as we head to my wing of the mansion. As soon as we're in the bedroom, I shove him against the door, my cock throbbing when he reaches for it, squeezing it painfully.

"This is what you wanted?" I bite out, anger suddenly running rife through my veins. As much as I would love the taste and feel of a slick, tight hole right now, I'm going to take my best friend and fuck away the agony gripping my chest.

Over the years, we've shared women. I've watched him fuck guys and women, but he's never spent more than one or two nights with someone, and deep down, I know it's due to his feelings for me. River has loved me for most of our lives together.

"You want to take out your anger on me?" he rumbles, causing me to snap my gaze to him. "Do it." It's a challenge. It burns in his eyes, and I want to extinguish the flame with fire of my own. I crash my mouth to his, our lips molding to each other's.

My hands are on his belt, tugging it from the loops. Freeing his zipper, I shove his slacks down and find his bulge throbbing beneath my hand.

Tears sting my eyes. I can't let them fall. My emotions are all over the place. It's the first time I've killed a woman, and the darkness seems to be dragging me under. River's tongue licks into my mouth, tasting of smoke and whiskey. Spicy and sweet mingled together to create a fucking intoxicating mix of want and need.

His hands grip my crisp white shirt, and he rips it harshly. Buttons pop against every surface within reach. The sound pinging like a warning siren in the darkness of the room.

"Don't let them win," he tells me when I suck on the flesh of his neck. His skin is soft, pliable, and my teeth sink in, causing him to groan. He rolls his hips against me, and it's my turn to grunt in pleasure. Our cocks rubbing against each other, we're dry humping like fucking teenagers, and I'm so close to blowing my load in my boxers.

"They'll lose. Every one of them," I inform him. Practically tearing at his underwear, I drop to my knees and take his cock in my mouth. River's fingers tangle in my hair, pulling me closer, causing me to choke on his thickness as I swallow my best friend. His eyes glower down at me, watching me like he would anyone else, but the smirk on his lips tells me this is what he's always wanted. Me, Drake Savage, on my knees for him.

It's the first time I've ever tasted him, and I revel in it. Licking slowly, dragging my teeth over the shaft, eliciting groans from deep in his throat.

"Fuck, Drake," he hisses, his head dropping back against the door as he plunges himself into my throat. His hips move in unison with his hands, and I allow him control. Suddenly, he pulls me off him. "Time to go to bed."

I rise, following him, watching as he perches on the edge of the mattress. His beautiful, naked body is sculpted to perfection, and in the dim light, the scars on his back are only just visible.

"Are you just going to stand there?" he questions, a smirk playing on his lips, the same lips I want to devour. Offering him a smile, I shove my boxers down and join him. Kneeling behind him, I grip his shoulders, feeling the tight muscles beneath my fingers.

Leaning in closer, I trail my lips along his neck. "I don't know how you do it, River," I whisper. "But each time you touch me, kiss me, I feel almost normal."

He turns in my grip, my hands falling away when he gets up onto the mattress in front of me. We're both naked. Our scars clear, matching. The pain we've both endured has been something we haven't spoken about, but we both understand it's there.

"You're not almost normal, Drake," he says, reaching for my neck, gripping it tightly as he presses his mouth to mine. "You're fucked up. So am I." I hear the click of the door, and I know who's entered. I don't look at him, but I feel him. The electricity in the room is at an all-time high.

Two bodies move in my peripheral, and I cast a quick glance their way. The girl is blindfolded. My brother leads her to the chaise near the window, making her kneel on the velvet material. Her body is covered in black lace. River's hand finds my cock, stroking it slowly as I watch Dante undress slowly.

"Where am I?" The girl giggles, but he doesn't respond. Once he's naked, I take note of his eyes boring into mine. He guides himself into her, causing a soft gasp to fall from her lips. His hips slam against her ass as she grips onto the back of the seat.

River's hand moves faster on my dick, and I know I won't last long watching the scene. Four of us in the room is more than I can handle. Watching my brother, having my best friend jerking me off, I'll soon be lost to it. To the darkness.

"Listen to her moans," River whispers in my ear, careful not to disturb the bodies before us. I reach for him, his hardness in my fist, throbbing, pulsing.

"Get on all fours," I bite out, and he obeys. This is what he lives for. To be mine. To be owned by me and my dick. Opening the drawer beside the bed, I pull out the lube. Snapping the cap open, I drench River in the cold liquid along with my cock. The slippery lube glistens on my shaft. Gripping myself, I guide the tip to River's ass, and as I slowly penetrate his tight ring of muscle, we all groan in unison. Sounds of sex echo through my bedroom.

River's hands grip the sheets, and inch by inch, I sink into him, taking him like he wants me to. Dante looks over at me as he pulls himself from the girl's sloppy cunt and positions his cock at her ass.

"You ever do this, baby?" He chuckles, dark and menacing, and I know he doesn't care if she hurts. My brother is cold, heartless, just like me. She whimpers a tentative *yes*, but I have a feeling she's lying. Dante spits down on her hole, circling it with his thumb before he thrusts balls-deep inside her, eliciting a screech so loud it bounces off the walls, and I'm almost certain it would've cracked the windows if we didn't have bulletproof glass in place.

"It hurts," she mutters, attempting to get away from him, but Dante doesn't care. His pleasure is all he cares about. His hips pull away from her, then drive back in. I match his thrusts, fucking River harder and faster. Moans and whimpers, squeals and grunts.

"Take it," Dante groans. "Take my fucking dick." He

continues fucking her wildly, and soon, she's bucking into him. Her tits bounce with every thrust, and I shut my eyes, picturing Caia. How much I wanted to use her body, to feel her cunt, to have her choke on my dick.

Darkness swirls through me. Desire so potent I can't help groaning as it heats my blood and burns through my veins. River moans, low and gravelly, and I know he's found his release. Moments later, as the pretty whore my brother is fucking cries out, I join him in euphoria and empty myself inside my best friend.

In the moments of my coming down from the high, I know I can't keep doing this, but there's no way out for me. Tomorrow, I'll tell River to leave. I'll give Dante his way out. And I'll finish this alone.

CHAPTER FOUR
DRAKE

"Drake." My brother saunters into the office where I'm sitting behind our father's desk. "I found something." It's been years since he's come to me with a job, or with news, but when I meet his gaze, there's emotion flickering in his expression.

"What?"

He throws the file on the desk, causing it to slide through the documents I've been working on. The yellow manila file has the words SPECIAL ASSIGNMENT emblazoned in black ink on the front. I lift my eyes, meeting his arching eyebrow in question.

"Just open the fucking thing," he bites out. I watch Dante settle in the chair near the desk, crossing one ankle on the opposite leg. He pulls out a cigarette, lighting it and inhaling a long draw before looking at me again. "If you don't want to find her, I'll go."

"Find who?" I chuckle, flipping the cover open to find a photo that grips my lungs, forcing all the air from them. Big eyes meet mine from the image of a girl, a ghost. Her hair is matted to her forehead. She's older. About twenty-two or so, I'm not sure. Her lips are still as pouty as I remember, but the dark circle under her left eye is new. It's purple-blue, darkened by someone's fist, or foot. A small scar along her cheek reminds me of the moments I held her trembling body against mine as she bled out.

Her neck is covered in ink, a tattoo which makes me wonder if she has any others on her porcelain skin. She's still as beautiful as I recall in my mind. Even though I haven't seen her in so long, it's as if I'm back in that room, holding her, bathing her.

"Is this some kind of joke?" My voice is raspy when I finally look at Dante again.

He shakes his head. "She's been bought. According to the research Hunter found, when they removed her from our compound, Thanos bought her from Malcolm." He spits our father's name, and I don't fucking blame him. I've hated the man all my life. The only good thing he ever did was bring River into my life.

"So, you mean to tell me she's alive?"

"Indeed, dear brother, and tonight we're heading to the club to find out where Thanos is," Dante smirks. "And once we get the location, we can find your girl."

"She's not mine." It's a lie. Dante knows it; I know it. I claimed her without a second thought, and I'd do it again and again if it meant I get to hear her voice one more time.

"Look, Drake, you've beat yourself up about this for far too long," my brother sighs. "It's time we finish this once and for all. We all have our lives to live. We're not even thirty yet. We have our lives ahead of us. We can move on."

Sighing, I run my fingers through my hair. Dante is adamant. His expression tells me that much. I lift the photo, my eyes glued to the girl staring back at me. If she's still alive, I can finally save her. I can do the one thing I promised before I lose who I am.

THE CLUB WHERE WE'RE MEETING THANOS IS WELL GUARDED, AND I know this because I've scoped it out each time I've been here. There's no way to take the fucker down on his home turf. If he really has Caia, I'll get her back. One way or another.

River is beside me as always, but he hasn't said a word since we left home. Dante opted to come alone, and I know it's because he's planning on taking one of the girl's home tonight. We're the only clients of Thanos's allowed to do so.

Each girl who works for the asshole can do what they want onsite, but going home with a customer is forbidden. Since Malcolm was good friends with Thanos, we're always allowed special privileges in his clubs. They're dotted across the country, and what goes on inside is nothing short of a porn set.

"What's wrong with you tonight?" River final questions.

"Nothing." My response is clipped, signaling end of the story. Pulling into the parking lot, I turn off the engine and exit the car before he can get into the emotional shit I don't want. I didn't tell him Caia could still be alive. I also didn't tell him I think she's working for Thanos. From the photo, I picked up tattoos all over her porcelain skin. Her hair is a deep red, clearly different from what I recall. And she's grown up. Older. More beautiful than before.

As we near the door, I notice the entrance is guarded by

two bouncers dressed like CIA agents. When we reach them, I offer a nod, and one of them opens the metal door, allowing us entrance. I've been here a few times before. Even helped them stop fights, so when I walk into the VIP area, I'm welcomed.

"Drake Savage." The sultry tone of Alysia comes from behind me. When I turn to find the beautiful brunette, her big blue eyes take note of the shirt I'm wearing, trailing down to my crotch, then snapping back to my cobalt gaze. "How are you, handsome?"

"Good." I smile, lifting the bottle one of the barmen sets on the counter. Taking a long gulp, I watch her sidle over to River. His blond hair and tanned skin always have the ladies fawning over his surfer looks. When they hear his British accent, I've all but lost their interest to my best friend.

Then they find out we fuck together, or not at all, and it's as if we've won the jackpot. I watch Alysia and River while I down my drink in a few gulps. My gaze rakes over the club, taking in everyone within.

"Hello." A gentle tone comes from beside me. The large brown eyes I find remind me of a girl I lost a long while ago peer up at me with an innocent smile.

"Darling," I respond. Setting the bottle on the bar, I signal for another drink. "Are you old enough to be here?"

She blushes, dropping her gaze to the floor, then she drags her huge eyes to mine. "You're Drake Savage," she tells me earnestly, and I'm immediately on edge.

"And you are?" Arching an eyebrow, I watch her for a moment before leaning in closer. "I don't fuck unless I know your name." My whisper elicits a shiver from her slim frame, and I smile.

"Malcolm Savage was the one who got me this job, before he died." Her words send ice trickling through my veins. Mentioning my father's name is what catches my attention though, and I know that's what she's looking for.

"Who the fuck are you?" I hiss, gripping her bicep, dragging her up the steps that take us to the private VIP booths. Shoving her into one, I tug the curtain closed and pin her with a glare. "I asked you a fucking question, little girl."

"I'm Harper," she murmurs, a blush still evident on her face. The name she offers means nothing to me. Fuck all. I don't know how she knows me or my father, but I'll soon find out, even if I have to get violent.

"And your name should mean something to me?" Crossing my arms in front of my chest, I watch her flinch at my harsh tone. Perhaps I'm being too hard on her, but I have to be wary. Especially if I'm taking out my father's partners in the organization. It's not easy, and it's far from safe.

"My sister . . . She was taken four years ago," the girl tells me. "She had just turned eighteen, so she'd gone out with some friends to a party. I couldn't go with her because I was only sixteen at the time. I told her to stay home, that our father would be furious if he found out she wasn't at home. I waited up until I couldn't keep my eyes open anymore. I wasn't sure what had happened, but my father came home and told me my sister had to go away for a while. She . . ." Her words fall silent, and I realize I know exactly what she's trying to tell me.

"She didn't come home. Did she?" My question causes her to shake her head *no*. I already knew the answer, but I wanted confirmation.

So much for a good fuck tonight.

"What's your sister's name?" I ask, hoping I've at least heard of the girl. I can find out if Thanos has her working one of his clubs. But I'm not prepared for her answer. Not at all.

"Caia Amoretto."

Opening my mouth to respond, I can't find words. Caia's sister is standing in front of me, and all I want to do is help her, but she can't know her sister is in the same club she's standing in. Or at least, in the same city. For her to be here is dangerous, especially if she's working undercover. Thanos is not a good man on a normal day, but if he finds out Harper is looking for her sister, he'll kill her.

"I know who took her," Harper continues when I don't respond to her. Those big eyes meet my inquisitive gaze. There's so much truth in her gentle stare that I want to delve into them and bask in it, just like her sister's.

"You're here looking for Caia?" She nods. "You could get yourself killed. This man is not someone who plays games," I warn her.

"Will you help me get her back?" Her eyes glisten with unshed tears, and as much as I want to walk away, I know I can't. I promised to save Caia once before, and I need to keep that. At least if there's one good thing I do with my life, it's to give her back hers.

"You'll need to tell me everything," I inform her, settling in the booth opposite her. The curtain opens, and in walks River with a bottle of tequila and three shot glasses.

"I think we need these," he says, shoving me farther into the bench seat. He pours three shots and offers Harper one. She looks sixteen, but from what she's just told me, I know she's twenty.

"Tell me why you're here."

She nods and starts her story. I listen intently, lifting the shot glass, downing one after the other as I listen to the story about the girl I'll soon be meeting.

"How do you know she's here?"

Harper sighs. "A man called Thanos," she utters the name that's been top of my list. "I overheard Daddy talking to him when I snuck into his office years ago. At the time, I didn't know what it meant. But, two weeks ago, I overheard him on a call. Daddy told the man, Thanos, that he can keep Caia to pay off his debt."

"What debt?" River questions, but she shakes her head.

"I don't know. She's been here for four years, Drake. I don't even know if she's alive." Her voice breaks on the last word, and I know I have to shift Thanos up my list. He's next. "Drake, my sister isn't the only girl that's been missing. Caia's best friend was kidnapped over eight years ago. I remember my sister was distraught about it. When they took her, she was only fourteen at the time." Harper's words only cement my resolve. "There's one more thing."

"What?" River asks before I can.

"I ran away from home. My father . . .," she whispers. "He's done things. Bad things."

I know exactly what she means. When Malcolm died, we found the videos he had on all his clients. And Caia's father is one of them. I didn't know his name at the time, but now everything is falling into place. My father had marked the videos by initial and a number. Her father's video was labeled A457 for Amoretto. I never did find out what the numbers were, they didn't have any rhyme or reason.

I didn't even recognize Harper, but when she blinks and

the tears trickle down her cheeks, I see it. I see the girl from the video, and the alcohol turns in my stomach, causing bile to rise into my throat.

Meeting River's gaze, I nod. Offering him the signal he needs to set our plan in motion, I turn to Harper. "We'll get her back."

"Promise?"

Her voice is timid, her eyes round with fear, and there's an innocence to her even though she's lived through those videos that have gotten my father's clients jerking their dicks. She looks just like her sister; the only difference is she's not the one my body aches for.

"I swear."

My words are a vow. A promise. And I never break my promises.

CHAPTER FIVE
CAIA

The shadows hold me in their warmth.

At the moment, I'm safe.

Alone. But I know it won't last long.

My eyes blink in the dim light. Cold trickles through me from the chilly breeze sweeping through the room, causing me to shiver.

My skin, bare to the cold, dots with goosebumps. It's the same every night. Each time the moon rises and the sun falls, I feel the cold more than I do in the daytime. But the only reason I know night is falling is from the small hole in the wall that tells me so.

It's been four years since that day. When time stilled, and I was left with the darkness I wanted to escape. The moment I was taken from one hell and brought to another.

When I awoke, I was in this cell with no one to tell me what had happened. Scared, alone, and filled with anxiety, I cried until my tears ran dry. I recall the boy with the blue eyes. The one who looked like he was going to save me. I remember bleeding, his hands holding onto me like I was his lifeline, but I slipped through his fingers. I thought I would be free, but now I'm here, still caught in the dark.

The moment I woke up in this cell, my body had shuddered violently. So much so, I had puked all over my clothes, which he left me in for a week. When I finally got a chance to change into the small white nightdress they offered me, the dress Drake had put me in was crusted with my week-old vomit.

My captor allows me into his club. He's given me clothes to wear, made sure my body is inked so the scars below are hidden. My hair is no longer brown; it's a deep red. And soon, I know he'll get tired of me because I'm getting older.

Each day got more difficult. More painful. I was taken into rooms where there were men who would watch me. Some of the men didn't touch me, but they didn't need to because their eyes invaded every part of me. Between my legs, my budding chest, they looked at me like I was a meal for them to feast on. But it was the moment I was no longer just on show, that I was a toy to be used, that my mind clicked off, and I no longer felt anything. And I'm numb, turned off from the world surrounding me.

Each day turned into another, and another.

And now, four years later, I'm twenty-two, and still, I have no way of getting out. When I *work* in the club, he doesn't allow me to talk to anyone. I tried it once, and when he noticed, I was taken into a room and beaten until I passed out. Now, all I do is smile and allow them to do whatever they want. I don't ask for help. Hope is a fleeting emotion, one I no longer allow myself to feel.

Broken. Tormented. Angry.

My captor told me I had an anger problem. There were

times I'd fly into a rage. I'd hurt myself. When he saw the cuts on my arms, he whipped me until I couldn't sit down. That's when he put the camera in the cell I'm caged in. I know there's someone watching. I can feel their hungry eyes on me.

My body shivers once more when I roll over. The red blinking light is bright in the darkness as I stare up at it from the bed. I don't know when they'll come for me again, or when I'll be allowed to go upstairs and be taken to the club, but I have a feeling it will be soon.

Every time I'm transported there, they knock me out. I know it's because they don't want me to see where I am or where we're going. All I remember is the smell. A cloth drenched in foul-smelling liquid covering my mouth and nose, and I sleep.

When I get back here, I scream to be let out again, just to be a normal person. I shout and screech until all that's left is the raw, burning sensation that makes it feel as if I've been swallowing razor blades, and I half expect there to be blood coming from my mouth.

I've been in hell for four years, forced to do things I'd never wish on my worst enemy. I only know how long my time here has been because as the sun sets and rises, I count. The stony walls of concrete are my paper, the nail I pulled from the metal frame of the bed is my pen. I make my markings where they can't see them. Because if they did, I'd be in trouble. Perhaps they'll finally kill me, but something tells me I'm alive for a reason. I just wish I knew what that was.

I haven't been allowed outside, but he has let me go to his dinner parties. But no one there would help me. When I tried begging a guest to save me, they laughed in my face and told him his doll was being annoying. That night was the worst of all. He's always violent, but after that one night, I didn't leave my cell for four days because I almost bled out on my thin mattress.

THE PEOPLE ARE DRESSED IN THEIR FINEST CLOTHES. I'M DRAPED IN silk as if I'm one of them. I'm not. I'm merely a plaything for the man beside me. He uses me as his nark. I go in, meet with the men he points out, and I get the information he wants from them.

I don't want to do it, but I have no choice. If I refuse, he tells me exactly what he'll do to Harper. And that in itself is reason enough for me to do what he wants.

"The man at the table with the silver tie," William whispers to me. His mouth only inches from my ear. "He'll be tonight's target. You'll find out about his plans to unite the two merging companies he owns."

"Yes, William," I offer.

Moments later, I'm in the meeting room, as William calls it, with the man with the silver tie.

"You're quite the sweet thing," the stranger utters.

"Thank you." Being coy doesn't come easy to me. Neither does this game I'm meant to play with them. "Would you . . .?" I allow my words to trail off, wondering if this man would be the one who helps me. I allow my bright red fingernail to toy with his tie. Lifting my gaze, I meet his eyes and smile. "Would you help me leave here?"

He chuckles. The sound is dark and foreboding, and as soon as it leaves his mouth, I realize my mistake. He shoves me backward. Stalking to the door, he tugs it open to find William on the other side.

"Your little whore is trying to weasel her way into my house?"

William's dark gaze lands on me as he shoves the man from the room and shuts the door with a loud thud. My heart hammers wildly in my chest. Breathing is difficult as I try to suck in breaths.

"You're a conniving little slut," he barks, shoving me onto the table face first. The impact causes my body to turn rigid. There's a soft whooshing sound, and I don't need to turn around to know what it is.

The red-hot sting on my skin is evidence that his thick leather belt is licking my ass. Again, and again. He's grunting with every exertion of the smooth weapon of choice this time. He whips me countless times. I can't feel anything but burning, the heat of liquid trickling down my thighs, and I know I'm bleeding.

I don't cry.

I can't.

My eyes are dry.

My lips are parted in a silent scream.

He rips the elegant dress I'm wearing from my curves, and then I'm filled painfully with his thick cock. He's rock-hard, sliding into my dry entrance, causing a lone tear to trickle from me.

Three, four, five.

On the sixth plunge into my body, he groans as pleasure rockets through him. When he pulls from my body, he grips my hair in a harsh hold and shoves me to my knees. His cock, dripping with his sticky white release and the crimson liquid from my body, he shoves into my mouth.

"Clean me." His words are venomous. "You deserve this for

trying to leave me. Stupid little cunt thinks she's too good for me."

He fucks my face, the tip of his cock sliding into my throat over and over again until he slaps me to the ground and stuffs his shrinking, almost flaccid dick into his slacks. Before he leaves, he spits on my face and chuckles when cower.

"That will teach you."

And then I'm alone.

I WATCH AS THE SUN SLOWLY SETS FROM THE SMALL HOLE AGAINST the far wall, the orange glow turning to a deep red then purple. The colors like an artist's brush on a canvas. It only reminds me how far I am from my old life. I don't remember much. It's been far too long since I've seen someone who I recognized as something other than a monster — someone other than him, Drake Savage.

His father, Malcolm, was the reincarnation of the devil himself. I remember the old man who made me watch those videos. The horrific scenes still haunt me, playing in my mind like movies on a never-ending loop.

Then I remember Drake, and I wish he were here. For some reason, he offered me solace in his cold, harsh words. And I wonder if he'll ever find me again.

My captor, William Thanos, has given one of the guards an order to teach me to fight. I wondered why he'd do that until I realized it wasn't to protect myself, but to hurt others he brings down here. Last week, it was an eighteen-year-old boy.

William threatened to steal my sister and make her do things that made me sick to my stomach if I didn't comply.

So, I did. I slit the throat of an innocent teenager because the man who holds me prisoner told me to.

So many days have passed, and I wonder just what month or year it really is. All I want is to spend time with my sister, to see her again. Harper was my light. All I wanted was for her to be safe. But when I saw the video of her and our father . . .

I'M BOUND TO THE CHAIR. MY HEAD IS SECURE, AND I CAN'T TURN away from what's happening on the computer before me. My mouth is gagged, so no sound can escape besides my mumbling.

The wand vibrates against my clit as I'm forced to stare at the white images onscreen. It doesn't take long before the video plays, and I realize I'm being tortured once more.

A man walks onscreen, but I can't see his face. Slowly, he unbuttons his shirt. And as he removes more of his clothes, my tormentor's low rumble is sadistic as he laughs, while the vibration is still poised at my clit, which sparks every nerve in my body.

The object being forced into me is rough, and I can't help crying out around the gag that's bound around my head keeping my lips parted. The sound is accompanied by the video playing before me.

When the sound is turned up, it's all I can hear, as if it's in surround sound. I want to block it out, but I'm unable to. My eyes are wide with shock as I take in the horrific scene before me.

I'm met with the sounds of the old man onscreen as he grunts in pleasure while he violently forces himself inside the throat of a girl who looks so familiar. It's a girl I've known my whole life. And as if my eyes are glued open, they tear up, and the image onscreen blurs, but nothing can stop me seeing it. Nothing can stop me recognizing the girl whose teary gaze meets the lens. The man moves to offer us a view of her pretty brown eyes—the image of my sister. It's Harper. There's no mistaking her beautiful eyes that shimmer with pained tears.

There's blood dripping from her nose, and she's lying upside down. Her head hanging over the edge of the bed. Her bed. I know the blanket my mother bought her when we were younger.

I watch in horror as she's violated once more by the old man. When he slowly turns to the camera and chuckles as his cock is lodged in her throat, bile rises from my stomach, but because of the ball gag in my mouth, there's nowhere for it to go but spill over the sides.

My heart catapults wildly when his face comes onscreen, and the vibrator against my clit is turned up harshly, causing pleasure and pain to skitter through me like a ten-pound weight.

An orgasm rocks me when I look into the eyes of my father, and all I can do is succumb to the force of agony that I'm thoroughly fucking broken.

I've been torn from a normal life.

I'm severed.

IT WAS AT THAT MOMENT I KNEW THERE WASN'T ANY HOPE FOR her. Unless she ran. I pray every day that she managed to get away from him. Deep down, I wish she killed him. Every day since that one, I've prayed my sister killed my father for what he did. Because I know if she didn't, I would do it. And I wouldn't feel an ounce of guilt for it.

He deserves to be tortured. To be maimed while he slowly bleeds out. My blood is on fire, and the need to slice him limb to limb runs rife through my veins. And in this moment, I realize what Drake felt all those years ago. That's how he spent his life, wanting to kill the man who was meant to love and guide him through life.

I saw it in his eyes. Each time he came for me, when those blue eyes met mine, I would see deep into his tortured soul. All the time I spent in that hellhole, I never believed Drake was anything like Malcolm. And even now, I know he's nothing like the monster who tried to kill me.

Something tells me that since I've passed twenty-one, I'll no longer be needed, and I'll find my end in this hell. The men here aren't fond of older girls. I've met one other girl since I've been here. She is twenty-one, and I know she's been here since she was very young. The thought has my body trembling in fear and revulsion.

But for me, the girl who had everything in a life that's now a distant memory, I now have nothing. My father gave me all my heart desired. The eldest of two, I was generally the one everyone focused on. Harper would hide in my shadow. Sadness envelops me at the thought of her being hurt in any way. I couldn't protect her.

It's so silent in this basement I wonder where he is. Will he come down here tonight and take me? Or will I have a reprieve from the torment? I never try to fight him anymore; he enjoys it when I do. So, I lie there. A doll. Taking what he gives. The pain, the force he grunts into me with, and the grip on my flesh that leaves blue and purple bruises over my body.

I'm no longer the princess of an upcoming empire. I'm now a fuck-toy for a man who enjoys depraved, vile things. And I'm his vessel for that. Nothing worth more than he offers. My mind has almost cracked. It's what he wants. He told me so.

All this time, I thought I'd be able to get out. All my life,

I thought I was strong, that nothing in this world could ever make me lose hope, but this is different. The monsters I'm held by are far worse than anything I've ever encountered in my short life outside this place. The agony I've been forced to endure has broken my soul. I've given up after all this time, because there's no way I'll ever be able to survive much longer.

My body is weak. They don't feed me enough to be able to fight my way out. The water I drink is murky, clouded over with whatever drugs they're feeding into my system. I swallow every drop because it's the only sustenance I get. My fight is slowly fading.

Sounds echo when the keys enter the keyhole to the door which allows them to enter the basement where I've lived for four years. I flinch when I hear their footfalls, heavy and ominous. Two sets. I can still count the way I was taught. In this hell, I try to keep my mind busy, but it's difficult when there's nothing to offer stimulus.

"The little one is awake." His voice comes from the other side of the cell before he appears at the bars. I scoot up the bed, pulling my knees to my chest, wrapping my arms around my calves. It's pointless hiding. He's already seen me naked, but each time he comes here, I try to conceal myself. All I'm wearing is a pair of white cotton panties they've allowed me to cover up with. I'm not allowed a blanket. There's one pillow, which feels like it's made of stone.

"She's been quiet this evening, sir," the man who feeds me says. He's bulky, with dark skin, which reminds me of coffee. His eyes are black, penetrating. Pools of tar which hypnotize me. The man who took me stares at me for a moment. He's taken me to lavish parties, allowed me to eat the most decadent meals, but as soon as the lights go down, he drags me kicking and screaming to this pit and leaves me alone in the dark like a dog that's being punished.

"Hello, little one," William smirks. His eyes are the color of onyx. An abyss of treachery and torment shimmer as they pierce me. "Are you talking today?" he asks. I should answer. If I don't, I'll be punished. I know this, but I can't. My throat burns with the agony of knowing he can hurt me so much more than he already has. Even so, I don't reply.

His eyes roam over me for a moment, taking in my appearance. My red hair is long because he prefers it that way, so he can tug at it. His fist clenches around the locks, pulling my head up and toward him. I don't know why I'm still here, still alive. I honestly have no idea.

"Not talking tonight?" he questions. His head tips to the side as he regards me with a satisfied smirk. Perhaps if I play the broken doll, he'll let me go. But I know it's wishful thinking. The thing about it is, I've seen his face. I know what he looks like, and he knows the first thing I'd do as soon as he let me go is talk to the police.

"What do you want to do with her, sir?" *Coffee* says. His voice is a deep rumble, reminding me of thunder rolling through the sky, alerting everyone a storm is on the way.

"Let's see if she wants to tell me anything today," the man with eyes the color of onyx tells *Coffee*. "I think it's time we got her to open up about all those secrets in her pretty little head. Perhaps if it wasn't so pretty, she'd tell us more. Wouldn't you, little one?" Each day, they ask me a series of questions that I don't know the answer to. With each incorrect answer, they shock me with the electric

Taser. Either that, or if *he's* here, he hurts me in other violent, immoral ways.

"I . . ." My voice is croaky as I try to respond. My throat burns when I clear it, as if there's sandpaper moving back and forth over my vocal cords. "I really don't know." I hate that I sound weak. Like a stupid little girl. I suppose I am. Young and stupid. That's why he likes me. He enjoys hurting me because he knows he shouldn't.

His hair is graying at the sides, hinting at his age. An older man with a penchant for girls young enough to be his daughter. I know for a fact he's got tightly packed muscle under the suit he wears. A businessman with a darkness he hides from his clients, but his friends are well-versed in his sick desires.

"I think there's so much more you know. All we have to do is unlock it. Reveal everything I need to know and then you can go home. Doesn't that sound nice?" His sneer sends fear racing through me. It's never going to stop.

Most men are power hungry. They'll stop at nothing to be gods. They have a penchant for taking what's not theirs to take. I know this because the man before me, the one who was once a stranger with the black eyes, stole everything from me until I had nothing left to give.

"Do what you must." My words aren't angry; they're defeated. I'm broken. There's nothing more left inside me, and it scares me. I feel as if I'll never be whole again. A phone vibrates and sings somewhere on one of the men, and my heart leaps into my throat. But as much as I'd like to scream for help, if I do, I'll be dead before whoever is on the other line arrives.

"Yes." His gruff voice sounds even more foreboding when he answers. While he listens to the caller with intrigue etched on his face, he watches me. Taunting me, waiting for me to try and act brave. But I'm not. Even though escaping is the only thing on my mind, I know it's futile. "I'll have my men bring her up. I think that would be splendid. Tonight, at nine is perfect. We'll have dinner, and you're welcome to try your luck with the stupid little toy."

When he hangs up, he meets my gaze. The darkness only makes him look more ominous. He reminds me of the monsters that starred in my childhood nightmares.

"Looks like you've hit the jackpot, little one. Tonight, you'll go to your new home. I'm sorry you can't see your precious daddy, but perhaps one day when you're both dead, rotting in hell, you'll meet again."

"Fuck you!" I don't know where my voice comes from, but the mention of my father only spurs me on. I've been silent for a long while. It's been two weeks since I spoke to him like this. Each time I've been questioned, it's been by *Coffee*.

His dark eyes seem to light up at my words. "Open your goddamn mouth," he hisses at me. I know what I've done. I've angered him, and there's only one way he handles that. Once the door is shut, he smirks down at me evilly. His eyes glower with rage.

His hands fist my red tresses in a violent grip. The hold so tight I cry out in pain. I must look like a forgotten toy on the side of the road. He shoves his zipper down and pulls out his flaccid dick. It's not small by any means. You'd think an asshole like this would be, but no, even soft he's able to choke me. He drops me on the floor, against the cold concrete wall. My head slams into the stone so hard I see stars.

"I said, open your fucking mouth," he grunts, and I do.

There's nothing I can say to stop this. As soon as my lips part, his cock slams into my mouth. I feel it jolt and thicken as he assaults my face. Back and forth, until moments later, he's rock-hard.

The tip hits the back of my throat, sliding farther, and I'm sure they can see the shape of it in my throat. He grunts and groans above me, one hand holding onto my hair, the other bracing himself against the wall. His hips piston into me painfully as he fucks my throat, and I feel it, the bile rising. I try to push him away, but I can't. He's too strong.

He grips my nose closed and forces his cock so far down my throat I retch violently. My stomach convulses. I see stars. It's dark, but the white pinpricks that dance behind my eyelids taunt me. The burning liquid, which was the meagre lunch I was fed only four hours ago, falls from my mouth and drenches my bare skin.

Tears stream down my cheeks, and I fall limp against the wall.

"You filthy bitch," he barks at me. Pulling his cock from my mouth, he jerks himself while he insults me. "You love being fucked, don't you? Little slut." His words are painful, vile, and degrading. "Stupid bitch likes me using her holes." I know why he's doing this. He can't get off without being an evil piece of shit. Then I feel the jets of hot semen painting my broken body. I curl up as he turns to walk out of the cell. "Clean her up for tonight."

It's the last thing I remember as I pass out.

CHAPTER SIX
DRAKE

As soon as I hang up from the call with Thanos, I smile up at River. After what Harper told us, I knew there was only one thing I could do, and that's buy her sister from the man who stole her from me. The plan is set in motion. We're scheduled to meet with William for a dinner, and he confirmed what we already knew — he's holding the girl there.

Soon, I'll gut the fucker, and Caia will be safe with her sister. *And me.* The thought leaps into my mind unbidden. Do I really want to keep her for myself? Will she even want me? No, it's stupid to think she'll choose to stay with me. My father hurt her far beyond repair, and I stood by and watched it happen. The only thing I can do once I've freed her is to let her go. To allow her to live the life she missed out on.

"It's all set up?" River questions.

Nodding, I pick up the tumbler and swallow the liquid. "Yes. We'll get her out of there and then we'll give both girls new identities. Set that up and get the passports ready."

My best friend nods. "Sure, that's the easy part. If Thanos's guards—"

"I'll kill the lot of them." I'm adamant my plan won't fail. William Thanos will never see the light of day again; I'll ensure that. And those assholes that follow him around like puppies will meet their maker as well.

"I know you will. I don't doubt you, but I want to be there," River tells me. When I meet his gaze, I know why he wants to be there. The man we're about to take down stole a lot from us.

The day my father died, I knew River felt a sense of peace. I could see it in his eyes. The past will soon be behind us, a distant memory, and I'll ensure my best friend gets his vengeance.

"We'll go together," I tell him.

Tonight, I'll ensure one of his greatest enemies meets a horrible death. It may not be the last one on the list that River and I plan to take down. But it will certainly not stop us from exacting justice.

When I reach the last name on my list, I don't know what I'll do. Perhaps take a vacation. Maybe I'll find peace in knowing they're all dead and buried. And maybe, just maybe, I'll find a way to move on.

Thanos sounded excited when I spoke to him about the girl he's got hold up in a cell. He thinks I'm meeting him for her. Perhaps I am. It's been years since I laid eyes on the pretty girl. Years since I've wanted her, needed her to the point of being paralyzed with desire.

For a long time, I thought of myself as her savior. The sad thing is, she's been there far longer than I care to think about. I know why he took her. She's beautiful, or at least, from what I remember, she was pure and beautiful. Even though she was bleeding out on me, I knew I'd want her for the rest of my godforsaken life.

However, what intrigues me is why Thanos wanted her. Why he kept her for all this time, and he hasn't yet killed her or worse. There were many girls who passed through our organization, but none of them ever grabbed his attention. I know he runs his own underground shithole, but I doubt it's anything like my father's.

Four years.

Long, lonely years.

It never stopped them before. But Caia Amoretto was stronger than the others. The thought causes bile to rise in my throat because I know what strong girls suffer. Shaking my head, I swallow my hatred down. Keeping a level head is the only thing I need to do.

Thanos is convinced I'll be there to put money on the table to take her away, but I'll be there to ensure he bleeds out all over his designer suit.

I make my way to the bedroom, grab my suit jacket, and shrug it on. A glance in the mirror reflects my raven-colored hair, blue eyes, and the cigarette hanging from my mouth.

"I'll give you fifteen minutes from the moment you enter his house to the second me and the team sweep the dungeon and rooms," River says. I glance up, and I see it in his eyes. The emotion he holds for me. Each time I head out on a job, he's beside me. And as much as I don't want him to care for me, he does.

It's unwarranted. He knows it as well as I do, but that doesn't stop him from showing it, feeling it. I don't blame him, but I can't offer it in return. Not right now.

"Is the room set up for her when we get back?" He nods in response. "I have no idea of her state of mind. Four years is a long time, and that asshole is a vile piece of work," I tell him, and the recognition flickers in his green gaze.

"Are you talking about us or her?"

Turning to him, I find myself speechless for a moment. Thanos was one of the first clients my father introduced us to. River and I had to show him what we were capable of. Needless to say, it's a memory I don't often revisit.

"DRAKE, RIVER, COME IN HERE," FATHER CALLS TO US. He's meeting with one of his newest clients, and I should've hidden in my room with my best friend, but stupidly, I didn't think he'd want us here for the contract signing.

"Yes, Father." I offer a smile, but it's fake, like so many things in this house.

"This is one of my newest partners," Malcolm smirks. "He's just invested fifteen million for two products."

I know what that means. Those products will soon be brought in to the dungeons below and tortured.

"I'd like you to show him how well you're doing within the organization." My father's expression is one of no nonsense. I can't refuse him. If I do, he'll hurt River. I think he knows about my feelings for my best friend. And that's a dangerous thing.

"I . . . I'm not sure . . ."

The thunderous expression stills my mouth. My words fail in the moment my father rises and stalks toward me. His hand grips my throat, shoving me to my knees. He leans in, sneering as he hisses, "This is your future. I trust you'll behave, Drake."

Spittle flies from his mouth. I nod slowly. My heart thudding wildly in my chest, it's beating a rhythm of agony and fear. A song I've heard far too many times.

"Or would you like me to call Dante in here?"

"No, I can do it," I utter swiftly. Knowing that my brother would be hurt makes me confirm that I choose my life to be snuffed before his.

"Good boy. You and River can entertain William while I get the maid to set up lunch." Malcolm chuckles, leaving me at the hands of the man who's now risen from the armchair and is slowly unzipping his slacks.

"Both of you, on your knees," William orders, and River joins me on the carpet. The old man tugs his cock, fisting the flaccid shaft as he grips my hair, slapping me in the face with his now hardening dick. "That's it."

I can't move. His hold on me is tight. In an attempt to save my sanity, I close my eyes and picture something else. I go to a place inside my mind. An island where it's only me, my brother, and River.

My best friend's fingers find mine in a show of solidarity. We're in this together. My mouth is invaded in the next instant. The tip of William's dick is lodged in my throat, causing my body to shudder as revulsion trails through me like a freight train.

He continues violating my mouth until suddenly he stills. I think it's over, but it most certainly isn't. He saunters over to where River is kneeling and continues his assault.

In this moment, I wish for death. I want my best friend and me to both find it, to die together and be free of this nightmare. But I know it won't come.

William pulls his now steel shaft from River's mouth and makes his way back to the chair. When he settles in it, he smirks over at us, barking another order.

"Fuck each other," he tells us. "I want to watch you." He points at me. "Suck him till he's about to burst." He gestures to River. This I can do. Can't I? Glancing at my best friend, I notice the slight nod he offers, and I know he'd prefer me doing this than the vile asshole who's sitting on the chair feet away. I move quickly.

I'm about to tug my boxer briefs down when the door flies open and my brother is shoved into the room. My heart aches when I notice the pain in his eyes.

"Ah, there we go. I requested him earlier," Thanos offers. "On your knees. You'll be part of my little fantasy." The old man chuckles. "On your knees, boy. Drake, here, will be pleasuring you both."

My hardened gaze snaps to the old man who laughs at my mouth falling open in shock. I'm shaking my head before I realize what I'm doing. But he's having none of it. Pulling a gun from the back of his trousers, he points it at Dante.

"Do it, or your brother will die with his dick in your mouth."

The shame of what I'm forced to do, forced to act out, burns through me. Yes, I want my best friend, but not like this. Not being held at gunpoint. Not being here for someone's sick pleasure. And I know my life is completely severed from anything normal again.

"HER. WE . . . WE'VE BEEN THROUGH IT ALL, BUT WE'RE STILL here. Working our way through the pain. She will too. I'll make sure of that," I vow.

"But how much longer are you going to hide your feelings?" he asks, and I know I deserve it. I should tell him I love him. And I do. But I can't bring myself to admit it. Not because I don't want to, but because the confusion that settles in my mind when I think about Caia and River makes me wonder how I can love two people equally. Is that even possible?

"Let's get this done, River. I'm not in the mood for this emotional shit," I tell him as I rise and grab my black combat boots. Shoving my feet into them, I ensure they're laced and stalk by him into the foyer.

"Listen to me," River says, closing the distance between us. His hand settles on my shoulder. It's confirmation that he's worried, but he has no need to be. I can do this. "This asshole isn't some fly-by-night buyer. He's trained. I'll be in the background. The team will be too, if you need anything."

"When I walk out of his house drenched in blood, with the girl in my arms, that's when I want you to worry about me." Casting a glance over my shoulder, I offer him a smile. One that tells him *I'm okay.*

He responds with one of his signature grins. It's sincere, handsome, everything I want from River. Then he murmurs, "I'll always worry about you."

"I know." My words are harsher than I expect, but he doesn't notice. He's too concerned about my well-being. The first time I kissed him was like being electrocuted. I was merely a vessel, and his warmth invaded me, filled me. When I was with women, I didn't feel that same emotion. Until Caia, and that's what scares the shit out of me.

"Just come back to me, Drake," he finally mutters.

Those five words are what he's always uttered to me. Each *meeting* I've been on, he'd always tell me to come back, and I've always returned. Nothing can ever take me away from him. Our past is riddled with excruciating pain, vile acts, and images that would haunt even the darkest souls, but it's ours. Something we share, and nobody can take that away.

I lean in, giving him some of the affection I know he craves. Our lips touch, his mold to mine, and I grip his hair, holding him steady as I dip my tongue into his mouth. He groans when I suck his tongue hard, biting down on the flesh, which causes another soft grunt to rumble through his chest.

The kiss heats when his hand finds my thigh. His touch isn't gentle, not like a woman's. It's rough, needy, and it matches my own desire. Our tongues duel for control, the taste of him overwhelming me, and I know I need to stop it. I need to put an end to this, or I'll never leave. And we'll end up on the floor with my cock inside his ass.

Pulling away, I stare at him for a moment. "This . . . We need to stop this, River," I tell him breathlessly. He nods. He knows I'm lying. Every day, without fail, I tell him the same thing. I don't want him waiting for me if I don't come back. It doesn't matter who was sitting in the seat beside me, I could never ask someone to pray for my return, not when I didn't want to return anyway.

"See you later," he concedes, knowing there's no way I will admit my feelings.

I head out the door with my phone and keys. Ensuring my smokes are in the inner pocket of my jacket, along with the holster holding my Glock. My sweet baby I never leave home without.

It's an hour's drive to the estate on the outskirts of town. A place where men do as they please. And I know one of those men used to be my father. All the truths that spilled from the pages of his dossiers sickened me. Granted, I'm an asshole, but the things I did were by force. I never had a choice. Except for the moment I first sunk my dick into Caia's mouth. The moment I felt heaven for the first time.

There's a limit to the damage you incite on someone, and I know the only people I would ever find pleasure in killing are the ones on my list.

My father didn't stop at nameless girls. He tortured his own sons. He did it to River, the boy who became more like family. I recall the moment he entered our home with his mother. The woman who left him there.

"HEY," THE BOY WITH THE GREEN EYES SAYS TO ME. THERE'S confidence radiating off him, but there's also something I've come to learn is happiness. I don't often allow kids in my space, but he doesn't ask permission when he leaps onto my bed. He shuffles himself against the headboard, then watches me.

"What are you doing?"

"I'm new here. My mom says I'm going to stay with you while she goes to work," his innocent voice offers as he smiles at me, and I find myself staring in shock and awe at him. He's pretty. Can you call a boy pretty? Maybe not, but he is.

"I don't want you in my room." I sound so angry. I hate being like this, but I can't help it. Not even Dante, my brother, comes in here. He knows my rules. Nobody is allowed in my space. But this boy . . . "What's your name?"

"River." He smiles.

"What kind of fucking name is that?"

His eyes widen at my curse word. We're only ten, but that doesn't matter. I can say anything I want. My dad doesn't care

142

what happens to me as long as I do what he says when he sends me to the dungeon.

"It's the best fucking name. What's yours?" He lifts his chin, folding his hands behind his head as if he's never been more comfortable, and it bothers me. I don't want him here, but I can't tell him to leave.

"Drake," I tell him, shrugging off his chuckle.

"I like it," he tells me with a grin so wide I can't stop the one that curls my lips. This boy is bad news. "My mom said your dad is helping her with work."

My body stills. An icy chill makes me shiver at his words, and I realize that this isn't "work." This is something else. I don't know what his mother told him, but I have a feeling River will be spending a lot more time here than he thinks.

"You're going to need a room," I tell him.

"Thanks, mate."

And as he follows me down the hallway, I shove open the door beside mine. If he's going to be stuck in this place, he might as well be next door to me.

HIS MOTHER LEFT THAT DAY AND NEVER CAME BACK. SHE WAS ONE of Malcolm's most esteemed clients, but I would never tell River that. He thinks she's dead. Murdered by some stranger in the night. I'm still not sure where she is; we haven't found her yet. Perhaps my father pulled the trigger while he was balls-deep inside her whore cunt.

Tonight, I take out the man who stole our innocence, along with the man who seeded my mother's womb. Thanos wrenched the purity from River and me, and there was nothing we could do about it. Helpless is something I'll never be again, not when it comes to the monsters who haunted my childhood nightmares.

A while ago, River asked me what I'd do once the list was complete. I couldn't answer him because as much as I wanted to tell him I'd move to London and be with him, I knew my heart wasn't there. Not at the time.

After I've completed my mission, maybe I'll find purpose again. But right now, there's no way I'll walk away from what I know I need to do. Keeping Dante, Caia, and River safe is my number-one priority. Second is exacting my revenge and finding my mother. I believed she died long ago, but when Malcolm knew when he took his last breath that I'd find the one last damning secret he'd been keeping all this time — she's alive somewhere.

Once I find her, perhaps then I'll be able to let go of the anger I hold close to my chest. Maybe then my life will feel like it matters, because right now, it's a maelstrom of darkness and destruction.

Memories of my past invade my mind. The father I thought was meant to care for Dante and me only used us as pawns in his game. He created me. His most loyal follower. The son he tormented for years before turning me into a toy for his own sick pleasure.

His love for power, desire for money, and hunger for respect made him a monster. I never thought I'd hate anyone, but as time passed, Malcolm became more engrossed in the darkness. He ensured I would be what he needed.

I think the moment he lost our mother he no longer cared. She was his light, and when the light diminished and went out forever, evil enveloped him.

Sadness grips me for a moment, but I push it down. I

hide it from view because the last thing I need is for this asshole to see my weakness. If there's one good thing I did learn from dear old Dad, it's that you should never let your enemy see your weakness.

It's the one thing that can get you killed.

CHAPTER SEVEN
DRAKE

The city lights speed by as I put my foot down on the gas pedal. My onyx Audi R8 zips through the near-enough empty streets as I make my way farther out of the city and closer toward the final stage of my plan. Dante has no idea what I lived through, and he doesn't know why I'm so adamant to complete this list of names. I can't tell him. Nobody, besides River, can ever know.

I couldn't tell my brother. The truth would only hurt him. As much as I fought my brother through our years of growing up, I love him and would do anything to ensure his safety. And now, the safety of Caia.

I still think about the one girl who meant something to me for the time she was locked in a cell in the dungeon. She was the first girl I'd thought of keeping for myself, who I wanted to love. But she was broken, so much so that I knew deep down there no turning back. Sometimes, when you want someone as much as I wanted her, it's best to walk away. She shattered before me. Her small body bleeding out as I attempted to pray to a god that doesn't exist. For years I thought she had died. But now, there's hope. Something I didn't think I would ever feel again. She isn't dead; she was just bought like an object.

I don't know what her state of mind will be when I finally lay my eyes on her again. After being here for so long, I'm certain she's so broken she doesn't even remember me. Or she could be working for Thanos and has finally given up on freeing herself, and she's planning to kill us all for what she's been through — giving in to the anger and vengeance that most probably fills her heart.

That night will forever stay with me. Haunt me. The nightmares I still have where she inhales broken breaths while blood spurts from her chest visit me every damn night. But the moment they wrenched her from my arms, the flicker of hope I had for the short time she was in my life went out, never to be lit again. It was something I had to come to terms with.

A memory assaults me as the road darkens, turning black before my very eyes.

"Dr-Drake," she sputters in blood from her lips. It makes her look deathly beautiful. I lean in, planting a kiss on her mouth, tasting the metallic liquid. I know he's watching. He knew I'd fallen for her. And this is his lesson. I'm not allowed to feel.

All she is now is a pretty, broken toy. There's nothing left, her body draining itself in front of me.

"I-I lo-loved you." Her words are filled with emotion. The real, heart-stopping kind. I nod. I know she did, but the problem is I was too focused on revenge, and I'd forgotten that all we

needed was each other to get through the dark. Not even Dante knew. She was mine. My secret.

I wanted to steal her away, and instead, I'm stuck here without her. "You need to close your eyes now, Caia. I'll find you. I'll save you." My words are low. I don't want him to hear me, but when Malcolm drops to his knees beside her, she glances back and forth between us.

It takes everything inside me to not attack him for doing this, but when I look at what I've turned into, I know it was the only choice. I would've killed her in my madness. With the sickness riddling my brain, there's no telling what I could have put her through.

"This is for the best, son." He slaps a hand on my shoulder as if he's just told me he's proud of me. Perhaps he is. Maybe he's not angry at all and he'll forget that my plan to stop them from hurting her would've jeopardized everything he worked so hard for. I was supposed to be the good son, but instead, I'm going to be the one who turns into him, the monster I've spent my life hating.

I watch as one of my father's guards lifts her limp form in his arms, and jealousy rages through me. I saw him with her. In the darkness of her cell, I watched how he hurt her, and I didn't do anything to save her. Guilt surges through me. She didn't know I was there, watching from the shadows as he took her, again and again.

Eighteen, and she's dead because I couldn't stop myself from loving her. Our game has ended, and we both lost. There'll be no more talking, touching, me watching her.

"I love you, Caia. Even in this darkness," I whisper to her, my lips not moving, so only I know what I've uttered. Her body jerks, blood oozes from her, and I watch as the white button-up the asshole wears is drenched in it. The pretty crimson fluid that

I've reveled in so many times now flows from the one woman I love.

That emotion will never again take anything from me. Because I will never give my heart to another. I'll never let anyone get close enough to see my now-blackened heart. As the life finally dissipates from her eyes, I vow that my emotions will die with Caia. My heart will be buried in her hands, with no chance of being recovered.

SHAKING MY HEAD, HOPING TO RID THE MEMORY FROM THE forefront of my mind, I make the left turn leading to the large monstrosity sitting on the hill overlooking the city.

The gates are lit by two yellow gargoyle lamps which illuminate the lions' heads on the ebony metal. Since the house sits outside the city, there are no other lights for miles.

Enveloped in darkness, the three-floor mansion looms over hills of greenery. A buzzer sits at the entrance to the drive, beckoning me to make contact. Inhaling a steadying breath, I push the button, and a camera appears in the black screen.

"Yes?" a deep, gruff tone comes in greeting from the speaker.

"Mr. Savage to see Mr. Thanos," I tell him. A soft buzzing sounds through the speaker, and the large iron gates slide open, allowing me entrance to Hell. This is the one place that's always left me with a sense of forbidding. I know what happens behind the high walls. I've seen the dinner parties and poker evenings run by Thanos and my father. Anxiety grips my chest painfully at the memories that flit through my mind as I am granted entrance.

The driveway is long. It offers me the chance to remember the times we'd come here. As it winds, I realize this could be the last time I drive up to this place. Dante and I will shut down everything my father had built. When I finally get a glimpse of the house, all the lights shimmer like a beacon, and I wonder what exactly awaits me on the other side of those walls.

As the car inches up the pavement and the mansion comes into view, I can't help the excitement at finally getting my revenge on the man who helped my father all these years. And at finding the girl who stole my heart without even knowing it.

Thanos will meet his maker tonight. He needs to pay for his sins. I look forward to driving a blade through his chest, twisting it while his blood seeps from the wound.

It's been a while since I've been around him. Most of the months since Malcolm died, I've avoided him. The others we took down dealt in drugs, weapons, but Thanos is special. He buys young girls and boys — and I mean *young* — for pleasure. He uses them, breaks them, then discards them like damaged toys. I know, because I've seen it.

When I exit the car, I stroll toward the door I hope doesn't open, but I know it will. He wants my money. He promised to sell me the doll he's currently playing with in order for me to extract the information he needs from her. Only, he doesn't realize he's made a deal with the fucking devil.

Upon reaching the door, I don't have to knock because it slides open, and on the other side is a woman who must be in her early twenties. She looks as lost as I feel. Her blonde hair is pinned behind her head in a low ponytail. Dressed in a matching, form-fitting top and skirt, I notice how skinny she is, but her tits are spilling from the top of the material. Her big brown eyes are dull, lifeless, as if her soul is dead. She's a walking shell, and I know exactly why.

"Good evening, sir. May I take—?"

"Show me to the dining room," I tell her without so much as a greeting. I'm not here for pleasantries. I'm here to extract the girl, kill the asshole, and have River clean up the mess.

The skeletal hostess leads me through the large home and into a room decked out in silver and the finest china. This isn't who I am, and this asshole knows it. But he's trying to impress me because he's under the impression I've taken over the organization from my father. Since we've kept Malcolm's death from his associates, telling them that he's stepped down offered me the opportunity to let them think I'm in charge. He's attempting to ensure my allegiance to his business. But there's nothing that could make me want to give this asshole anything.

"Drake Savage." His gruff tone comes from behind me, and I turn to find Thanos strolling in with a smirk of satisfaction on his face. He's old, even though his hair is still dark, there's gray on either side of his face, and I know he's in his early fifties now.

"William Thanos," I greet, shaking his hand.

His expression is pleasant, but his eyes conceal hidden truths far too terrifying for anyone to fathom. Something must have happened prior to my arrival. There's something about him I can't pinpoint, but I notice the sick satisfaction emanating from him.

"The little toy is getting cleaned up. She was misbehaving, and I had to teach her a lesson," he informs me, settling himself in the chair at the head of the table.

Bile rises into my throat, burning its way into my mouth, and I have to fight to swallow it down. A waiter with the same lifeless eyes as the hostess enters with a bottle of red wine. I can't see the label, but he fills my glass, then Thanos's. With a swift bow, he leaves us.

"And what exactly do you feel is proper training for toys?" I question, lifting the wine to my lips, taking a long gulp. My gaze never leaves the monster that sits on his throne.

"I went easy on her tonight. She threw up on my dick. She has to learn never to do that again. When you take her this evening, I trust she'll behave." He chuckles, and it takes all my restraint not to shove the glass in his face and cut him a new fucking hole to spurt shit from.

"I see. And you haven't thought about giving her a lashing?" I question, playing his game, and I know he'll fall into my trap. My gaze doesn't leave his over the rim of the crystal wine glass.

"Oh, she's had plenty of those. Tonight, though, I wanted to ensure her porcelain skin is unmarked. You are welcome to inspect her. I'm intrigued to see your methods."

Of course, you are.

"I look forward to meeting this beauty you've been telling me about," I say. The doors slide open, causing me to shut my mouth. Two staff members walk in — both dressed in black slacks and white shirts — a boy and girl, who can't be older than sixteen.

They set our plates down. Steaming food, which normally would have me salivating, now only makes me nauseated. A steak, rare from the blood dripping from it, along with a large green salad, sits on the expensive crockery.

I'm about to thank him when the air changes and the hairs on the back of my neck stand on end. Lifting my gaze, I turn to find a girl standing in the doorway. Her body is boyish in the clothes they've dressed her in, showing off her tits which are a handful, if that, along with slim hips and bare feet.

But when I lift my gaze to her face, that's when my heart stops. Her big, hazel eyes are glaring at me. Her full, darkened, pink lips are plump, causing my dick to stir in response. They're perfection, and I know they'll look incredible sliding up and down my shaft. The memory of the night she took me in her mouth — well, the night I fed her my dick — runs wildly in my mind. I stifle a groan at the image and take her in.

Her dark red hair is long, hanging on her bony shoulders in waves of silk. Tattoos now mark her arms, neck, and I wonder where else she's inked that I can't see. She's beautiful but broken. I know it's because he's been fucking her. Rage heats my blood, trickling through my veins at an alarming rate.

It's been a long time since I laid eyes on her, and now that she's standing before me, I don't know how to form words. Normally with girls I take home, it's an easy, emotionless fuck. Afterward, I leave them without needing to even know their name, but for some reason, the girl looking at me like I'm a monster has hooked me.

"Ah, there she is," Thanos chuckles, crooking his finger to call her over.

She pads toward us, and I can't help staring. Underneath her brokenness, she's exquisite. When she reaches the table, I watch in awe as she stands, waiting for his order. He grips her hair, tugging it in his fist and shoves her to her knees. They hit the cold wooden floor with a thud so loud, but all she does is whimper.

Her strength steals my attention, holding it hostage. She's always been strong. Even at eighteen, she was one of the feistiest girls in our dungeon. Now at twenty-two, she's just as resilient.

It's wrong. It's so fucking wrong, but all I want right now is to take her and claim her. To make her mine. To fuck her into oblivion until all she knows is me.

It's ridiculous.

Shaking my head, I bring my wine back to my mouth. She watches my every move as I gulp the liquid down. I tip my head to the side, wanting to question her, but that's when Thanos makes his fatal move. The glint of the knife in his hand alerts me he's about to hurt her, and against my better judgement, I jump to my feet.

"I think it's time for me to inspect her. Then we'll need to be on our way," I say before he has a moment to get near her with the weapon.

His gaze flicks to me. Forgetting about his earlier plan, he sets the knife down on the white tablecloth that will soon be stained with his blood. I can feel her confused gaze burning into me at that moment. I just saved her, but I'm here to buy her. I wonder if she recognizes me. If she does, she hasn't made it known.

"You're not staying for dinner?" he questions. There's curiosity in both his and her stares, but I school my features to keep this game going.

"Well, the quicker I start with this job, the faster you'll have your money," I tell him, knowing that the only thing he wants from me is the cash.

He flits his gaze over to her. Reaching for her hand, he

tugs her toward the table. My body is alert, ready to attack the fucker, but I can't do anything until River has taken out every one of the guards outside.

"Yes, you're right. No sense in wasting time. I trust you'll enjoy this one, Savage." Once again, he utters my last name like we're friends. We are so far from ever being anything close to that, but I nod in agreement.

CHAPTER EIGHT
CAIA

He stares at me.

A familiar stranger.

His eyes hold secrets when he looks at me. Hidden in the depths of the ocean of his gaze. I feel like drowning in the waves that crest in his irises. Anger and hatred emanate from him like a cologne. It's been years since a man looked at me that way. Like he does. There's no malice there, and I wonder how I know him. His hair is dark, which is a stark contrast to his ice-blue eyes. He tips his head to the side, the corner of his mouth lifting, and that's when I see it.

Recognition flurries wildly in my mind when I'm transported back to a time when I was nothing more than a pawn in a sick and twisted game. The man before me may have darker hair, he may be dressed in an immaculate suit, but I know him. The first man to ever touch me and make me feel pleasure rather than pain.

Drake Savage.

Confused emotions swirl through me. Anger. Sadness.

Curiosity. And one that's stronger than all of those, one I need to tamper down — desire.

I don't know if I should be thankful or saddened he's here, but I don't allow my expression to falter. It's indifferent. And I watch as his shoulders relax from the tension radiating from him. Even though he's playing it cool, I pick up every nuance of this man.

No matter what his plan for me is, there's nothing I can say to him now. Thanos will know he's someone from my past, and something tells me that he doesn't want him to know. So, I play along, the obedient toy I've been trained to be.

His head tips slightly to the side with an inquisitive arch to his dark eyebrow, which makes me want to talk to him. To beg him to free me, to steal me from my hell. But where would he take me? To the awful dungeon where I'll do his bidding instead of Thanos's? Perhaps I should be afraid, but Drake doesn't scare me.

Why has he come for me after all this time?

What is he planning on doing with me?

He offers a smile, tips the glass of wine to his lips, and gulps a mouthful, swallowing the alcohol before turning fully to me. "You're rather exquisite," he utters, and his voice takes me back to the night in the library where we spoke like equals.

"I took your beautiful cunt last night," Drake says as he shoves me into the chair. I have a feeling we're being watched because he's aloof, closed off.

"You did."

"That's the last time it will ever happen. If I'm found out . . ."

He doesn't need to finish his sentence because I know exactly what would happen. Neither of us would survive, but then again . . . Am I surviving?

"They'll do horrific things to you," he tells me. Gripping the edge of the desk, his fingers turn white with frustration.

"It's not like they haven't already."

"You keep fighting them, Caia." His shoulders slump, but he doesn't look at me. Instead, he lowers his head as if he's been defeated. "I can't keep you safe."

"Why would you?"

Either my eyes are playing tricks on me, or Drake's body really is vibrating with barely contained rage. I wish he would look at me. I silently plead for those blue orbs to pierce me, to steal my soul.

"Tell me, Drake?" I force. Shoving up from the chair he just put me in, I place a hand on his shoulder, causing him to tense under my touch. "Tell me what it is about them hurting me that pains you so?"

He spins on his heel, and I can't stop the shocked gasp that falls from my lips. As if something has taken over him, he is furious. There's venom in his eyes. Pure, violent, and unrestrained.

His hand grips my arm, the other wrapping around my neck. When he squeezes, a sound tumbles from my parted lips. His glare falls to my mouth, watching as I struggle to suck in deep breaths. Attempting to pull air into my lungs.

"Is this what you wanted? Them to choke the life from you? Because if it is, I can do it. I'll happily kill you before they do."

I can't respond. My eyes tear up, but it's not because of sadness. Instead, it's fear that he's right. They will kill me. And *the realization slams into me that I'd rather have him do it than them.*

"This is no game, Caia. It's life or death."

He releases me suddenly, running his fingers through his hair, tugging at the strands in frustration.

"Fuck this," he hisses. "I want you again. I'm torn between wanting to fuck you and kill you. Between wanting to steal your lips or stealing your life."

"You're not one of them, Drake." Coughing the words, I turn away from him, not wanting him to see me struggle with my own thoughts, my own emotions. I want him. I shouldn't. But I can't stop my traitorous heart from feeling something for the man who holds me hostage.

"No, I wasn't one of them. It's been years though. There's only so much I can take," he confesses with his back to me.

"They hurt you too. Don't they?"

"They hurt us all."

And that moment is when I realize I'm falling in love with the man before me. When I realize Drake Savage not only owns my body, he owns my heart too.

IT'S SO STRANGE SEEING HIM AGAIN. HE LOOKS OLDER, MORE mature than the time I was first thrown into the hell where his father tortured me. I can't tell his age, but I would guess he's nearing thirty. All the visitors that have attended parties were older — men with gray hair and beards and women whose faces were wrinkle-free, but the rest of their bodies showed their real age.

"Thank you."

He smiles, crinkling the corner of his eyes, and the color of the sea twinkles. His almost-black hair is short, but there are some strands hanging over his forehead, reaching his eyes. The darker hair suits his tanned skin, making him almost human. His lips are a dull pink, but they're full, plump. My eyes travel over the black suit he wears, which hugs his muscles.

Perhaps he's not real. An apparition in my mind. And just maybe I'm imagining him being here. It's been four long years, and the last time I laid eyes on him, I was bleeding out.

The one thing I learn by assessing him is that it's clear he doesn't like the man who's taken me, but what I don't understand is why he's having dinner with my owner.

I notice his hands next. Long fingers, with a tattoo peeking under the cuff of his shirt, and I wonder if he has any more ink that I can't see. The two men stare at each other for a moment before my owner glares at me.

"Take that dress off," Mr. Thanos orders me in a tone which scrapes against my skin, reminding me that I'm here because he's allowing it. Not of my own free will. For years, this has been my life. It's ingrained in me, and there's nothing I can do about it.

Drake's eyes burn into me as I lift the hem of the dress they've put me in. Once it's over my head and pooling on the floor beside me, I meet those blue eyes that pierce me in a moment of heat.

He trails his gaze from my bare feet up my thin legs, stopping at the apex between my thighs. I know he sees the bruises. It's not like I can hide them. I don't cower. He lifts his stare up to my small breasts, over the lashes, scars, and black-and-blue marks on my flesh. The ink only hides so much. It's visible only for the occasions when I'm dressed up like a doll for the parties I am forced to attend.

When he meets my eyes, there's an emotion I didn't expect. Guilt. He didn't do this, but for some reason, he looks even more remorseful than the man who inflicted the wounds on me. He lifts his hand, causing me to wince, but he doesn't strike me as I thought he would. Instead, his fingers pull a packet of cigarettes from his pocket. He taps one out, pressing it between his full lips, his eyes never leaving my face.

The lighter flicks to life, allowing the flame to dance wildly as it ignites the tip of the white stick. The silence from the man inspecting me is heavy, hanging in the air like a weight. He pulls a long drag on the cigarette, inhaling the nicotine, then a cloud of smoke billows around him.

"She's perfect." Two words, and my heart stutters. "I'll make the payment right now," he says. *He's here to buy me.*

"Good. Would you like her to do anything else? I want all those secrets she's hiding in her pretty little head, Savage," my owner says.

Savage.

The name may mean violence, but the man before me is far from it. He looks nothing like a barbarian. Far too poised, too calm and collected. I bite the inside of my cheek to keep from pleading for him to take me now, before Thanos changes his mind.

"Put your dress on. We're leaving," Drake grunts around the smoke hanging from his lips. His one eye narrows as he regards me in a sideways glance while he pulls on the cigarette.

I don't respond. I obey him.

"You should've stayed for the meal," Mr. Thanos utters, his tone tight with confusion. Something shifts in the air as the material slips over my slim frame. Once I'm clothed,

Savage pulls his phone from his pocket, and I realize it's been vibrating.

He puts it to his ear, then utters one word. "Now."

Suddenly, the dining room doors fly open, and I'm on the floor in an instant with a heavy body cocooning me. A cry is wrenched from my throat. All I see is a swift movement of black, heavy boots thud on the floor. There's a grunt, screams from the staff, and I feel dizzy. Everything moves too fast for me to figure out where the blood that's drenching me is coming from, but the slick fluid is staining my skin.

My eyes snap up to find Mr. Thanos gripping the handle of a blade. Crimson liquid spurts from his body as his wide eyes glare at the man who's dropped the smoke he was just enjoying on the body of my owner.

A grip on my arm is harsh, but I'm on my feet in seconds.

"Take this." He hands me a smaller knife, which I grip, but stare at him in shock, not knowing what he wants me to do with it. "He's all yours."

My head turns to see the man who's hurt me all these years I've been here watch me. The blade that's already inside him isn't there to kill him. It's to slow him down. I realize what Drake means. Stepping closer to the man on his knees, I smirk. The satisfaction in my expression must alarm him because that's when he pleads with me.

"Think about this. You don't know what you're doing," he tells me. The man who bought me, violated me, and broke me in ways I'd rather not think about, is now pleading for his life.

Lifting the knife, I press it to his mouth, trailing the tip of the blade over his lower lip. My eyes meet his, and I finally say everything I wanted to tell him all this time.

"You're a sick fuck. This is mercy," I bite out. Spitting in his face, I smile. Blood trickles from his mouth where I slice into his bottom lip, causing him to cry out, and I revel in the agony I'm causing him.

Two men dressed in black grip his wrists behind his back as I push the sleek silver onto his tongue. "Time for you to learn how to swallow this," I spit his words back to him with venom lacing every syllable. Pushing the long silver blade into his mouth, I feel flesh squelch as the blood seeps from him. My whole hand is in his mouth as I watch his eyes roll back, and the scarlet fluid rushes like a waterfall down his chin as I throat-fuck him with the weapon I've been gifted.

I feel Drake's eyes on me as I pull my arm back and shove it back in, again and again. I've never felt such intense satisfaction as I do in this moment when I watch the life drain from his eyes. When I finally rip my arm away, there's no longer silver or black on the weapon; it's red, shimmering in the low light like a beacon.

Vengeance feels good.

Turning to my savior, I see the smile on his face, and for the first time in a long time, I grin back. He's handsome in a dark, dangerous way, but I find myself magnetized to him. I don't know what his plan for me is, but for now, I'm happy.

CHAPTER NINE
CAIA

His blue eyes leave mine, and he gestures with his head to the other man who just walked in. "River," he says to the male I recognize instantly. "Take her to the car. We'll get her cleaned up and head to the house."

"I can speak for myself," I say confidently, causing his stare to snap to mine. "Why did you let me do that?" I ask.

"Because you needed revenge. Now let's go. I want to learn all there is to know about you." He winks, the corner of his mouth tipping up into a smirk so sinful I know I've just met the devil himself. He hands me a lit cigarette. "Smoke that. It'll calm you," he orders, and I place the smoke between my lips, pulling the nerve-calming drug into my system.

My lungs fill with nicotine, and my eyes flutter closed in satisfaction. When I look at Drake again, there's a storm in his eyes. It dances like a hurricane ready to wipe out a town, a city, or even the world, and I wonder just how dangerous my knight in shining armor is.

"Let's go," he tells me.

"Why should I trust you?" My question feels pointless. He's just given me a weapon, which I used to kill a man. He watched, smiled, and waited until I was ready before touching me. And even so, his touch was as gentle as it was commanding.

"I don't expect you to trust me, or forgive me for what happened in the past," he tells me with a shrug. "But we need to get out of this house before the police pull up. River and his men will clean the mess, and we'll be safe at the house before dawn."

"And . . .?"

"And you'll be able to shower, sleep, and decide what it is you want to do next. But you don't have to decide right now. All I want to do is get you out of here safely." There's a glimmer of affection in his eyes as he regards me warily. He doesn't trust me, and I don't trust him. We're at an impasse.

I nod. His fingers find the small of my back. Immediately, a slight shiver races over my body. It's involuntary, but the fear of being hurt is still there. "Look at me," he utters. An order which causes me to stop, my eyes meeting his. "I'll never fucking hurt you like he did."

I look at him for a long while. Is he a wolf in sheep's clothing? No. There's brutal honesty in his gaze. I know one fact, and that's Drake Savage is indeed a devil in angel's finery. He smiles once more. That same intense grin makes my stomach flip-flop and my heart beat wildly in my chest. Nodding slowly, I respond, "Fine."

This feels too easy. Almost. There are two men dressed in black cleaning the mess I made. Thanos's body is gone, and I notice River is watching another two men from their team work around the room, invading the cabinets. I'm unsure of what they're looking for, but I keep my mouth shut.

"Sir, we've found the basement where he kept the—" The young man's words halt when his eyes land on me. No doubt he found my cage.

"What is it, Crow?" River questions, insistence in his tone.

"There's something you need to see."

"I'll be there in a moment," he responds, then turns to Drake, questioning with a serious expression that only serves to make my anxiety twist low in my gut. "See you at the house?"

"Yes." One word, and Drake's fingers find my back as he guides me from my hell. Being here was the worst nightmare I'd ever lived through, and as we walk out of the mansion, I inhale fresh air for the first time in almost four years.

"Wait here. I'll be back in a moment. The men here will keep you safe," Drake tells me earnestly. I want to answer him, to give him my voice, but all I can do is nod. I thought I was stronger, but I realize in the moment his cerulean orbs meet mine, I'm not. The girl who first fell for those big blue eyes is back, and I can't tamper down the feelings.

I was eighteen when I arrived at the Savage Mansion and met Drake. The private school girl who was lost to her family for so long I'm sure they think I'm dead. My chest tightens painfully, reminding me that my old life is gone. I'm no longer that innocent girl.

I'm new.

Reborn.

I've given up trying to find her. Deep down, no matter how long I search, I know she's a stranger to me. My heart is no longer filled with happiness and affection. And I've done something I never thought I could ever do. I've stabbed someone. I'm a killer. A murderer who's lost everything. As I step out into my new life, I make a choice.

I'm stronger.

I'm no longer Caia, the toy.

I'm Caia Amoretto, the survivor.

DRAKE

As soon as I reach the cells, we find three other girls hidden in the corners of each room. They're cold, malnourished, and one is bleeding profusely.

"Get them to the hospital," I order Crow, one of the best men on my team. River joins me, his eyes dark filled with hatred and anger. "This is . . ." I turn to the last cell and find a familiar face that is the spitting image of River. The big green eyes, the dark hair, and pouty lips of Rayne Atwood. She looks exactly like her brother. As if they were twins, but I know she's younger.

My body turns cold, rigid with confusion and rage. She's skinny, sickly, and pale. There are black rims under her big eyes; those that used to shine with life are now lifeless and dead. Everything has been stolen from her.

"Rayne?" My best friend's voice is nothing more than a shocked whisper, but the pain it drips when he utters her name grips my chest. His sister's eyes are wide when she takes us both in. I haven't seen her since she was two, maybe three-years-old. River never spoke of her since the day their mother disappeared with her. We thought they were both killed. But the girl before us is very much alive.

"Get her out of here," I utter at Crow as soon as he returns. But as soon as two men reach for her, she loses her fucking mind. Her screech is ear-piercing. "Do it!" I command, and as they move closer to her, I notice one of the men has a syringe.

"It's an injection that will help calm her," I inform River when his stare zeros in on the needle, but he knows this. It's his own concoction of drugs that we've used before.

As soon as it pierces her flesh, she goes down like a fucking rag doll. She's naked, and I can't help taking in the blue and purple bruises on her body. There are cuts and scabs on her knees. A botch job of stitches on her lower abdomen is visible when they move by us with her limp form.

"What the fuck did they do to her?" My voice sounds hoarse and raspy. She's probably so fucked up, so shattered that she doesn't know what's real and what's not. I wonder if she even recognized her brother. Innocence stolen by force, and her mind has been broken.

That wasn't Rayne in there. It was a rabid animal.

"We'll fix her," I tell him as we head toward the steps that lead to the main floor of the house. I'm not sure we can, but I don't tell him about my doubt. I hide it where my best friend can never see it.

All these years, River thought his sister was dead, but she isn't. Which leads me to the question . . . *What the fuck happened to her?*

Stalking toward the cars parked out front, I find Caia sitting on a concrete bench overlooking the fountain. The gardens of this estate are vast, beautiful, but the horrors

that hide within the walls of the mansion are better left
untold.

"We should go," I tell her.

She turns her gaze on me. In the dark, she's exquisite.
Even though she'll probably never trust another man ever
again, I can't help the need to protect her. I may not be able
to love, or show affection, but I can offer her friendship.

"This is it," she utters. "No more hide and seek," her
voice rasps.

"What?" I'm the one confused now.

"He used to love to play hide and seek with us. He'd
have these parties." Even as she speaks, her voice is
faraway. As if she's not really here, beside me. Her mind is
long gone, still within the confines of the house.

"You can tell me about it another time," I offer, reaching
for her. I notice her flinch when I press a hand gently on her
shoulder. "My car is over there." I point as she rises. Quietly,
she follows me, settling in the seat when I open the door
for her.

Once I'm in the driver's seat, I start the engine, pulling
down the drive and toward her freedom. There's nothing
but silence surrounding us. The roads are pitch black, bar
from my headlights. It's eerie, but it would be safest to keep
her from the city.

"Thank you," she whispers into the darkness.

"It's my pleasure," I respond, not daring to look at her. I
wonder if she remembers me. If she does, she doesn't say it.
She doesn't ask about Malcolm, about the mansion. Surely
she must have questions?

Her heated gaze burns into my skin. I feel it as she
watches me intently. A soft sigh from her lips causes my
dick to twitch in response, but I breathe it out, hoping to

calm my desire for her. She doesn't need some fucking asshole trying shit with her after all she's been through.

The house we rented as a hideaway for this job is ten miles from here, and I know she'll be asleep by the time we reach halfway. I wanted to take her back to the mansion, but it's too dangerous. If one of the clients sees her, or if she loses her shit and tries to run away, it could be detrimental. If the parties she attended with Thanos were filled with buyers, they'll recognize her the moment she steps foot in the city.

The stench of blood is rife, but when she opens the window, I smile. She sticks her head out of the space, allowing the wind to flick her hair around her head. There's something so innocent about it. Childlike. When she finally sits back, she turns her attention toward me. I can feel her gaze on my right side, but I don't look at her. I've learned how to deal with people who've been through trauma, but for the first time, I want to learn everything about her.

The promise I made her has turned into something else. It's no longer one to just find her; it's one that I'm making wordlessly to keep her safe. Whether that be in my arms or not.

Four years is a long time to feel something for someone. But when I saw her tonight, it was if I was transported back to the first day I laid eyes on her.

"Sir," I call to my father. In here, we're not related, merely boss and slave. That's how I see it anyway. "We have contact," I tell him, knowing he'll be happy about that.

"And they know what we have?"

I nod.

"*Good. Get her ready.*"

As soon as I step into the room, I'm stunned by the pretty little thing curled up on the bed. She looks so delicate. Tiny. Almost fragile. And I wonder how much it would take for me to break her.

My cock agrees. It wants to see how much she can take. Smirking, I stroll farther into the room. Her big eyes peek up at me from under long, dark lashes, and I envision them tearing up from her position on the floor while I order her to do what I want. Anything I want.

Ignoring her, I grab the bucket and fill it at the sink, which is situated in the corner of her room. For some reason, I can't bring myself to talk to her. It's stupid, but there's something far too innocent about this beauty.

"*I need . . .,*" she whispers, her voice raspy and melodic. Once again, my cock agrees, because it jolts at the sound of her. I spin on my heel, glaring at her, causing her to cower under my ferocious stare. "*I, uhm, need to pee.*"

Her cheeks darken, a dusty rose which makes me lick my lips. Her skin is smooth, unblemished, and she's free of any makeup. Too fucking innocent.

I want to be nice to her, to offer her a kind word, but the mental image of what my father is about to do to her reminds me that no one in this shithole can be saved.

"*Piss yourself on the mattress. The next girl won't be here till it's dry.*"

Her mouth falls open, and I'm tempted to use the opportunity to fill it. To see those plump lips slide over my shaft.

"*Don't mind me, doll, I've seen much worse.*" I chuckle. "*Working with him, I've cleaned piss, blood, and shit when he's finished with one of you, so you're definitely not special.*" I don't look at her, but her gaze ignites every inch of my skin. It's as if

she can see into my soul, and I'm afraid she'll see the black that
taints me.

"I haven't been outdoors in years." Her words are wistful, as if she'd just said she was craving ice cream or something trivial, but the reality is this girl has been locked up in a dark, cold cell, only allowed out when Thanos wanted to use her as bait, I'm guessing.

I've always been one to admit my wrongs. To give brutal honesty. And now, I know that from the moment she walked into the room, I wanted her. Being alone in the car with her doesn't help the need I feel for her. It also doesn't dissipate the image I have of her naked, showing her body to me because that asshole ordered her to.

The road ahead is dark. In both the literal and the figurative sense. Her gaze is intense, as if there's a fucking strobe light on me. It's electric, burning my flesh.

"I'm sorry," I utter. My words drip with guilt knowing my father is responsible for the life she's lived. For what she's been through. And I realize nothing can ever replace what was taken from her.

For years, I felt the world owed me something. I was an asshole to everyone I came into contact with. Only one person knew what I'd been through — River. There wasn't a girl whom I'd fucked who knew what I'd survived. None of them got close enough.

Sadly, not even my brother knows. I spent my life ashamed of what I became. Needing the darkness to enjoy a simple pleasure most people take for granted.

"It's not your fault," Caia says, causing me to finally glance her way. There's so much innocence in her eyes, but also warring with the beauty of her sweetness is a glint of a warrior. Her eyes hold a fire within them, one that can be trained into a killer.

"Oh, little raven, most of the bad things that happen are my fault," I tell her.

"Little raven?" She smiles, gifting me a flash of happiness in the sordid world she's just been freed from.

"You remind me of the bird. Beautiful, yet darkness seems to consume you. Exquisite, but can be as violent as a bird of prey. It can devour the dead, but also shimmer in the sunlight."

"You're quite the poet, Drake." She utters my name with an affection I don't deserve. The sound so familiar, so intricately woven into the fabric of my veins. She finally reveals the truth. She does recognize me. I knew she couldn't forget me, even though I've changed, hardened to a man rather than the boy I was when we first met.

"Caia, words are merely that. It's actions that speak a thousand times louder than any utterance can," I inform her.

"Perhaps," she sighs. "But there are also words that can heal, that can offer solace in times where actions are futile."

"Maybe one day you can show me," I respond, knowing I want her to be here tomorrow, the next day, next month, and year. I don't want to lose her again, but that's up to her.

"You know me," her voice confident. "These have been long, lonely years, Drake Savage." There's sadness lacing each word she utters. It matches the emotion that's waging war in my chest. I want her. I crave her. But I don't want her to live in this life of darkness that's got hold of me.

"Memories can be tragic things," I tell her.

"I suppose you remember those moments as well," she says quietly. It's not a question, merely an observation.

"Always, Caia."

"Drake." She tastes the word. The tone of her voice and the way she utters my name once again has need racing through me like I've never felt before. "Where is your father?"

"Dead."

A gasp falls from her lips at my answer. I wait for her to question me, to ask if I was the one who dealt the fatal blow, but she doesn't. What she does say shocks me.

"I wish I was the one to do it."

The road opens up onto a dirt track, the conversation halting as I slow to a crawl as we head up the bumpy path to a house hidden by forest. River left the lights on, so when we pass the smattering of trees, we come to a double-story, wooden cabin, which looks like it should be featured on America's Most Beautiful Homes or some shit. It's illuminated by the golden bulbs, giving it a feel of home and safety.

Her words play on a loop in my mind. She wants to kill. I don't blame her for that because it's something I've wanted as well. "If that's something you feel you need for closure, I can offer you a way to do it. Obviously not my father, but . . ." I turn to her as soon as I kill the engine. "Others like him."

"Really?"

I nod but offer nothing more. Not tonight. She needs rest.

"Is this the safe house?" The wonder and awe in her voice makes me smile. It's like watching a bird take flight.

The fear and anxiety that once tightened her expression is now curved into a beautiful smile.

"It is. You'll stay here for a few days until we can ensure your documents are in order. You'll receive a new passport and driver's license."

"I . . . I can't drive." Her voice fills with sadness.

"I'll teach you," I promise. My hand reaches for her, and I wait for the flinch, only this time, it doesn't come. We sit there for a moment. Waiting. Silent.

She sighs, turns, and pushes the car door open. I follow suit. Rounding the front, I reach her, and for some inexplicable reason, pull her into my arms. It's been a long while since I've held a woman. Much less cared enough to offer her driving lessons.

Her body shudders in my hold, and I tighten it. As if I can keep her from drowning in the sea of emotion I know is trying to swallow her whole.

I remember the time I broke down. How vulnerable I felt. I recall the moment my mind finally completely shattered, and I didn't know which way was up. I was sinking in a turbulent ocean, flailing around until I found my solace in blood. In death. Taking the lives of those who wronged me.

"It's going to be okay," I tell her, the promise clear in my voice. No matter what she's been through, I'll ensure she walks out the other side.

"Why did you save me?" Her question turns me cold. I don't want to talk about it. To tell her what I've seen and why I allowed her to kill Thanos. "I'm not an innocent. I've seen things many girls wouldn't have survived. Unless you're too afraid to confess," she taunts. Her words lighten the mood, but not by much. She doesn't know it yet, but nothing can ever be light between us. However, her teasing only serves to make me want to show her exactly what I can do to her.

"Little raven, be careful of what you say to me," I bite out, my fingers fisting, tensing, and releasing. There's a fire that suddenly blazes in her eyes at my threat.

"Oh?" she quips. The playful tone of her voice makes me smile. Shaking my head in awe at this woman, I take her in. After everything she's been through, she's still smiling.

"I'm not any different than the last time you saw me," I tell her.

"And you forget, I'm the one who has been through similar horrors you have," she tells me. "I'm still here, Drake."

"I'm not doing this now. You need to get some rest. I need to make sure Thanos's men aren't on the hunt for his killers. You'll stay here because it's safe and I can keep an eye on you. There's food downstairs, clothes in the closet, and anything else you need in the bathroom." When I finish my instructions, I glance at her again, unable to take my eyes off the woman who's become so much more to me than I'd anticipated.

"Thank you . . . for saving me." She smiles then. It's small, but I notice it because I can't help staring at her, meeting those intense hazel eyes. Even in the darkness, she seems to shine like a strike of lightning through a darkened sky. And that burns me more than anything I've ever encountered.

"I'm not a knight in shining armor. I'm not here to give you a castle and a white horse, little bird."

"No, you're not the good guy; you've made that abundantly clear. But you're not the bad guy either. You're somewhere in between, and perhaps that's why you can't come to terms with this." She gestures between us with her finger, and I'm tempted to grab it between my teeth and bite on it just to hear her yelp.

"I've spent my life not knowing who or what I am. Another few years won't make a difference."

She stills, and I take a step back. Her eyes shimmer with emotion. "I'm sorry," she says timidly, and my chest tightens. This is exactly why I've stayed away from connections. Even the one I have with River shouldn't happen, but the asshole is stubborn, and he doesn't want to admit I'm bad news.

"Never apologize again. You're . . ." *Mine.* "Safe." I don't tell her what I think. The word that sprang up in my thoughts in those few seconds, I shove into the recesses of my mind, because as much as I'd love to claim her, I can't.

She's perfect.

Wrong in every way. Because when I'm near her, all I want to do is fuck her. Seeing her kill Thanos was enough to have my cock throbbing behind my zipper. I've seen assassins trained to do this shit, but when this beauty's hand shoved the knife into the throat of the man who hurt her, it was utter perfection.

I turn and lead her into the building that will be our home for the next three weeks. It's situated close to three of the names on our list. And that's the reason I chose it, because while Caia can heal, I can kill.

CHAPTER ELEVEN
CAIA

I t's the second day in the house he's brought me to. It's a comfortable log cabin in the middle of nowhere. I haven't left the room in all the time I've been here, still unsure as to what he wants from me. Even though they haven't hurt me, I find that being wary is the only way I will survive this.

Seeing him again has brought back memories of what I went through when I was locked up in the Savage dungeon, but it's also brought back the memory of what I begged him to do. What he took from me, violently and without remorse.

I MEET THOSE BLUE EYES, THE PLEA CLEAR IN MY HAZEL ONES AS *I watch him. There's a war raging through him, the good and bad of Drake Savage.*

"I'm going to fuck you. I'm going to take your virginity and own it. And when I do, you'll be mine." His voice is gravelly as he promises me what I've just asked him for. It's a vow. And I know

if he makes good on this, if he really steals my virginity, I'll belong to him. No matter what those men do to me, I'll always be his.

"Then do it," I challenge him, praying he'll take the bait and do the one thing he's not supposed to do. "I don't want them to have it. Please?"

The corner of his mouth tilts up when he leans in closer. His lips shimmer with the saliva his tongue paints them with, and I follow the action.

"Hearing you beg me to do it makes me even harder for you. It makes me want to rip into you and make you cry," he growls, and as he utters the words, he's already pushing his slacks down those long, muscled thighs. His hand grips the hard, angry erection jutting from his hips. Seconds later, I'm lifted against the wall and he's driving into my wet, tight heat.

I cry out as agonizing pain burns through me, and I know there's no going back now. I belong to him. He owns me. And there's nothing I can do about it.

IT'S SILENT IN THE HOUSE, BUT I KNOW HE'S STILL HERE. IT'S AS IF I can feel him. He ordered me to come up here and shower, to change into some fresh clothes, and sleep. My body is still aching from the hard mattress I was allowed when I was in Thanos's house, and the bed I'm now lying on is a stark contrast. Staring up at the ceiling, I wonder what Drake's plan for me is. Will he keep me? Or will he let me loose on the world?

When I laid eyes on him again, my heart stuttered wildly in my chest, reminding me of the night he took my virginity in that office after I'd begged him to. But when he looked at me, there was no affection in his gaze. Perhaps my stupid, young heart wanted more, wanted him to care.

I never thought I'd see him again, yet here he is. He promised to save me, and he did. It took him four years, but he made good on a promise. Sighing, I roll over onto my side and close my eyes, wishing for sleep to steal me away.

———

"Wake up." The gritty tone of Drake's voice startles me awake. When I open my eyes, I notice he's dressed casually in a pair of dark jeans and a black T-shirt that hugs his frame. "We need to talk," he tells me, then leaves me in the room once more.

The sun streams through the small window opposite the bed, warming the room. It's been so long since I'd seen the sun, it seems almost foreign to me. The artificial lights in the mansion were something I'd become accustomed to.

Rising from the bed, I slip on the sandals I'd found in the small closet the first night I stayed here and make my way downstairs to find River, Drake, and Dante. I recall meeting Dante years ago, the twins who look so alike but are so very different in personality.

"There she is." River smiles, but the two Savage men just glare at me as if I'm a problem they need to sort out. "Sit," River says, pushing a chair toward me.

Perching myself on the stool, I open my mouth to speak but realize I have no idea what to say, so I utter the words I've wanted to since they stole me from Thanos. "Thank you," I rasp, glancing at each man.

"No need to thank us," Dante smirks. "Perhaps you'd want to hear us out before you say those two words, because we're not saviors, gorgeous." A cold shiver races down my spine at his words, and I wonder then if they're going to kill me.

"Ignore my brother," Drake finally speaks. "We need to know what happened to you in there. We need names of the men you saw and met while living with Thanos." He's all business, lifting a mug of steaming liquid to his lips, and I find myself licking my own in response. The boy who took my virginity is gone, replaced with a man who's cold and closed off.

But then again, he always was like that.

"I can't remember them all. There . . . There were a lot of parties." Dropping my gaze, I focus on the countertop instead of looking into those blue eyes that have pierced my heart so many times before. I should never have let my emotions get the best of me, but there was something about Drake that made me want more. That made me want *him*. Even in his anger, he's handsome. Even in his darkness, he's light.

"Well, then tell us what you do remember," he responds, sighing as he sets a mug of coffee in front of me. "Drink that. It will warm you up." Snapping my gaze to his, I offer a small smile and accept the hot drink. It's the first time in years I've tasted coffee, and I gulp the scorching liquid, ignoring the burn on my tongue and down my throat as I swallow it.

"There were four men who were there every time he had those dinner parties. One was a friend of my father, Leonard Harrelson. The CEO of LH Corporation. They deal in computer hardware."

"We know him," Drake says, then glances at Dante. "Get info on him. I want everything, all those dirty secrets.

We'll pay him a visit tomorrow." Dante nods, pulling out his cellphone and leaving the room as he says *hello* to someone on the other end of the line.

"And the other three?" River questions, placing a hand on mine.

My gaze flits between the two men who remain in the room. "What are you going to do to them?"

Drake sets his mug down, leaning on his elbows. His face is merely inches from mine. His hot breath fans over my mouth, and I want to lean into him. "We're going to gut the fuckers until they're nothing more than roach food."

River chuckles beside me, and Drake straightens to full height, leaving me cold, not only from his words, but also from the absence of his mouth close to mine.

"What are you going to do with me?" I whisper, my voice raspy with fear at what Drake's intentions are. He turns to fill his mug, his back to me for a moment before he pivots and glances at me with an arched brow.

"That all depends on you."

Straightening my spine, I question, "What do you mean?"

"You can either walk away from this with a new identity," he tells me easily, waving his hand at River who places a yellow folder before me.

My trembling fingers tug at the tape holding it closed. Opening it, I find a passport with my photo and a name that's not mine. "What's the other option?" I question, tracing my index finger over the image of me in the small blue book.

"You can work with us to take everyone down."

Shock races through me as I lift my gaze to his. "Work with you?"

"Yes. Kill the assholes. Shut down the operation my father started," he says. "The problem is, since Thanos is dead, the other clients would've heard about it through the grapevine. We need to plan this so they don't suspect I'm the one killing each of them off."

"What's the catch?" I ask, setting the fake passport on the counter. I pick up the mug and round the counter to get a refill, which puts me right beside the man affecting me more than anyone ever has.

He watches me pour the coffee but doesn't respond until I meet his blue eyes. The corner of his mouth tilts into a sinfully dark smirk.

"The catch is you get to work alongside me, little raven," he whispers. "If you can handle being around me and not think about how I took your purity."

"You're still the asshole I remember from four years ago," I bite back, my voice not wavering with fear this time, but burning hot with anger.

"I'm even worse now, little bird," he tells me confidently. "I'm far from asshole, more like . . ." He purses his lips as if he's thinking about what to tell me. "Satan himself."

"Does that mean you turned into your asshole monster of a father?" I retort, not sure where my confidence is coming from, and I realize that remark could get me killed. He may need me, but once he's done, he could easily murder me. Drake snaps his hard glare on me, his hand gripping my neck and squeezing, causing me to cough. In shock, the mug slips from my hands, falling to the floor with a loud shattering crash.

He leans in close, so close I can taste him. "If you ever say that again, I won't think twice about ripping you apart, little raven," he bites out, anger vibrating through him into me. "I'm nothing like that monster." Tears prick my eyes as my blood turns cold. My lungs protesting, needing air.

"Drake." River's voice is distant as he calls to his volatile best friend. "Dude, let her up. She's just trying to piss you off."

I reach for Drake's wrist, my nails digging in deep, feeling his flesh tear as I scratch into him. That only makes him smile. He brushes his lips over my ear and whispers, "Remember, little raven, I love it rough. I love when you draw blood from me while I make you wet with my dick. Do you remember that night, little one? Because I do. I remember every wet, slick, tight part of you." He releases me, stalking from the kitchen, leaving me gulping in air.

"Ignore him. He's just going through shit," River says, as if his best friend wasn't just choking the life from me.

"He's a monster," I grit out, my throat burning.

"That he is, but he's as broken as you and me, babe," River offers, rising and leaving me in the kitchen to seek out Drake. I don't know what to do. Without them, I'm not sure I'll be able to survive. But with them, I may be broken even more. I just need to decide which is the lesser of two evils.

CHAPTER TWELVE

DRAKE

"Did you enjoy that?" River questions when he finds me outside smoking. My body is still vibrating with a rage I never thought I'd feel again. When Malcolm died, it finally eased up, the anger that's so palpable it runs through my veins. It ate away at me for years.

Alongside the rage was the fear that I'd turn into him. It was a constant reminder that it could so easily happen. I worked hard to fix myself, to focus on the end goal, to be free of the organization he started. But with each step forward, there were two back.

"I did," I finally respond to my best friend. I can feel his gaze burning a fucking hole through me, and I know why. He's angry with me for hurting Caia. I'm angry at myself for what I did, but there was fire dancing in her eyes as she struggled to suck in breaths. I wanted to steal them, to swallow them and bask in her warmth.

"You're an asshole." He tells me something I've known all my life. He pulls out a packet of cigarettes, lighting one while staring at me.

"Tell me something I don't know, River."

He sighs, blowing out a lungful of smoke, the white cloud billowing around him. Dante is just off the porch talking to someone on his phone, and I know he'll soon have the info we need. My brother paces back and forth, something he does when he's nervous or when he's ready to blow a gasket. I wonder which one it is this time.

"She has feelings for you," River mutters around the smoke hanging from his lips. I didn't want to admit it, to acknowledge it, but he's right. I saw it in her eyes. It's clear as day when she looks at me. Needless to say, I've still got some fucked-up feelings for her too. Only, I can't act on it. She needs to be free of this life and me as soon as I've gotten all the names from her. Seeing her alive is strange, especially after I thought she'd died along with my soul.

But I can't deny my mind has been on her since she went to bed last night. I watched her sleep for a while. Seeing the rise and fall of her breaths calmed me somewhat.

"You know, Drake—"

"River, I don't need your fucking pep talk right now," I bite out my frustration, pinning my best friend with a glare. It's not his fault; I've done this to myself. Let her in, and now I'm lost in the feelings that are taking over me. This is why I never let anyone in before. Emotions are murderous vultures that peck at your life. They devour you as you lie dying once you've offered your heart to someone.

"Jesus, you're really hung up on her," he says. Stepping up to me, he leans in, whispering, "If you want her so much, then fucking take her."

My hand grips his hair, tugging him closer as I crash my mouth to his. Groaning when our tongues make contact, I bite down on his lip, causing him to grunt against me. I want to kiss her. I want to kiss him. I'm so fucked up I can't even get hard without hurting the person I love so much.

The thought invades my mind as River's tongue invades my mouth. His lips are hot against mine, the warmth snaking its way through me, but it can never melt my ice-cold heart. The image of Caia beside me, her hands on both our dicks while she watches us runs rampant through my mind, and I know I have to have them both.

"Get a room." Dante's gruff voice breaks through the haze of need burning me alive, and I have to pull away from River. "I have a positive location on our guy. He's scheduled to have a dinner date this evening with his wife. It's their anniversary."

"Looks like we'll have to deliver our gift in person." I smile, knowing how this is going to play out. "Where is the dinner?"

"Gorlois, that place down on the west side of town."

Nodding, I make my way inside to find the woman who's fucking with my head and my heart. Taking the steps two at a time, I shove open the bedroom door only to find her naked as she's pulling up a pair of white panties.

"Jesus," she grits out angrily. "Can't you knock?"

"No." Entering the room, I settle on the dressing table, ignoring the fact that she's attempting to get dressed. Her tiny tits jiggle with every movement, and my kiss earlier with River is only serving to make me harder than a fucking steel pole. "Have you decided what you want to do?" I question her.

She stills, taking me in for a moment before she tugs on the jeans I'd bought and placed in the room this morning. She doesn't know I left her alone for a few hours earlier and bought her enough clothes, toiletries, and underwear to last her a year. When I walked into the store, I found myself wanting to spoil her, to see her smile, but all I'm getting now is a scowl. Not that I blame her. Perhaps it's better that she hates me.

"I want revenge," she finally answers once she's fully dressed. The blue top she's wearing makes the dark ink on her skin pop against the light color.

"Oh?" I arch a brow at her.

"Yes. I want to kill my father," she tells me with confidence in her voice. There are fine red marks on her neck along with the butterfly tattoo that covers her flesh. The marks are mine. She's mine. She always has been.

"That's a rather valiant remark, Caia," I tell her. I wonder if she knows her father sold her to us when she turned eighteen. She must if she wants to kill him, or it might be that she witnessed what a monster he truly is.

"I've seen what he did to my sister. She may be dead now, but I need to avenge her somehow."

She doesn't yet know that her sister is at my house. And she doesn't know that her father is looking for his youngest daughter. "Harper is alive," I tell her, hoping to put her at ease.

Her body goes rigid, her face a picture of shock and confusion. "What?" she utters.

I rise from the bed, stalking toward her. "I found her; or she found me," I whisper. "She's safe at the mansion." Caia shakes her head, disbelieving me for a moment before I grip her chin between my thumb and index finger. "She's alive. Now, tell me what your choice is?"

She lifts her gaze to meet mine, her plump lips parted as she takes shallow breaths. Every time I'm near her, all I want to do is make her mine, to feel her body mold around mine as I claim her, but I have so much to do before I can ever venture into the unknown with her.

"Will you hurt me?" She finally voices her concern. Her tongue darts out, swiping along her lower lip, making it glisten with saliva, and I can't help leaning in, allowing myself to taste her. The flavor of coffee is still on her, and I lick along the plump flesh, savoring her sweetness with the bitterness of the caffeine.

"I will." My promise has her gasping. "But when I do hurt you, little raven, you'll love it. You'll beg me for more. Just like you pleaded with me to steal your virginity all those years ago."

I watch her now, intrigued by the change in her. There was fear in her eyes when I found her, but now I look at her, and that's been diminished. In its place is a fire so fierce I want to burn in her wreckage.

"Then take me to your house. I want to train with your men, because I need to make my father suffer for what he's done. And I need to see Harper."

I always knew Caia was strong. Resilient. And as she learns more about who she is, she'll see that she was destined to walk beside me. I've spent four long years fighting my need for her, but her choice is to go with me. Since that's the case, I know I'll not be able to deny her when she begs for me again.

I won't touch her until she asks for it. And I know, if she feels anything like I do, she will ask for it. For me. I nod. "Fine. Then you'll train with me. You'll play along with my rules because the men I'm about to take down along with your father are not stupid. This is your choice. Once you step foot on the Savage compound again, you cannot leave unless you're..."

"Killed?"

I nod once more.

"Take me there."

"Okay," I agree. "Get some more sleep, then pack your shit. We'll leave this evening. I have things to do first. We'll come back for you in a few hours." I turn and leave her in the bedroom. Finding River in the living room, I offer him a smile. "She's agreed."

His eyes widen as if he's shocked, but I know he isn't. He knew she would go with us. And deep down, I think he wants her too. We'll fix this. One way or another.

CHAPTER THIRTEEN
CAIA

The car ride is silent. There's nothing left to say because Drake has already warned me about what's coming. I'll be working alongside him to take down the assholes that have been clients of his father.

Lights shine through our car from River and Dante in the car behind us. They are illuminating Drake in the driver's seat as we make our way to the Savage Mansion. With the light shining on him, I take note of his white-knuckle grip on the steering wheel but say nothing.

I focus on the road. Even though it's dark, I notice the trees as we drive through the town, heading toward the mansion I left four years ago. When we pull up to the estate an hour later, I glance up at the place that will be my new home for the next few weeks, months. Who knows how long it will take for me to finally get the revenge I've been craving all this time. To finally drain my father of every drop of blood, to watch him breathe his last breath.

I follow Drake silently. The bag I packed with the

clothes he bought me hangs from my left shoulder. River and Dante are flanking me, and I wonder if they're worried I'm going to run away. Would I? No, I don't think I could ever run from them, not when they saved me. But then again, Drake has hurt me before.

The memory of him choking me in the kitchen swirls together with the feeling of him taking me that night. I begged him for it, and his confidence is clear. He thinks I still want him. Sadly, it's true. I can't *not* want him.

"Follow me," Drake orders me, then sets his blue gaze on his brother. "Call the team. I want them ready." Dante nods and disappears down the hallway into the darkness of what I'm guessing is a living room.

"I'll see you in the office once you've gotten our lovely guest settled." River offers me a nod and makes his way into the bowels of the home in the opposite direction than Dante went.

"Come." He doesn't wait for me as he heads up the staircase that sweeps in a wide arc, taking us to the second level of the house. "Your sister is probably asleep, or in her room." He talks to me but doesn't glance my way. The thick, plush carpets make our footfalls silent in the enormous space.

He stops suddenly, causing me to crash into his back. The muscles tense when my palm lands on his shoulder. Stepping backward, I allow the space between us to calm my erratic heartbeat. The door we're standing in front of is dark wood, and I'm certain my sister is on the other side.

Tears burn my eyes, attempting to spill onto my cheeks. My heart is in my throat, threatening to choke me, just like Drake did hours ago.

"She's inside. Tomorrow, you'll be attending a gala

event with me. One of the men my father worked for is hosting. I'll have my shopper get a dress for you to wear," he smirks, raking his gaze over me. "And I suppose I'll have to get you something sexy to wear underneath as well. Be ready at six," he says finally, leaving me at the entrance to my future. To see the girl, I've watched being hurt. Tortured. I'm finally going to look into her eyes again. And I've never been more afraid in my whole life.

Pushing the door open, I step inside the room. There's a large four-poster bed to the right with dark sheets and my sister curled up under them. She's all grown up, an adult, and my chest tightens with sadness realizing I wasn't there for her when she needed me most.

Even though I was stolen, severed from the family I grew up with, I feel the guilt sitting heavily in my gut. I set the bag down gently. Toeing off my shoes, I pad closer to the bed, not taking any notice of the room itself, but the girl who's sleeping soundly.

I want to talk to her, to wake her and hold her in my arms, but fear holds me back. The anxiety that she'll hate me for leaving her in that house with the monster we called Dad. Sighing, I lean forward, pressing a hand to Harper's shoulder, which wakes her immediately. She scurries away from me, fear written all over her face. But when our eyes meet, she stills, staring at me as if I'm an apparition.

"Caia?" I nod at her query, knowing that seeing me after all this time must be strange. "It's really you?" She moves closer, slowly, but she comes toward me, taking in the sister she most certainly won't recognize. I have ink on most of my visible skin, my hair is a deep red, and I'm certain my eyes are no longer shiny and glistening with happiness.

"It's me, Harper," I tell her, hoping she'll see through

the façade of who *he* made me into and find the sister beneath the mask.

"Oh God," she cries, flinging herself on me, causing us both to topple onto the thick carpet. Her arms are wrapped around my neck, holding onto me as if I'm her lifeline. "I've been searching all over for you." Her words still me, ice racing through my veins.

"What do you mean?"

We're sitting on the floor, my sister curled in my lap, our arms wrapped around each other. Harper lifts her gaze to meet mine and confesses, "I ran away from home. As soon as I could, I packed a small rucksack and ran. Malcolm found me at a club and got me a job at a nightclub that was owned by his associate, Thanos." There's so much sadness in her eyes; those beautiful pools hold the agony of what she's been through.

"And he hasn't looked for you?" I question, causing her to still, her body rigid with anxiety. It's thick and heavy in the air between us. "I'm sorry. I'm so goddamn sorry." This time, I blink, and the tears I can no longer hold back spill down my cheeks.

"It's not your fault. When I found out you didn't leave by choice I knew I needed to find you," Harper whispers. Her voice cracks, and soon, we're both crying. She shakes, trembling in my hold, and I can't stop my own frame from shivering. "I missed you," she tells me. "All I wanted was to see you again, to know you were safe from whatever . . . from whoever . . ."

Her body wracks with sobs, and I hold onto my little sister so tight I'm sure I'm cutting off her air supply, but in this moment, all I want is to feel her in my arms. She's safe, alive. She's no longer being hurt. I know she should talk about what happened, but right now is not the time. Right now, we need to let the pain flow by crying out the agony from the past few years that I know will soon be haunting us once we fall asleep.

CHAPTER FOURTEEN
DRAKE

"So, you're going to have her working with us?" River questions as I light a cigarette, pulling the smoke into my lungs, praying it calms me. But nothing can calm me now. The girl is in my house, only a floor up, but it's as if she's right beside me. Four years is not long enough to forget how she made me feel. It's also not long enough to make me forget how tight her virgin cunt felt gripping my dick as I slammed into her. Most of all, it's not been long enough for me to stop the way my heart aches to be hers.

"Once we're done, she'll leave," I lie to River.

He pins me with a glare so fierce I wait for the desk I'm sitting behind to catch fire. My best friend rises, rounding the one thing that separates us, and crouches between my spread thighs. His hands on either one, the heat of his touch makes me groan in response. The memory of how Caia tasted still taints my lips when River leans in close. Our mouths are inches apart. My cock thickens, ready to feel him, feel her, either one of them. I'll gladly take them.

"Bend over the desk," I tell him.

River rises, watching me as he unbuttons his shirt, tugging it from his frame, gifting me a view of his toned chest. The muscles are corded in his arms, tense, yet the bulge in his slacks tell me he's as ready as I am. Following his lead, I stand, tugging my T-shirt up and over my head.

My best friend is soon naked, offering me his body to use as I need. I want to get lost in him. I need to forget Caia because there's no way she would be with a monster like me. Opening the drawer, I grab the lube. Trickling a generous amount between River's cheeks, I drop my boxers and slowly massage him, from his shoulders down to the place I'm about to fuck. The tight ring of muscle around my one finger pulses, the sound of his groan evidence of his need for me.

I pull the foil packet from my desk drawer and rip it open with my teeth. Once I've sheathed my cock, I fist myself, positioning the tip at his entrance. Inch by inch, I slide into River, fucking myself deep in his ass.

His hands grip the edge of my desk, holding on, as my own fingers dig into his hips. A soft click steals my attention from him, and when I lift my eyes, I find Caia at the door. She's standing there, dressed in a small pair of shorts and a tight tank top. Her nipples are hard. Even in the dim light, I can see the peaks of her tits, needy for my mouth. Lifting one hand, I crook my finger, calling her to us.

Her bare feet pad shyly as she makes her way into the room, the door shutting behind her. I fist River's hair, tugging his head up so he can see her watch us fuck.

"Looks like we have a voyeur in our midst," I smirk, balls-deep inside River's ass.

"Come closer, princess," he calls to her. I can hear the

smile in his voice. She does. Slowly but surely, she nears us, and I watch as her eyes are glued to the scene before her. "Take your top off."

"I . . . I . . . can't." Her voice is barely a whisper.

I pull out slowly, slamming back in deep. River's pleasured groans echo around us as Caia's lips part in a gasp. Her chest rises and falls faster and faster as I move my hips, thrusting against River's body.

"Touch yourself, little raven. I want to watch you fly," I tell her, staring at her slight frame. She hesitates for a moment, as if she's unsure of her next movement. It's like I can see the wheels turning in her head, then she smiles shyly, settling herself on the chair opposite my desk, and slowly teases her nipples through the material of her top.

"Good girl," River hisses in pleasure as I pull out, thrusting harder and faster against him. Fucking into him with animalistic desire. The two people who hold my heart before me, their pleasured moans turning me wild.

Caia takes the lead, her hand dropping between her thighs as she gently touches her core. I'm sure the material is wet, drenched with her sweet, slick juices. Her head drops back, her whimpers louder as I continue driving into River's ass.

My best friend begs for more, for me. "Fuck, do it, Drake." His voice is raspy as I pull out, then thrust in deep. My body shudders with need, with desire burning through me, and I find pleasure and euphoria as River moans, Caia cries out, and I fill the condom with jets of hot release.

I pull out, slipping the rubber from my softening dick. Disposing of the condom, I pull on my boxer briefs and meet Caia's wide eyes.

"Come here, little bird." I smile. She slides from the

chair, rising silently. As she nears me, the scent of her sweetness invades my nostrils. Her head tips back so she can look up at me. Without shoes, she's even shorter, and I love how small she is compared to me.

"Did you like the show?" River questions, his cock hard, jutting from between his thighs. Thick, hard, and pierced, the silver ring at the tip shines in the light from the desk lamp.

"I've never . . . I mean . . ."

"Shh," I whisper, running my knuckles over her cheek. Lowering myself to my knees, I pull her with me. Nodding up at my best friend, he leans against the desk. "Are we going to do this together?" I question her, my hand gripping River's hard erection. Slowly, I stroke it, jerking him against my lips as I lean in, taking him into my mouth, my eyes locked on Caia's as she watches me.

I never told her about my past. She doesn't know the things I've done, how I've been conditioned to find pleasure, to find the release most people can without the sick needs in their heads. I need it. I've been broken. My mind severed from the normal desires of the human mind.

I don't think she'll do anything. She sits quietly for a long while as I suck River deeper into my throat. But then she shocks the shit out of me when she leans in closer as soon as I pull his cock from my mouth, and she takes him into hers.

"Sweet fucking Christ," River hisses low and gravelly, and I know my girl, our girl, will be just fine working with us to take down the assholes who hurt her, who hurt me, and most importantly, who hurt her sister.

We continue pleasuring my best friend, taking turns

sucking and licking him until he grunts his release, painting her tongue alongside mine with his sticky release.

We move fluidly, my lips molding to Caia's as we share River's seed, tasting and reveling in the juices, and she swallows what's left after I break the kiss.

"You're ready," I tell her, confident that she doesn't need to be trained. She has been trained all her life. It's time for her to shine. To take back the life that was stolen from her.

"For what?"

"To be ours."

CHAPTER FIFTEEN
CAIA

A soft humming wakes me from a dreamless sleep. When I open my eyes, I find my sister sitting on the window seat with a book in her lap. She's focused on the pages, her gaze locked on the words. She's wordlessly singing a song I don't recognize.

I can't move. Listening to her melody makes me sad. The pain in the song grips my heart, squeezing it until my breaths become uncomfortable.

"Hey," I say, pushing up against the headboard.

Harper's head whips my way. Her eyes crinkle at the sides as she strolls toward me. "Hey, sis." She smiles, gifting me one of those special grins that only my sister can offer.

"What are you doing?" Swinging my legs over the edge of the bed, I push off the mattress. Once I near Harper, I notice the book she's holding. I've not heard of it, but then again, I've not been allowed to read books of my choosing, watch television, or anything else.

"Dante had a box of books delivered for me." She smiles

sweetly. There's a softness to the way she mentions his name, and I wonder if my sister wants Drake's brother.

"I see." Settling on the seat beside her, I lean in on her folded legs, placing my cheek on her knees. Closing my eyes, I focus on the warmth of my sister. "Do you like him?" I question, unsure what my sister is feeling or going through. I don't doubt that Dante would keep her safe, but for some reason, I want to know if my sister is falling for the brother of the man who holds my heart.

After last night, I'm confused about my feelings. With River and Drake, everything blew up into something I'd never experienced. Having them both there, watching them, sharing pleasure with Drake and River, was so far outside my comfort zone, but the difference was I wasn't forced to do anything. They allowed me to be me. To enjoy them without any rules, any restrictions. It was purely based on need. Drake has never told me about his past, but something inside, something deep down in my gut reminds me that his father was Malcolm Savage.

"I do like Dante, but . . ." Harper finally responds, dragging me from the turmoil in my mind and in my heart. When I meet her gaze, I know there's so much more to her feelings for Dante. I don't know how long they've been close or how long she's been here, but something must've shifted in that time.

"Harper—"

"He has never touched me. Nothing's happened. I just . . . I just like him," she tells me wistfully, and I realize my sister has a crush. She's not a teenager anymore, but the way she's acting it's as if she's still sixteen. Sadness once again lances me, slicing through my chest.

I lift my head, looking at my sister, noticing her

sweetness and innocence. Even though she's been through so much before, she's still a girl. A young woman who experiences life the way she should.

"Do you like Drake?" She smiles, tipping her head to the side. Her gaze pierces me with curiosity as she regards me with a knowing smile.

"This is where I was brought when I was stolen," I finally confess. "Drake was the first man to . . . I begged him to take my virginity so the assholes who were going to buy me didn't claim it." I don't know why I just told her that, but I needed to finally voice it out loud. Not once since I met Drake to the moment he saved me have I confessed what I did that night in his office. I pleaded with the blue-eyed devil to take the one thing I held dear.

Do I regret it?

No.

Would I do it again?

Yes.

"And he did it?" Harper's eyes are wide with shock as she regards me. I nod in response. "What was it like?" she asks, causing me to look at her with confusion. "I . . . mine was . . . I didn't have a choice." Her voice drips with sadness, and my heart is finally crushed into pieces I'm not sure I can ever put back together. While I was lucky to have Drake, my sister wasn't that lucky, and I feel like it's my fault for being stolen. It's stupid. I shouldn't feel guilt, but I can't stop the emotion taking hold of me.

A knock at the door startles us. When it opens slowly, a young woman strolls inside. She smiles, setting a garment bag on the bed. She doesn't tell us anything, or even utter a hello, merely nods, then she's gone.

"I guess that's mine," I finally say. We're both sitting

there staring at the object as if it's about to attack us. But I know what it is. The dress Drake told me he'd have delivered. "What's the time?" I question, glancing at my sister.

She smiles. "It's after noon. You got to bed really late last night." It's not an accusation, merely an observation. I nod in agreement, remembering what happened when I sought out Drake and instead found him and River and joined in their erotic and sensual display.

"I had to meet with Drake. I'm going to be working with them soon," I tell Harper. She may be young, but she's not stupid.

"It's dangerous," my sister offers, and I dip my chin in agreement again. It is indeed, but this is something I need. Something I've been fighting for all my life since the day I was stolen. I wanted to give up, but what kept me going was the image of my father lying dead in a pool of blood.

"I know, Harper, but" — I offer her a reassuring squeeze on the leg — "this is something I need to do. And I need you to understand."

She watches me rise from the seat, padding my way to the bag on the bed. After the zipper hisses, I pull out the hanger, finding a dress more suited to a fashion model. Floor-length, bright-red silk hangs in soft waves.

The neckline is cut low in the back, hitting the bottom of my spine. The front would sit just between my breasts. The soft material is gentle to the touch, delicate, and I know he picked this out for a reason.

"He loves you." My sister's voice cuts through my thoughts.

"What?"

She shrugs nonchalantly as she drops her gaze back to

the book she's been reading. "He loves you. I can tell." Harper doesn't look at me, but her observation makes my skin tingle with awareness. I watch my baby sister focus back on her book, and I know, deep down, she's not the girl I remember. She's a broken, shattered young woman I may never get back.

CAIA

The dress Drake chose hangs over my slight frame, with slits up to each thigh, hinting at the skin beneath. The neckline offers a view of the ink that now adorns my skin. Since the cut is so revealing, I can't wear a bra, but he made good on another promise — the panties he chose are exquisite black lace.

Harper helped me tie my hair into a tight chignon, and my makeup accentuates my cheekbones and the dark shade of my eyes. My lips are stained a cherry red, matching the dress. My shoes offer me height; the four-inch heels are a deep red, and I know Drake chose these for a reason. One I won't think about right now.

Stepping from the room, I wander down the hallway. When I near the living room, I hear the gentle giggle of my sister. Upon entering the space, I find her sitting beside Dante at the grand piano positioned in the far corner. They're tinkling on the keys, playing something random, but the smile on her face seems to light up the entire room.

"Oh wow," she gasps when she glances my way. "You look amazing. That dress is made for you."

Nodding, I offer a smile. "Thanks, sis. It's a perfect fit."

"My brother has exquisite taste," Dante offers. Rising from the seat, he stalks closer to me. "I think he forgot to deliver this to your room." He makes his way to the cabinet, opening a small drawer. He hands me a sleek black box, allowing me to open the top. Inside, lying on the velvet, is a silver necklace. The dainty design shimmers in the light. A pendant is attached to the chain — a bird, a small onyx raven with a tiny diamond as the eye. Ever watchful.

"This is incredible."

"As are you, Caia." The voice from behind me has me spinning on my heel to meet the blue gaze of Drake Savage. Dressed in a black suit, white button-up, and a cherry-red tie, he looks immaculate. His dark hair is tousled, perfectly messy, but elegantly styled. He hasn't shaved, and the stubble on his jaw is thicker, making him look more distinguished than ever before.

He closes the distance between us, plucking the necklace from the velvet and helping me lock the clasp in place around my neck. The raven sits between my small breasts, glinting in the low light.

"Dante, you'll stay here with Harper." It's not a question. It's an order.

"I'll keep the young princess company." Dante turns to my sister who's blushing furiously. I'm not sure she should be involved with Dante Savage. There's something dangerous about him. But then again, I'm falling for a man who I know could hurt me more than anyone ever has.

"Let's go." Drake turns and struts from the living room. Quickly, I make my way to Harper, giving her a hug before following my date for the evening. I've played the arm-candy role so many times over the past few years, but all those times I was forced into it. Now, I'm willingly walking beside a man to be shown off like a piece of art.

Drake opens the door of the midnight blue Maserati GranCabrio. Taking my hand, he helps me slip into the passenger seat. The material of my dress falls open, the slit offering him a generous view of my thighs.

"You do look exquisite." He smiles, shutting the door and rounding the front of the vehicle. As soon as the engine purrs to life, Drake glances my way. "I trust you enjoyed last night?"

I can't help blushing at the question. The memory so fresh in my mind. My stomach somersaults at the desire that overtook me with him and River.

"Perhaps." I smile, turning my attention to the window instead of meeting his penetrating gaze. It burns me. It digs into my soul and disarms me. Drake can see all the darkness lurking beneath the surface, all those needs I've hidden away come to the outside when he is near. We drive off the property onto the dark road before he speaks again.

"Tonight, you'll be a toy. My toy. They'll not touch you; I'll make sure of it. But whatever I do to you, I'll need you to allow it." He doesn't look my way, instead focusing on the road ahead. "The man we're meeting is volatile."

"I understand."

"Good."

The rest of the drive is silent. We don't talk about what happened, and all the questions I wanted to voice no longer find their way from my tongue. I reach for the pendant, holding onto it as if it's going to give me strength for what's to come. I'll be his tonight, but my traitorous heart wants more than one night. It wants to belong to him.

Drake pulls up to large gate moments later. There are four men with guns on either side of the car, and my heart gallops wildly in my chest at the sight of them.

"Good evening," Drake greets one of the men confidently. "We're here for the gala." He hands a card, which I can only guess is the invite, to the security guard who nods swiftly, and the gates glide open allowing us onto the enormous property.

Once we're parked, a young man opens my door, assisting me with an offered hand. I walk beside Drake as if we were a couple. It feels real, and just for a moment, I smile.

"I think you like role playing," Drake whispers in my ear, sending heated shivers through me.

"I think you just like watching me submit to your needs."

The large wooden door slides open, and we're welcomed into a stunning entrance hallway. "I do. But I also revel in seeing my little bird fly," he finally responds, but I have no time to give him a retort because we're led deeper into the house where we find more couples mingling as if it were a normal dinner party.

The room they walk us into is exquisite, just like I thought the house would be. There are a few men I recognize, but none of them pay me any mind. Thankfully, I'm forgettable to them.

I follow Drake as he weaves his way through the crowd, my gaze flitting over each of the young girls dressed in expensive gowns. Seating myself beside Drake at one of the tables, I watch as he grabs two flutes of bubbly golden alcohol.

"Drink this," Drake offers. "So, you see anyone you know?"

"A couple of the men in the corner at the bar," I whisper, sipping the champagne slowly. I've not eaten much today, and I need to be aware of my surroundings. Setting the glass down, I settle back in the chair, waiting for Drake's next order.

One of the men I recognize from my time with Thanos strolls up to the podium, his hands shaking as he holds onto the wooden surface. He looks older, frail almost compared to the last time I'd seen him. A cold shiver trickles down my spine, reminding me of what he did to me.

My skin burns, but I don't turn to Drake. I can feel his stare locked on me, and I know he's trying to grab my attention, but I'm slowly drowning in the darkness of the night this man took me into the room Thanos had set up for his parties.

THE ELEGANT ROOM IS LIT WITH THE LARGE CRYSTAL CHANDELIER *hanging in the middle of the ceiling. The women and men are dressed in their fineries. It's a party for royalty, only the people here are nothing to be worshipped. They're creatures with animalistic needs that only violate others.*

"This," the man by my side whispers, "is your future. You're only nineteen, but you'll learn." He places a kiss on my cheek as if we're a couple. But revulsion skitters through me, causing my throat to burn with bile.

His hand on my lower back isn't gentlemanly; it's an order, a warning. *I need to obey, or I'll hurt more than what he has in store for me.*

He allows me to walk in front of him, and I'm caught between his hard body and the man who steps in front of me.

"This is an exquisite little toy," the man before me utters, lifting his hand to my chin, his thumb and forefinger catching it in his hold.

"She's our entertainment for the evening," Yeoman, that's his name if I recall correctly, says.

"Good." The response is all the man in front of me offers before he pulls me closer. Then, as if it's merely a flimsy piece of paper, my dress is shredded, and I'm left naked in front of the two men.

They move closer, hands and fingers exploring me, probing me painfully as they dip into me forcefully. My knees tremble as pain sears me when Yeoman, who's behind me, shoves two fingers into the tight ring of muscle of my ass.

"She's perfectly tight. Practically a virgin," he tells his friend.

"Then we'll happily break her until she's bleeding."

I blank out then. Darkness consumes me, and I'm breathing through the agony that grips me from the front and back.

Closing my eyes, I pray for death. I will it to steal me. But I'm not that lucky.

DRAKE'S HAND SUDDENLY FINDS MY THIGH, CAUSING ME TO JOLT IN surprise. His lips brush along my ear, and he whispers, "I'm right here beside you. They're not going to touch you." A reminder. A promise.

I attempt a nod, but I'm still cold from being thrust back into this world.

"Good evening, ladies and gentlemen." The man smiles.

"Tonight, we have a special treat for you. One of our girls has just turned twenty-one, and we're going to give a lovely gift." His words turn my blood to ice, and Drake's fingers only tighten their hold on me.

The monster before me smirks before he continues his speech.

"I know there have been many of you applying to be a part of this evening's festivities, but sadly we could only choose five." There's a murmur around the room, and I have to wonder what that means. This is certainly different from the events I've been a part of, but the fear of my memories grips me in their fierce hold.

Another older man, who looks like he's in his fifties, saunters up onto the podium and offers a smile at the crowd watching him. "Tonight, we'll be in the viewing dungeon. Make sure to bring your toys along. They'll want to see what happens when they disobey."

"Stay here." Drake's voice is low, urgent, causing me to tremble. With that, a flurry of activity takes hold of the room. Drake rises, sauntering toward the front of the room that's set up like an award ceremony with security dotted around the perimeter, along with a few other men in expensive suits and graying hair, looking pleased with themselves. He offers a few handshakes, and while I'm alone watching him from a distance, I recall those moments when I bled out all over him, how warm his hands felt. How his promises were whispered over the screams and shouting of that night.

He told me he'd find me. If only he knew how much I waited for him to come for me, to leave this world and be with him; but now I know why he didn't. He had to take over from his father. When he offers a goodbye to the men,

he finally casts a glance my way. Those eyes lock on mine, and I'm sucked into his orbit.

I take note of their faces from where I'm seated, locking them to memory, because soon enough, we'll go after each one of them, and when we do, I'll enjoy every bloody moment they offer me. Drake returns, offering me his hand, which I accept. He pulls me to my feet, his body flush with mine, and his mouth finds my ear once more.

"We need to go down to the viewing room. I'm going to make a call to River to let him know to bring the team now. Stay calm. Don't be alarmed if I do anything out of character. I will not hurt you."

My mouth falls open, but no words come out. I jerk my chin down once in silent agreement, attempting to swallow the lump of fear sitting in my throat. I follow the man I'm entrusting my life to as we make our way into the depths of another hell.

The room we enter is less opulent — a stark contrast to where we just were. There are seats set out as if we're in a cinema. Drake pulls me toward him; settling himself in one of the luxurious seats, he tugs me onto his lap.

"I want you close," he tells me in a hushed tone that skitters over my skin. His arm lazily drapes over my lap, and the other wraps around my middle. The room fills up quickly, and soon enough, the black curtains are opened onto a scene that's straight from a horror show. On the stage is a girl bound by her wrists. She's naked except for a pair of panties that hug her slight frame.

My eyes prick with tears when I take her in, when the memories assault me with a vengeance so fierce I want to throw up. Drake's gentle touch grips me tight, his fingers holding onto me as if I'm spinning and can't stop, and he's the only thing grounding me.

"Focus," he whispers. He pulls out his phone, tapping a message I can't see. Once he's done, he slides the device into his pocket. The footfalls of men sound from the stage, and I glance up to see five men circling the girl like vultures about to feast on the decaying meat of a carcass.

"Good evening, gentleman, and a special good evening to the beautiful Ms. Easton, whose birthday it is today," Yeoman, the man who attended the dinner parties with Thanos says, his gaze lingering on the girl for far too long. Three women dressed all in black enter. They're all made up with hair and makeup that looks professionally done, joining the men on stage.

CHAPTER SEVENTEEN
DRAKE

Caia is shaking on my lap. I know fear has a hold of her, but if she can't get through this, she'll never be able to kill her father in cold blood. She needs to learn to be stronger, to be tougher. My hands on her body hold her steady, keeping her from toppling from my lap as one of the women on stage walks up to the girl, pulling her underwear from her hips.

Once she's completely naked, one of the men kneels, spreading the slim legs of the girl and leans in. Running his nose up and down her inner thighs, we hear the groan that his action elicits as it rumbles through his chest.

"Perfect purity," he utters when he rises. My stomach turns with acidic bile, but I can't stop my cock from throbbing. I've been conditioned, and it saddens me that I can't stop it. Caia glances at me, and I know she can feel my erection against her ass.

"I'm sorry," I tell her soundlessly. My lips moving, but my voice is hidden from the assholes we're surrounded by. I don't know why I'm apologizing; Caia knows I'm a monster, but I don't want her to hate me. My anger gets the better of me most times, and I know I'm volatile.

She leans in and whispers in my ear, "I understand." There's a screech from the stage, and all I see is blood trickling down the girl's thighs, down to her calves. I notice one of the guests chuckling beside Ms. Easton holding onto a long, thick dildo which has spikes protruding from the shaft.

The crimson liquid stains her porcelain flesh, and my cock shamelessly hardens, pressing against Caia, wanting entrance, needing slick warmth.

Shutting my eyes, my fingers dig into my little bird's thigh in an attempt to shove the image from my mind. A soft whimper from her doesn't help when her lips graze my ear. Her heated breath sending my need skyrocketing. My blood burns for her; it's at boiling point, and I'm praying, I'm fucking praying for salvation, because all I want to do is fuck Caia while watching the horrific scene on the stage.

And the god I didn't believe in offers me grace, because River and the team slam through the room with guns blazing. I lift Caia from my lap, pulling out my 9mm from the holster hidden by my suit jacket. I hand it to her, wrapping her fingers around the metal.

"Get in the corner," I order, guiding her to the safest area. Bodies are dropping fast, and I need to get to River. Casting a glance around, I find him nearing me. He throws another weapon at me, which I catch, and soon I'm right beside him in war. The girls are being ushered out of the room, and the men are being slain with guns and knives.

Racing through the room, I grip the shirt of the asshole Caia pointed out. His face is right in mine as he rears back, slamming his fist into my jaw, causing me to stumble backward. Tasting the blood on my lip, I smirk at him, raising the gun River handed me.

"It's time for you to pay for your sins," I tell him. That's when I feel her. The warmth of Caia is right at my back. His eyes dart to her, narrowing as he takes her in.

"You're the little bitch I fucked at Thanos's party," he chuckles, then lands his dark eyes on me. "You buy this toy from him? You're killing me for her?"

Tipping my head to the side, I laugh. A loud, maniacal guffaw. "I'm killing you because you deserve to die." My words are a violent hiss. Rage billows through me, a storm thundering through every inch of my body. But before I can pull the trigger, Caia steps forward, closing the distance between her and the asshole I want to drop to the ground.

"You're the devil," she tells him, tilting her head upward, meeting his inquisitive gaze. The tiny girl taking on a man double her size. He sneers, slapping her, and my body is propelled forward.

Knocking him to the ground, I straddle his middle, my fists raining down on him, again and again. Blood splatters everywhere as I take out the rage I feel on his face. A loud crack tells me I've broken his nose.

Caia's hand on my shoulder is the only thing that breaks through the darkness consuming me, and I still. The wrinkled skin of the man on the floor beneath me is bloodied, his teeth red, his nose at a strange angle, but he's still alive.

My sweet little bird crouches down, a smile on her face, causing me to frown. She looks at the man for a long while, then pushes the gun I gave her into his mouth and pulls the trigger, shocking me once more today.

"Goodbye, Mr. Yeoman," she utters, then glances at me.

"I'm ready, Drake. I can do this." Her confidence shines through her fear, and I rise, pulling her along with me. River sidles up to us. The eight men and three women who were here for the gala are all dead.

"This wasn't as much fun as our last kill, but I can safely say I'm hard as fuck right now," River chuckles beside me, winking at Caia who instantly blushes, and I'm certain she's recalling last night.

"Get the men to clean up. We'll head back to the house." My order is swift, and my best friend nods. Lacing my fingers through Caia's, I pull her along as we make our way down the long hallway toward the exit. We pass a few closed doors, and I wonder just what's inside them.

Before we hit the staircase, I shove one door open to find a bathroom. I tug my little raven into the space and shut the door, pressing her against the hard wood.

"What are you doing?" she questions breathlessly. The gentle sound is an aphrodisiac I didn't need, but welcome anyway. Lifting her dress, I tug her panties to the side and dip two fingers into her cunt. She's drenched, tight, pulsing around the digits.

"I'm going to fuck you." I don't ask; I don't need to, because she wants this as much as I do. Her delicate fingers fumble with my zipper, and soon, her fist is wrapped around my hard shaft. Pulling my fingers from her core, I place them in her mouth, shoving them into her throat, coating her tongue with the sweet essence of her pussy.

"We need to talk," she tells me as I sink into her body.

"Then talk," I smirk, rolling my hips, causing her to whimper. Her hands grip my shoulders, and I hold onto her pert little ass. My body fits within hers perfectly.

"Last night," she starts, then a soft moan falls from her

lips when I pull out and slam back in. "I want this." I still at her confession, her eyes wide with lust, emotion, and want.

"River and me?"

She shakes her head, then nods. "I'm intrigued. I'm . . . I'm new to so much, and last night was just the first taste of it. Drake, I'm not refusing, but I need time to get used to this life." She's right. But I shake my head and continue fucking her. I can't love her. This is just a fuck. "For now, though." She gazes at me with a plea in her eyes. "Hurt me," she begs, causing my dick to jolt inside her, thickening farther, stretching her.

Gripping her throat, I squeeze, and her cunt pulses around me. I choke her, reveling in her eyes tearing up as I use her for my pleasure, but I know it's not only mine. She's getting off on this. She loves the pain. I lean in, my mouth latching onto her fat bottom lip, and I bite down hard, drawing blood from her flesh. I savor her flavor.

"Please," she mumbles, her gagging, choking sounds make me harder than I've ever been before as I pump into her faster and faster. "Oh god, please." Her plea causes my balls to draw up, and I empty myself inside her.

I've marked her.

I've fucking claimed her.

And I have no idea how to undo it.

But I don't think I want to.

CHAPTER EIGHTEEN
CAIA

My nerves are shot. They're fucking obliterated. I'd never thought I could kill someone, let alone two people within a few days of each other. But the moment I looked into Yeoman's eyes, I felt it, the need to purge the filth from my body. And Drake was right there to give me what I needed after. He fucked me against a bathroom door, and I begged for more.

The house is silent when we enter, and I wonder where my sister is.

"Dante took Harper out," Drake tells me as if he can read my mind. I turn to him, meeting those blue eyes that disarm me. They look into my soul, they chip away at the walls I'd built to shield myself, and they see right through my pain.

"Where did they go?" I question, walking beside Drake into the living room.

He shrugs. "Not sure. He mentioned he wanted to get to know her." I watch as he strolls up to the bar, filling two glasses with a deep red wine. The color so dark it's almost black.

"I'm not sure it's a good idea," I tell him when he turns to me. He hands me the glass, which I gratefully accept. Alcohol will hopefully calm my nerves that are frazzled by this evening's events.

"They're both adults. We can't tell them what to do," Drake tells me, settling on the sofa. His suit is stained with blood, but he doesn't seem fazed by the fact. "I want to talk to you. About tonight," he says, gesturing for me to sit beside him.

Perching myself on the sofa, I wait for him to continue. I'm not sure what he wants me to say, and I certainly don't know how to explain what happened. Something took over me. Rage. The anger of years of abuse finally let itself out.

"You told me you wanted this, to get revenge on your father, and I will certainly help you with that," he starts. "But I need to know one thing before we continue here, Caia." His gaze pins me to the spot. It steals my breath and causes my heart rate to spike. "Since the moment I laid eyes on you, I wanted you. I was planning to steal you from my father all those years ago."

"I didn't—"

"I'm not done," he interrupts me, and I allow him to. "You told me while I was fucking you that you wanted this." He gestures around us. "Did you mean River and me, because we're a package deal, or did you mean you wanted the vengeance?"

What did I want? Him. If he and River are the only way I'll have Drake, then I'll have to live with it, because as scary as it is, I can't live without Drake.

"I'm not forcing you to do anything you don't want to, little bird," he tells me. Scooting forward, he takes my hand in his. "But you need to know, I'm indeed savage. I'm angry, I'm dangerous, and I like the darkness. I've become accustomed to it."

"I'm not sure of everything right now, Drake, but I just can't be alone. The world out there scares me. I've been afraid for so long I'm not sure how to be anything else."

"You're strong as well," he affirms, sipping his wine as he regards me. "I'm not sure how to be anything other than violent."

"I guess the namesake runs deep." I shrug, earning me a smile from his handsome mouth. His face lights up with the action, and I find myself entranced by him. "What happened to your father?"

He shakes his head, lowering his gaze to the glass. "He died. Breathed his last breath a six months ago. River, Dante, and I made sure he saw our faces the moment he died. He suffered. Each day I poisoned his whiskey until the day it finally ate away at him and he was bedridden. Then, we took the final step and killed him," Drake says proudly. "There are a few things he left me with though. Things I haven't told River or Dante."

"Why? Aren't they your only family? Surely they need to know if something is wrong."

He lifts his blue eyes to meet my hazel ones. There are so many emotions flickering in his gaze it's startling to see. The windows to Drake's soul are tarnished with pain and agony, with violence and mayhem, and I have no idea if he would ever be free of them.

"My father held so many secrets from us, from River, it's

worrying. We found his sister in Thanos's house," he tells me.

"The wild girl?" Drake nods. "She's not the only family he has, is she?"

"No. River's mother worked for my father. She was on his payroll, and she sold River to the Savage Organization in the hopes of getting her ass seated in the White House."

A shocked gasp comes from the doorway. Both our heads whip toward the entrance to find River staring straight at his best friend.

"Shit," Drake hisses, rising from his seat, but River is gone. I follow quickly, wanting to comfort the man who's slowly becoming part of my life. I watch him race up the stairs, ignoring Drake calling his name. "Fuck it."

"I'll go." Placing a hand on his shoulder, I press a kiss to his cheek and follow River up to the second level of the house. When I reach the door with the large, ornate R carved into it, I knock tentatively. It flies open, and I'm met with the striking gaze of River.

"Can we talk?"

He shrugs in response. Leaving the door open, he makes his way into the room. When I enter, I take in the rich browns and golds in the room. Deep, warm colors furnish the space, offering a homey feel. He turns to me, his green gaze penetrating mine with curiosity.

"He didn't want you to find out like this," I start, unsure of how to speak to him.

"And you know my best friend so well?" His voice is low, but I hear him. I don't respond, because I can't say I do. Drake is mostly a stranger to me, but I don't feel it. For some reason, it's as if we've known each other all our lives.

"Perhaps not as well as you, but I can see the pain he holds onto. This can't be easy for him," I implore, wishing he would see that this wasn't a plot to hurt him.

"You know," River breathes as he nears me. Our bodies inches apart, and the spark that ignites between us is something new.

Drake has always been the one to make my body come alive, but with what happened last night, it seems River can ignite my desire just as much.

He leans in, closing the distance between his mouth and my ear, before he whispers, "Drake didn't give up looking for you, even though I told him it was futile."

Even though the room is empty, I feel the nervous fear that I'll be ripped away from them both. That I'll be severed from my links to both men, and I'll once more be shoved into a hole in the ground.

"And each time he tried to find you, I watched the agony on his face when it was a dead end. I've seen his pain. I've tasted it, savored it. Don't tell me that you're the only one who sees it."

His words cause me to snap my gaze to his. "I want this," I tell him then, offering the same words I gave Drake moments ago. Placing my hand on River's chest, I smile up at him. "I told him as well. I want you both in my life. There isn't a fight for who he'll choose, because I don't want him losing either of us. This isn't a game, River."

"I know it's not, darling," he smirks. Lifting his hand, he trails his knuckles over my cheek, causing chill bumps to rise over my skin. "You see, Drake is all caught up over you, and that makes this vendetta dangerous for him, for me, and for you," he tells me, glancing behind me, and I wonder if there's someone there. If Drake has silently entered and he's watching our exchange. "Soon you'll learn all there is to know about Drake and me. Our past goes back so far into this shithole, we've survived so many things, and I just hope you're strong enough to stomach the truth." He shakes his head as if the memories are attempting to drag him under. When he meets my stare once more, he smiles sadly. "My best friend cares far too much about you."

"Are you jealous?" I bite out, confusion sizzling wildly in my chest.

River laughs, the sound almost melodic when he does. There's something he's not saying, and I know it's the fact that he's in love with his best friend. Green orbs trap me in a gaze so piercing I hold my breath for a moment.

"Caia, if I were jealous, I'd have ended you already. The thing is, I know you want him, and yes, he does want you as well. The way I see it, sweetheart, everything is better in threes," he tells me with a cocky wink, turning to walk away, but I grab his arm to halt his steps.

"Then accept me," I say. Right now, I know River is my only way to get Drake, his brother, and him out of here. To find the family they've lost, and to figure out how to end the monsters we all face.

"Are you sure you want this, Caia? Because once I agree, we will be bound by our promise." A dark brow arches at me in question.

"I do," I affirm with a nod. "You, Dante, and Drake have been in here for far too long. It's time to set yourselves free." This time my voice is a rushed whisper. "And your sister, we'll heal her somehow."

River nods once. Tugging his arm free, he smiles and

turns his back to me. I follow behind him as he heads out of his bedroom, and I know we're going to Drake. The plush carpet muffling our steps as we make our way down toward mahogany double doors. I know what's on the other side. The room where I lost my virginity. It's not the first time River is leading me here, and I know it won't be the last.

DRAKE

When the doors open and both River and Caia step inside, I offer them a smile. Thankfully, my best friend seems calmer than he did earlier.

"We need to talk," River says, settling on the antique leather sofa. Caia strolls over toward me, seating herself on the stool against the bar counter where I'm standing. I wait for River to start his demands. He'll want to know about his mother, his sister who we have in one of the cells downstairs. I don't know if he's been down there to talk to her, or try to at least, but if he has, he doesn't mention it.

"We do need to talk. There are things that I've kept from both you and Dante, and I think it's time we reveal the secrets that Malcolm kept."

He nods, watching me as I pour us all a drink. Setting his down on the table, I straighten and take a seat in the wingback chair that faces the door. Dante will be home soon, and I don't want him walking in on our conversation.

It's late. I can't deal with both River and my brother,

and after the night we've had, all I want is a shower and to sleep between Caia and River.

"Why did my mother leave me here? I want to know everything. Is she alive?"

"When Malcolm died, I found records, contracts between him and a lot of people I don't know. But there was one folder with your mother's name on it. When I opened it, there was a photo of you and her along with the agreement that she relinquishes all custody to Malcolm."

"But why would a mother do that?" Caia questions. Joining us, she settles beside River.

"To be honest, she was a power-hungry bitch." I shrug, not caring if it was my best friend's mother. It's the truth. And I'm not afraid to say it. "She'd asked my father to ensure her seat on the White House cabinet was confirmed, but when that didn't happen, she threatened to expose Savage Organization. That's when my father requested the gift of her daughter."

"But when I came here, I was young. I don't even remember Rayne being able to walk at that stage."

I nod at River's comment. "Yes, you came here at the age of ten. Rayne was about two-years-old, I think. At least that's what the paperwork says. She offered up her baby girl to Malcolm Savage for a CEO seat within the Organization, which she's currently running in Thailand. She left the US years ago," I tell him. Gulping down the drink, I set the empty glass on the table. I pull out a pack of cigarettes and light one before continuing. "I don't know if she's alive or not. She must've heard about Malcolm's death, because she's disappeared."

"So, my mother is a monster, just like the rest of them,"

River utters with so much sadness in his voice it grips my chest in a fierce hold.

"River, I—"

"No, it's fine," he says. Rising from the sofa, he stalks to the bar, refilling the glass I'd given him with a triple shot of whiskey. The amber liquid sloshes around the crystal as he swirls it. "I've lived with enough of this fucked-up shit in my life to know that having hope is pointless."

"That's not true," Caia pipes up. She's on her feet, closing the distance between her and my best friend. She gently places a hand on his shoulder, and I watch the scene play out before me. "Hope is something that may feel out of reach, but deep down, right here" — she places her finger tips on his chest, right where his heart is — "that's where you hold the people who matter, and they're the ones who offer you hope. Drake, Dante, and me." She whispers the last word, but I hear her. She's really in this. When she told me in the bathroom and then again in the living room that she wanted this, River and me, I didn't believe her. I'm not sure why, but I couldn't bring myself to hold out hope.

River nods, downing the alcohol in one long gulp. He winces, his face screwing up for a second. When he opens his eyes, he meets mine. "I'm going to bed. I need time."

"Okay." I only offer him one word because there's nothing more to say.

Once Caia and I are alone again, she sighs. "He'll need more than time."

"I know." My response earns me her stare. Those beautiful hazel eyes land on me as if she's seeking more from me right now. But I don't have anything to give. I've just fucked over my best friend with the news of his family, and now I have a girl I'm falling for looking for a knight.

I may have saved her, but I'm definitely not the good guy.

"I think I need to get some sleep," she tells me. Lowering her gaze to the floor, she smiles, twirling her toes into the carpet. "Thank you for keeping me."

"You're not a possession, Caia."

She doesn't respond. I watch her leave, the door clicking closed, and I'm alone once more. I wish I had time to do all the things I'd planned, but we don't have that luxury. My phone vibrates on the coffee table, and I pick it up to see Dante's name.

"Brother," I answer easily, leaning into the back of the chair.

"Saturday night, Amoretto is having a party. The list will be there. It could be the only chance we have to annihilate them all in one day."

"Killing a few birds with one stone," I offer with a satisfied smirk.

"Indeed, brother," Dante responds. "I have a show tonight; would you like to watch?"

This causes me to sit up straight. "Please don't tell me you're fucking around on Harper?"

"Not at all, dear brother. In fact, my little minx is going to be playing with a friend we found at the local club downtown." I consider it. A show would be fun, but my mind is filled with one girl and one only. And she's down the hall, within reaching distance. For the first time in my life, I might attempt to talk to her about my feelings.

"I'm busy tonight, but you enjoy yourself, Dante."

"Always do," he chuckles, then hangs up before I can get another word in.

Saturday. That's two days away. Tomorrow, we'll plan.

But tonight, I need to shower first, then perhaps pay my little bird a visit.

STROLLING THROUGH THE QUIET HOUSE, I HEAD INTO THE LIVING room, following the soft tinkling of the piano. Each moment I'm around Caia, I find myself more and more intrigued by her. I'm hungry, and she's the only thing that will satiate me. Leaning on the doorjamb, I watch her at the instrument. I bought it years ago, but never bothered learning to play. Dante is the one who enjoys it, who loves sitting on the bench and getting lost in the music.

I wanted to go to River, but I know he needs time to come to terms with everything he learned. The clock dings at three a.m., and I wonder why Caia is awake. A smile plays on my lips, and I find myself calmer than I've ever been. Perhaps on some level, I always knew I'd have her in my life.

Her delicate fingers dance across the keys — the expensive ebony and ivory — creating a melody that's both passionate and melancholic. A contrast. Just like the girl herself. She hums along with the song she's playing, and I don't recognize it. Her eyes are closed, and her head is bowed in concentration.

A memory of a song I'd like to play for her comes to mind. One that talks about devouring her. Where she's dressed in a pair of yellow cotton shorts, her long tanned legs hide under the piano. The black, form-fitting tank top hugging her soft frame makes my dick hard.

Only a few days have passed, but I can no longer deny it. All those years ago, I told myself she's just a new toy, but now I know she's so much more. Each night she was gone, I would still find myself stroking my shaft at night with her on my mind.

I pad into the room, trying to be quiet and not startle her. I know she realizes she's not alone because her finger hits the wrong note before once again finding her stride. I'm inches behind her when she finishes up the melody.

Silence engulfs us.

It holds us in its safety before she turns to face me over her shoulder. The pose innocent but sultry at the same time, and my dick responds in kind with a jolt.

"Do you do that on purpose?" I question, my eyes meeting hers. Those orbs that see right through my hardened exterior, right to my very core. The dark, depraved soul of who I am. And yet, she still wants it. She still wants to hold my evil in her angelic hands. She still wants to shield my dark heart in her light.

"Do you like watching me?" she asks with a knowing smile. I don't respond; instead, I hold out a hand to her, which she accepts. I pull her up from the small bench. Her frame is cocooned by mine.

Our bodies are inches apart when I lean in, feathering my lips over the shell of her ear. I can't stop my own desire burning me from the inside out, so I allow myself to let it consume me. Even for tonight, I just want to attempt to be normal.

"When you're alone at night hiding, you know I would seek you out. Don't you, little bird?" My words send a tremble over her frame. "Why don't you show me exactly what you do at night while you think of me?"

I step back, watching her. She stares at me for a moment, her lips parting with a soft gasp before hooking

SEVERED   233

her thumbs in the waistband of her shorts, shoving them down. Once they pool at her feet, she steps out them, and I notice she's naked beneath.

"Good little raven. A pretty bird, and I want to watch you fly," I say, never allowing my gaze to leave hers. I smile when she glares at me. I love when she's angry. There's something delicious, tempting, and alluring about the way she pins me with anger.

I had a plan. I ensured that there was nothing that could go wrong, but of course, when you allow emotions to get involved, there's always danger. When I first laid eyes on her, she was part of the hell. But now she's part of my salvation. She's become my light, and I no longer want to be in the dark. She may not need me, but I require her for much more than the jobs we will be doing together.

I was meant to save her, but it seems she was the one who saved me. She's become an endless shot of heroin to my veins. With every pull on my cigarette, each sip of alcohol, there's only one thing that can truly calm my anxiety.

Caia Amoretto.

CHAPTER TWENTY
CAIA

There were times in my life I knew what I wanted to do. When I was stolen, I didn't give up hope until I watched the blood draining from the wound that threatened to steal my life. Rolling over, I find the warm body of Drake Savage beside me.

He was the only sure thing I'd ever had. Even when I lived with Thanos, it was Drake who had given me hope. His long lashes flutter on his cheeks and his soft snores rumble through his chest. The smooth skin is enticing, and I can't stop my lips from pressing a kiss on the smooth curve of Drake's shoulder.

A click sounds from the entrance, and I turn to see River standing in the doorway. He smiles, entering and shutting the door without a sound. I take in every inch of him, the low hanging pajama pants he's wearing offer a glimpse of his hips, the dips of his oblique muscles clear as day. River is handsome. His eyes glint with mischief when he settles on the bed.

"We need to get planning," he tells me in a hushed

whisper.

I nod. I'm not sure what's going to happen in the next few days, or weeks even, but one thing is for sure. I want to be here, with them.

"Are you both here to piss me the fuck off?" Drake rumbles, his voice heavy with sleep, which makes me giggle. The sound is so foreign to me. And I let it take over, allowing myself to laugh for the first time in years. For the first time since I was stolen from my family, then severed from Drake.

I didn't know what was going to happen then either, and somehow, through all the darkness, I'm still here. "Don't be a grouch," I whisper, curling myself into his body. The heat of him makes me tingle on every inch of my skin.

"We do need to plan though," he responds, pulling me tighter in to his hold. "River, do we have the team on standby?"

"Yeah," River mutters, looking down at us both. "I've also got clean up ready. We need to tell them when and where to be."

Drake nods, groaning before planting a kiss on my head, then releases his hold on me. He swings his legs over the edge of the bed, rising from the mattress. His bare ass on view to both River and me.

"You're both fucking perverts," he chuckles, sauntering into the bathroom and shutting the door behind him. Every inch of Drake is hardened, toned, and muscled. And I can't help smiling at the thought of him being mine.

"He's an asshole at times," River tells me. "But I love him." Green eyes pin me to the bed when he looks at me. An inquisitive arching of his brow as he regards me. "Do you love him?"

I'm not sure what to say, how to tell him that I can certainly see myself falling for them both, but right now, I can't. "It's too soon for that," I respond. Scooting up the bed, I lean against the headboard as I regard him.

"I get that," he agrees. "But if you find at any point you can't love him, you need to walk away. I can't see him hurt again."

"I'll never hurt him." This time, my words are even more confident. "I just need time to come to terms with everything that's happened so far."

"Hey, you two need to stop with the emotional shit," Drake says, stalking closer to the bed. He's pulled on a pair of low-slung gray sweatpants and a white tank top that offers sneaky glimpses of his toned torso.

"Let's get to the office," River says, rising from the bed.

"I'll see you guys soon." They both nod in response, leaving me in the bedroom to mull over what River said. My feelings are all heightened. The fact that I've been here nearly a week now and I'm still jarred from being with Thanos, I'm unsure of my emotions.

Love.

It's a word I never thought I'd use again. Even considering it now, I'm fearful of the pain it could bring. There aren't any guarantees that this relationship between the three of us can work, but then again, you have to take a chance to find your happiness.

WALKING INTO THE OFFICE, I NOTICE DRAKE BEHIND HIS DESK before he looks up. His head is bowed over the iPad as he taps away on the screen. The room smells of his spicy cologne, which makes me smile. The man is an Adonis, with his almost-black, tousled hair, those ocean-blue eyes that seem to look right through you, and his sinful smirk that tilts just the corner of his mouth up.

As dangerous as he is, he's also pure sex.

Unadulterated, devilish, and he knows it.

"Are you going to stand there all day?" he questions without looking up. I don't respond. Instead, I shut the door and make my way toward the chair I sat in the other night while we had our filthy scene. Only, I'm no longer a stranger in his office. No. I've become more. I'm the girl he wants in his life.

"River is with the men. He's briefing them, and I'll be giving you the rules of what we're about to walk into." He doesn't look at me when he tells me this, but the tension in his shoulders seems to tighten with his confession. Finally, after a long moment, his eyes lift lazily up to me. From the black heels I'm wearing, up my bare legs, to the short black dress which hugs my slim frame, stopping momentarily on my breasts, then finding my hazel eyes.

"Sit," he orders, tipping his head to the side. The corner of his lips quirk, and I'm afforded a panty-melting grin. He sits back and regards me with those sky-blue eyes. I settle on the chair, relaxing back in the large wingback covered in a soft red leather.

"What is happening?"

"You play quite the innocent woman, little bird," Drake says with a soft smile.

"Perhaps," I grin, crossing my legs, one over the other. I know I'm taunting him. He expects me to be the broken girl. Maybe he wants me to be that, but I'm far from it. Something inside me clicked last night. Drake offered me the confidence I was sorely lacking. He's given me so much more than I've ever dreamed he could.

"This weekend, there's a party happening," he tells me. "Your father will be there, Caia." His words still me for a moment.

Swallowing the fear, I nod.

I rise. Stalking over to his desk, I lean my ass against it beside his chair. Gripping the edge, I lift myself onto the rich, varnished oak. He doesn't move. A statue. But I feel his eyes; they bore into me, burning me from the inside out.

That's when I spread my thighs, wide enough for him to see I'm not wearing anything under my skirt. No words, only a guttural sound resounds deep in his chest. The sky-blue that was present only second ago turns molten. They darken to a shade that reminds me of a stormy sea.

"Jesus," he growls, running his fingers through his dark hair. His other hand grips my thigh painfully as his fingers press into the soft skin. "You're a bad girl, Caia. Do you know what happens to girls like you?" he asks, snapping his glare to mine.

"They get what they want, Mr. Savage." The game I've played for four long years is ingrained in me. I've become something else. I've become something I no longer recognize, but I'm stronger for it.

"Very true, little bird. Very true," he agrees. "Tell me about the first time you had to use your body to get something from one of Thanos's clients. I need to know if you're ready for this weekend."

I close my eyes, sitting on his desk, and recall the moment I turned off all my emotions. The day I became a whore for Thanos. Not by choice, but because the moment I refused, I'd bleed, for days.

. . .

THE DRESS HE'S GIVEN ME TO WEAR IS LONG, FALLING TO THE
*floor. The material a soft silk that hugs my slim frame, and the
neckline is cut low in the front. He knows what his clients want,
and tonight, I'll be the pawn in the game this man plays.*

My owner.

*Strolling through the room, I exit and head into the hallway.
He's waiting at the end of the passage, dressed in an immaculate
suit.*

*I'm no longer scared. I spent far too long being afraid of
what was going to happen to me. But I've finally accepted that
this isn't going to change a thing. Thanos will still hurt me. He'll
use me like a toy, a piece in the puzzle game that will someday
come to an end.*

*Thanos smirks when I reach him. I can't cower, or he'll get
angry, so I straighten my spine and meet his stare. There's
nothing good inside this man. He's filth.*

*He reaches for me, his large hand gripping my arm, and my
stomach bottoms out. I recognize the feeling immediately —
rage.*

*"I trust you'll get the information from him this evening," he
says close to my ear, allowing his alcohol-scented breath to fan
over my face.*

*"As you wish," I tell him with a small smile. If I don't, he'll
hurt me. He gave me the rules early on, informing me of what
I'm here for. A whore for his needs. The men he brings here are
powerful, their positions in government and various businesses
give him the information he needs to blackmail them into doing
his bidding.*

*He leans in. His scent is heavy, surrounding me like a cloud,
making my stomach recoil. His mouth is on my neck, suckling*

the flesh, while his teeth bite down hard causing me to whimper. "I'm certain Harrison will show you what filthy little toys like you deserve." His promise triggers horrific images to race through my mind.

Without another word, he pulls me down the hallway and shoves me into the room. I can't help stumbling into a solid wall of a man on the other side of the threshold. When I lift my gaze, I find green eyes staring down at me. There's desire dancing in them, need for something I'm meant to offer.

"Such a pretty little whore," he smirks, then glances behind me, offering my owner a nod. He kicks the door shut behind me, and I know there's no escape. I don't respond. I'm not allowed to, so I follow him deeper into the room. There's a long table that sits only inches from where we stop, and he pushes me onto the surface. His hand on the middle of my back forces me down. My breasts squashed against the wooden top, while my ass juts out toward him.

"Open your legs." I do as he instructs. He lifts the skirts of my dress, bunching it around my hips, and then his hands are on the fleshy globes of my ass. He squeezes them harshly, spreading them open. "Filthy holes. Do you want them abused, fuck-toy?"

"If you wish." My words are broken, cracked with sadness.

I tremble with fear when a harsh spank on my ass causes me to yelp. Closing my eyes, I hear the shuffle of material, but he doesn't enter me. Instead, he wraps his tie around my head, the material pressing between my lips, making me gag.

"Your owner tells me you're obedient. I buy girls all the time, and some of them are far too annoying with their whining," he chuckles. That's all he says before he slams into me so fast it steals my breath. He slides out, and in. Back and forth. One long stroke after another. My cries are muffled by his tie. His grunts are low and feral. Basal. He's animalistic as he takes me. "Fucking little *slut. Coming in here, making me hard. This is what you wanted. Isn't it?" he hisses under his breath as he tugs me back by my hair.*

Our bodies slap together, echoing in the room. The burn of his cock inside me only makes me whimper in agony, which he thinks is pleasure. His hands grip me painfully, and I know I'll be bruised tomorrow. He suddenly pulls out of my body, the heat of his release splatters on my ass, running down my thighs.

Tears trickle down my cheeks as the agony takes hold. I'm about to rise when he presses a finger between the cheeks of my ass, forcing it into the tight entrance. My body tenses in shock. It's not the first time someone has touched me there. Thanos has been inside every part of me, but fear still grips me. He rips the tie from my mouth, and I'm free to cry out, but I don't. I've learned not to make a sound.

"You're tighter than my whore," he grunts.

"How many girls have you done this to?" I question, knowing my owner wants all the information I can get out of this man. "Does your wife not allow you to do this?"

He chuckles. "My wife is a frigid bitch. That's why I have you little sluts to give me what I need." His response drips with malice as he opens me, stretching the tight ring of muscle painfully. "So pretty." Another dark chuckle vibrates in his chest. Spit drips onto my ass while he uses two fingers to spread me. Seconds later, I'm filled, and it feels like I'm being torn in two.

My eyes shut tight as I cry out. I can no longer bite my tongue because the pain is far too much. Everything stills, and I feel him throb.

"I've paid a pretty penny for you to take my dick." He leans in, whispering in my ear. "But I didn't ask you to talk." His fat hand wraps around my delicate throat, and he squeezes. "You like this, don't you? A broken toy who gets off on being abused."

His words are vile, and my stomach turns. The bile that rises to my throat burns its way onto my tongue. That's when he pulls out of me and drags me to the floor. Shoving me to my knees, he grips his dick and forces it into my mouth. A groan of pleasure rockets through him as I choke and gag on the tip of his dick prodding my throat.

I wait for it. My hands gripping my ankles and soon enough, he empties another load of semen onto my tongue. The sour flavor causes my puke to overflow, and it hits the carpet in a splatter.

"Stupid bitch," the man groans. "Tell your owner that if he wants to partner with me, he needs to find younger, more useful toys."

He stalks from the room, leaving me reeling from what just happened. My knees hurt, my body aches, and my soul has darkened to the point that I no longer recognize who I am. Pushing from the floor, I rise onto wobbly legs and make my way to the small chair at the window. The curtains are drawn, and I don't open them. I don't want to see what's out there, what I can no longer have.

Thanos won't be happy about what happened. I'm meant to please the partners. To ensure they sign with him. And the man who just walked out didn't seem like he was happy. Tears stream down my face when I think about what my life has become.

The door opens, and my owner saunters in. His eyes burning through me with rage and hatred. I don't know why he doesn't just kill me. When he reaches me, his hand grips my hair, tugging me from the chair.

"Do you want me to hurt you?" Curiosity and confusion lace his words. "Do you want it like that, fuck-toy? Tell me."

I want to answer him, but bile rises in my throat again, causing me to swallow deeply. I've been conditioned to want to be hurt. The images that still play in my mind on a constant loop are evidence that I need the darkness to feel pleasure. But there's only one man I want to give it to me — Drake Savage.

"No, sir," I say before he retaliates with force.

"Go to your room. You're not allowed food today, and perhaps even tomorrow. You've disappointed me, toy." His voice is rough, almost raspy, and I wonder if he was thinking about fucking me. It's the only time he comes near me. When he releases his hold on me, I skitter away before he changes his mind.

I can't walk properly, but I make my way to my room safely without seeing anyone else in the hallways. The other doors are all locked, and I know they hide girls behind them. I curl up on the bed and sob. I allow all the pain from tonight to ebb away. But I know it's not the end. Not yet anyway.

WHEN I OPEN MY EYES, DRAKE IS STARING AT ME WITH BARELY controlled rage. His body is vibrating as if he's about to explode. The danger that emanates from him is stifling. But he doesn't respond. He doesn't say a word.

I want to walk away, but when I shift from his desk, he holds me still. Leaning in, he plants a soft kiss on my thigh, then mimics the action on my other leg. Again, and again. Gently, he moves up to my core, and his lips press against my bare pussy, causing me to whimper with need.

"Never again" — he whispers over the slick flesh — "will you be hurt. You belong to me now. And nothing will ever change that."

And that's how I know I'm never leaving Drake Savage again.

CHAPTER TWENTY-ONE
DRAKE

A week has passed since I found her. Since I stole her from the man who took her from me. Tonight, we'll enter a lion's den, and I can't promise that I'll save her from this. I've never been a nervous person, but this is something that scares me. Knowing all those men could kill us with merely a flick of their wrists because they're guarded by trained security.

Dangerous. Violent. Ruthless.

I've stayed strong over the past few days for Caia, not allowing her to see how I feel. I've never been one to show emotion. Instead, I keep the war waging through me deep inside. My father taught me to never let your adversary see your weakness, but tonight, I'll be walking alongside her — Caia, my weakness — into that house.

The mansion is silent as I make my way into the basement. It's cold tonight, and I wonder if it's a sign. Perhaps we should stop this charade. Maybe we should pack up and move to London, where I know we'll be far from this shit.

As much as I'd rather do that to keep Caia and River safe, I know it's not the answer. Running is a fool's errand; staying to fight to the end is what I need to do.

As I enter the hallway to find the cells, I recall the first time I walked down here with my father. He was so proud to show me the legacy that would fall on my shoulders one day. It was in that moment I considered running away. Taking my brother and my best friend and leaving this place.

I wonder each day if the girls ever survived once they'd been sent to their prospective owners. Shoving the office door open, I settle in the chair to see Rayne on the bed, curled up. We've made sure the room is as *normal* as we could make it. She's calmed down somewhat, but there's still a rabidity that explodes when she's angry.

Pulling the cigarette from the packet on the desk, I light one and pull in a deep lungful of smoke. The screen crackles, and I watch the girl roll over. She must be in pain because there's a wince on her face every time she moves.

Closing my eyes, I recall a memory of the moment I broke, just like Rayne is broken. Just like every child that passed through these walls had done.

"Drake." My father's voice comes from behind me. I've only just turned fourteen, and he's been bringing me down here every day. I've watched things that would make anyone have nightmares for the rest of their lives. Thankfully, he hasn't brought Dante down here.

I wonder if he remembers being a good person. It's as if someone else has taken over his body and my father is gone. It's only been a few short months since the first day he made sure I knew what he did and why the Savage name is so well respected. Men, women, all those in power pay my father a stupid amount of money to do things. Ugly things.

"I think it's time you and River help me down here," he tells me, causing my heart to leap into my throat. I wish it would kill me. I pray for death, but it never comes. "Bring him down here. We'll have a session where you'll get firsthand experience of the trade."

"Yes, Father." I nod, knowing I cannot deny him. If I do, I'll be whipped. Turning to the door, I race up the stairs to find my best friend in my bedroom. His big green eyes meet mine.

"Hey." He smiles, and my heart thuds happily. I love when he smiles. I don't understand why, but sometimes I think about him. Not like a friend, but more than that. And sometimes, I wonder what it would be like to kiss him. But he's not a girl, so I will never find out.

"My dad wants us in the dungeon," I tell him, not giving him a smile in return.

His face falls, and I know he's as afraid as I am. He sighs, nods, then rises from my bed. When he nears me, he catches my face in his hands, holding me steady. "We'll be okay," he affirms.

"I know," I tell him confidently. I know he can see past the lie. River can see everything. He's known me for years, and he can always call me out on my bullshit.

"Let's go."

We make our way silently to the dungeon to find my father and one of his men in white coats. They both look like doctors. I know what's going to happen. I've seen this before, but River hasn't. As much as I wanted to shield him, I knew it was only a matter of time.

"The boys." Dad smiles, gesturing for us to enter. When we

do, I notice a girl in the room lit with low, yellow light. There are two small bedrooms set up alongside the main area, and I know what happens in there. The bed she's sitting on is covered in a white sheet. "Today, you both will experience what it's like to be men," my father announces.

He shoves us into the room and shuts the door behind him. Settling himself on a small, two-seater sofa, he unbuckles his belt, watching the girl on the bed. My body is cold, rigid, I can't move, but when he crooks a finger at River, I step forward, shielding my best friend from my father.

"Don't fuck this up, son," he says in a gruff tone.

River places a hand on my shoulder. The touch calms me, but I know it's not going to last long. My father reaches for my best friend, shoving him to his knees before pointing in my direction.

"I want to see if you're a man yet," he chuckles darkly, then points to the girl on the bed. I have to do something. I know I have to move, but my feet no longer know how because I'm rooted to the spot. "If you don't fucking move now, I'll make you move."

His threat jolts me into action, and I turn to the shivering girl. She's pretty. With dark hair, and big blue eyes filled with innocence I know shines in my own. I step forward only to have her cower, scooting backward on the bed away from me. She's shivering, her skin almost blue, and her straggly hair is matted to her head.

"Get the fuck up," my father bites out.

I'm angry that she's so scared. If she would fight, perhaps he wouldn't hurt her, but I wouldn't put anything past Malcolm Savage. She doesn't move, merely trembles like a dog that's been kicked. Anger courses through me as I stalk toward her. As soon *as my hand grips her thin, waiflike arm, I tug her up onto her bare feet.*

"I've taught you how to handle the toys, Drake. Make me proud." The threat is thick in my father's voice. If I don't turn into him, into a monster, he'll hurt River.

Glancing over my shoulder, I notice my dad's hand in River's golden-brown hair, fisting it painfully, and my best friend winces. I have to choose — the boy I love or a girl I don't know.

"Please, don't hurt me," she mumbles, and I'm ready to rip into her until she lifts her gaze to mine. Soft blue eyes, the color of the sky on a spring morning, almost pastel in shade, peek up at me.

"I said get up. When I speak, you obey me. Am I understood?"

She tips her head up and down in agreement, and her fat bottom lip wobbles as she blinks back tears.

"You'll do what I want."

"Open your legs, toy," Malcolm grunts from behind me, and I don't want to see what he's doing. The image is burned into my mind. I've seen him do things with other captives in here, and it makes me ill. So, I focus on the girl who does as he asks and opens her legs. There's dark hair there, but I see the pink of her private place.

I swallow the lump in my throat, willing myself not to react to her, but my body betrays me, and I feel my cock throbbing.

"That's it. Use your fingers and show my son your cunt." Malcolm utters the word that makes my skin crawl. She doesn't deserve this. But neither do I. And neither does my best friend. The girl moves, opening herself to three of us who watch her intently. I don't want to look, but I can't turn away.

That's when she fights. When her fire burns, and she screams bloody fucking murder. My father is on his feet in seconds, his hand gripping her tiny throat as he pulls her body from the bed and drags it over to the sofa.

"Get on the bed," he orders River who quickly moves beside me. "Sit. Both of you."

We're both seated, unsure of what is about to happen, but still knowing exactly what my father will do to her. She's still trying to scream, but her voice is raspy because of Malcolm's hold on her. He pulls out his cock. It's thick, hard, and I don't know how he's going to get it inside her.

I don't have to wonder for too long, because suddenly, his hips lift, and the horrific scene of her body opening is all I can see.

"Touch him," Malcolm utters hoarsely, his free hand pointing at River, gesturing to me. "Do it, or I'll fuck you all till you're bleeding." My best friend is crying. Tears run down his cheeks as he reaches for me. "Pull his dick out and stroke him. Both of you."

I want to close my eyes, but I know if I do, we'll be in trouble. Once my hand is around River's cock, and his is fisting mine, my father continues his assault on the blue-eyed toy who's screaming so loud my ears ring. I don't want to get hard, I don't want to be turned on, but the way River's hand feels is too good, and I can't stop myself.

There's blood dripping from her body, and I watch it in awe wondering if my father really did break her. I realize then my father is Satan. He is the devil, and soon, he'll want me to be just like him.

Shaking my head, I sigh, running my fingers through my hair. "I'm a monster." It's mumbled to myself, but deep down, I know he's listening. The man who is using the beautiful girl for his pleasure. He's the one who breaks them.

He's no longer a father.

He's a monster.

And I wonder how long it will take for him to finally break me.

RIVER

Since we were young, we fell down a sordid path of self-destruction. It's not something we chose. It was forced upon us, and there was no way out. We waded through the darkest depths of depravity, and we basked in it. We found pleasure in the desires that kept us hooked on each other. Like a drug, he was my fix. And like a cure, I was his medication. Until I fell. The moment I looked into my best friend's eyes, I knew I loved him.

I see the depravity in his eyes — the yearning he exudes. Drake was shattered when he learned the truth about his family, but the moment it hurt him the most was the day his father broke me. When we had no choice but to allow Malcolm to play his games.

From then to now, nothing's changed. Outwardly. However, the person I knew is no longer who I'm looking at now. I watch Drake while he's busy in the office. He knows I can see him. The cameras around the house are set up to allow one person to see everything happening in any room.

His father used to sit here and watch us. I know he did;

that's how he found out about my relationship with his eldest son. The emotion I held for Drake was clear in my actions, in my words, and I was stupid enough to allow Malcolm to see it.

Sighing, I head down the hallway toward the staircase that will take me down to the cells. I need to try to talk to Rayne. My sister is a stranger to me. Sadly, she doesn't even remember who I am. Not that I blame her.

When I reach her cell, I watch her for a moment. Her small body is curled into a ball. A twenty-one-year-old woman, but she looks so much younger, and it hurts my heart.

Rayne glances up when I tap the bar. Her wide eyes meet mine. Hers shimmer with tears, and mine, they're cold and hardened by years of pain. I don't feel anything anymore. A boy broken. And a girl shattered.

"Who are you?" she questions in a raspy tone. "Let me out of here. They'll find me and hurt me. I need to run." My chest aches as she speaks. Her voice, so much like my mothers, from what I can remember. The woman who gave up her children.

Hatred coils in my veins, a sleeping serpent slowly waking from its slumber. Rayne rises from the bed, stalking closer to the bars. She smirks, attempting to seduce me with a sway in her hips. She lifts the tank top she's wearing, baring her tits to me.

She's transformed into the dark temptress right before me. Nothing like the delicate version of her that only moments ago begged to be set free. She seems almost virginal. I say almost because this woman is far from an angel. They've turned her into something vile.

"Let me out, big boy," she coos, running her fingertips over mine.

My white-knuckle grip on the bars only tighten at her touch. I want to slap her for being so stupid, for trying to use sex to get something.

"Rayne Steele," I utter her name.

Her lips part, in shock or something else, but she watches me with wide eyes. "How do you know my name?"

"My name is River Steele," I tell her. Her brows furrow in confusion at my admission. "Our mother, she was a bad person."

"I don't have a mother. She died when I was born." Her fiery confidence in what she's saying has been solidified by years of lies.

"How old are you?" I question.

She sighs, lowering her gaze to our hands. "I'm twenty-one." She's right. I worked out the years that have passed since I last laid eyes on her. My sister hasn't lived a normal life since she was too young to even remember our mother.

A ghost.

I allowed myself to believe she didn't truly exist.

I convinced myself I'd imagined her.

When Drake's father took me in as his own, I let my life become part of his game. He turned me into a pawn. He tortured me. Not with violence. No. He wasn't that type of monster. He broke my mind. My will to live was shattered, and if it wasn't for Drake, I wouldn't have made it through.

Years I spent in love with a man who is so cold he can't even show affection. But now that he has Caia and me, I hope that will thaw him. That he'll once more be the Drake I recall from our younger years, before the darkness consumed him.

"You were taken, a long time ago, Rayne."

She nods. She knows this. "They said I was special. That I would be made into the perfect toy. He kept telling me I was worth more than any of the others."

"If I let you out of here, will you allow me and my friends to help you?" Perhaps I shouldn't trust her, maybe I should leave her in here to simmer away in her fury and rage.

"Yes."

"Promise me, little sister," I implore her. Silence is thick in the air as I wait for her to vow that she'll allow us to help. To do something to ensure she can attempt having a normal life. To live in the sunshine and not the dark.

"I do. Please, River," she whispers, her big green eyes that match mine lift, and I'm certain she's in pain. Not physical, but emotional. There's nothing inside her anymore, and I can't blame her for shutting it out. I did, too, for a long time.

She looks at me for a moment, offers me a smile, but I see it — the brokenness. Brought forth over so many years. It dances in her eyes, it tugs and pulls at her like a war which rages within her. I understand her. She's just like me. A shell.

Fishing the key from my pocket, I unlock the cage we've kept her in and open the door. She steps tentatively over the threshold and falls into my arms. The softness of her body, the tremble that races through her makes me wrap my arms around her, holding her so close it's as if she's going to climb into me.

Her hair is matted, her sobs wrack through her, and I close my eyes to keep from tearing through the city on a wild rampage to kill every motherfucker in my path. Tonight though, tonight we'll take them all down.

"River." Dante's voice comes from behind me. Dragging my gaze over to him, I take in his expression, and I know immediately something is wrong.

"What is it?"

"APB is out on Rayne. I've just gotten word from our man on the inside. She's been reported as kidnapped by Amoretto," he informs me.

"No. No, you can't give me to him." My sister starts shaking violently. Shoving away from me, she moves back into the cell, scuttling onto the bed and curling into a ball.

"Rayne," I call to her, closing the distance between the bed and myself. "We're not giving you to him. Tell me what's wrong? Did he hurt you?"

She looks so small, so fragile as she cries on the bed. Her tiny frame even more delicate than before. Her fear is palpable. I feel it right down to my bones.

"Listen, little one," Dante says. "We're not sending you back there. You need to tell us what happened." He sounds so confident, so sure of himself. Dante was always the brother I knew would survive this better than Drake. He wasn't subjected to a lot that Drake and I were, but he knew what happened. He'd seen enough to know that his father was evil.

"He . . . That man is bad," Rayne finally whispers. "His house has a room hidden in the walls." The more she talks, the more my body vibrates with fury.

"What room?" This time, Dante is on the bed, attempting to pull her out of the ball she's curled herself into. I can't move. My body is frozen, and I know if I touch anyone right now, I'll kill. I'll rip them apart, so I allow Dante to take charge.

"It's a place like this," she tells us. "He does things in there, with . . ." Her voice tapers off, but my imagination is running rampant with horror-filled images.

"With?"

"He takes girls, or boys, in there."

Dante's hands are on her arms, holding her steady because it looks like she's about to pass out. His voice is composed, calm, but I can tell he is as angry as I am. "You've seen this?"

She nods.

The party is tonight. We need to get in there and find this room. There's no longer a doubt about when we'll take them down; it has to be tonight. Or we'll all be killed. Amoretto is a dangerous man. He's known to be connected to organizations that deal in guns, drugs, and children. He needed to die a long time ago, but I know Drake's focus was on Caia. He needed to find her. Now that she's here and helping us, we can finally put an end to this.

"Rayne," I finally utter her name again. "We're going there tonight. Can you explain where this room is? We're going to help those that are hidden in his home."

Her eyes land on mine. "He'll kill you."

"I have something to do. Dante, can you take her up to Caia and ask her to help my sister?"

"Yeah, man. Where are you going?"

"A place I know I'll find help for tonight." I push off the bed and head to the door. Without looking at my sister, I mutter, "I love you, Rayne." And then I walk out, leaving her with one of my best friends.

CHAPTER TWENTY-THREE
RIVER

The lights of Twisted & Shaken appear in my view ten minutes after I've left Rayne and Dante in the cell. I knew what I had to do. The luminous blue lights of the bar beckon me in the darkness. I found this place when I needed escape. When I needed to leave the Savage Mansion and take a breather from what I'd seen.

Stalking into the bar, I find the raven-haired woman I'm about to fuck into next week serving a beer to a burly biker. Her long dark locks are streaked with blues and purples. Her dark eyeliner is what you would call emo. A ripped black tank top hugs her curves but also teases the large tits I know are real because I asked her one night.

She's been a distraction for years. Drake and I had an understanding — if we needed time, we could go out and find someone to use for the night. It's how we've always lived. Guilt sits in my gut this time because I care about Caia, and I love Drake.

The woman smiles at me when she meets my eyes. "A double shot of whiskey," I tell her, dropping a fifty on the bar. "Keep the change." She sets the glass in front of me, her eyes shimmering with knowing. Every time I come in here, I've taken her in the back and fucked her.

"You're feeling generous," she remarks, lifting the bill from the counter. I shrug in response. Gulping down the amber liquid in one swallow, I feel the burn all the way down my throat and into my chest. "Something on your mind, River?"

"Another drink."

She nods. Moving to grab the bottle, she fills the shot glass and meets my gaze with a curious arched brow.

"Nothing you need to worry yourself with. Perhaps you can take a break soon?" I ask, lifting the drink to my lips. I need to release this tension Rayne has brought about. I don't know how I'm meant to get her to trust me. Love and rage are two very dangerous emotions. They're deadly, and tonight everything will finally come to a head.

"I can always take a break for you, River," she responds with a lift of her plump lips.

"Good. Give me five," I tell her as I drain my drink and head into the men's restroom to take a piss. Moments later, I'm back at the bar. "Let's go, baby girl." I don't wait for her. Instead, I stalk to the back of the bar and into the office where we've fucked more times than I care to count. The door clicks, and I settle in the large leather chair that sits behind the desk.

"Are you going to tell me why you're here?" she asks, but I shake my head in response. She knows I don't ever tell her about where I come from or why I need her. We've been through this before. Countless times. The problem is, she's the only person other than Drake I trust to just give me what I need.

I tug my belt from the loops, crooking my finger to call her over. She kneels between my open my legs. Once I've wrapped the leather around her neck, I tug it up, causing her to rise to her feet.

"I don't want to talk. Do you understand?"

She nods. So fucking obedient. I love it.

"Lift your skirt. Let me look at those beautiful holes." Trinity spins around, my belt tightening with each movement. She lifts the micro-mini she's wearing to show me the blue thong meant to cover her cunt. A thin string disappears between her pert cheeks, and I rain down a slap on each one.

I reach for the thin material and rip her thong from those beautiful hips.

"Bend over the desk," I order gruffly. I make quick work of my zipper and grip my cock, stroking it as I drink in the woman before me. My fingers taunt her slit; it's slick and needy. She's always ready for me. Perhaps that's why I lose interest. I want a challenge. I need someone who'll tell me no.

But I know it's more than that. It's because I'm in love with someone else. I crave him more than I do my next breath. And now, with Caia, I've been sucked into their world, and I hunger for her just as much.

Pulling a foil packet from my pocket, I rip it open, sheathing my dick. Once I'm covered, I thrust into Trinity's pussy, balls deep.

My body moves with hers, but I don't feel the gratification I want. The happiness I seek is not here. I'm so fucked up, so tortured, I'm here wanting to find sinful pleasure from someone I don't love.

I pull out of the woman before me, slumping down on

the chair, causing her to turn to face me. She has so many emotions flitting across her expression it makes me sick.

"I need your help," I tell her.

"Clearly." She rights herself, hiding her pussy from my view, and I'm thankful for it. Not because she's not beautiful, not because I don't find her attractive, but because I came here for something else.

"Tonight, I have an event, and I need a woman on my arm."

"That's new." She smiles.

I rise, stuffing my dick into my pants before I meet her gaze. "This isn't something fun. It's not a date. The home we're going to is owned by a dangerous man."

"And you need me to be . . . what?"

Running my fingers through my unruly hair, I meet her gaze and offer the truth. It's the only thing I have. "A toy. A whore on my arm."

"Let me get this straight. You're taking me to a house that could be a danger to me, and you want me to agree to it?" She sounds as incredulous as I thought she'd be. But I've known her for a while, and I thought it would be something she'd do for me. Granted, I didn't want to tell her the truth, but lies have been far too volatile in my life.

"I just need you on my arm. To be my escort tonight to a gala dinner with a few men I will be meeting with. We won't be alone. Drake and Dante will be there too."

She sighs, and I can see the resignation on her face. Trinity has met the twins before. She's seen what they're capable of, especially Dante. He has a violent streak when he's drunk.

"And if I agree to this, you'll pay me for my time?"

This is the reason I went to her. I know she's easy

pickings, and it might be wrong of me to put her in that situation, but with the party we're going to, each man needs a *toy* on his arm, and I'm not taking my sister into that house. She's far too volatile to be in a situation where she'll see men who've clearly hurt her before.

"You know I'm always good for it," I assure her. "I have a dress for you to wear. I need you to agree to it before I can offer you any more than what I have so far."

She watches me for a moment, and I'm certain she's about to deny me, but then, when I turn from her gaze, she utters, "I'll do it. But if anything happens to me—"

"Nothing will happen to you. I've never let anyone hurt you before, and I won't allow it now." As much as I voice the words, I know they're a lie. I've hurt her. I know it, and so does she. But that wasn't my choice; it was hers. I told her I can't love her, but she fell anyway.

"Okay."

"I'll pick you up in an hour."

I leave her to mull over it and head back to the car. It's done. I tap out a message to Drake and Dante informing them of our guest and make my way back to the house to get ready.

CHAPTER TWENTY-FOUR
CAIA

I glance at myself in the mirror. The dress Drake bought for me is more than beautiful. It's flawless. The silk hangs over my newly found curves, hugging each dip of my body.

"I know why I'm not allowed in there," Harper says from behind me. She's sitting on the bed, her legs crossed Buddha-style as she watches me. "But I wish I could be a fly on the wall when Dad sees you again."

"I doubt he'll recognize me," I tell her. I hardly recognize me. The tattoos have become a part of me. I see them as my strength. I survived hell. I wish I'd had a normal life. Every day, I wonder what would have happened if my father wasn't a monster. And each day, I realize I would never have Drake, nor River, in my life.

"You look so pretty," Rayne — the girl who was locked in Thanos's dungeon with me — offers. She's perched on the window seat. Her eyes are the same shade as her brother's. Dante brought her up here, told me to clean her up.

When she finally stepped out of the shower, I noticed all the bruises and scrapes on her porcelain skin. But it was when she was dressed in a pair of sweatpants and a tank top I noticed how pretty she is. Her hair, a golden blonde color, shimmers in the light, as if it's spun silk. Her curious gaze follows me everywhere within the confines of the room.

"Thank you, Rayne," I respond, offering her a kind smile. Her beauty is startling. When we found her, she was hidden behind layers of dirt, smudges of black on her face, her hair matted and knotted. She truly was a broken toy. I wonder why Thanos never gave her what he did me.

A knock on the door has me turning to face the entrance as Drake appears. He's dressed in an expensive black suit, the shirt underneath a dark red, with a silver tie. His hair is tousled, styled as if I'd just been running my fingers through it. I can't help admiring how handsome he is.

His tanned skin, the scruff on his jaw, and the dark suit are a stark contrast, making his bright blue eyes pop. They're incredible. "We best go. River is here with his date."

"Date?"

"These parties are couples only," Drake explains. "If a man walks in without a woman on his arm, they'll suspect something."

Nodding, I pick up the necklace from the vanity and hand it to him. Lifting my long hair, I offer my neck to Drake. The cool metal causes me to shiver when he fastens it. A diamond lands between my breasts.

"Perfect," he tells me, inspecting every inch of me with his gaze.

Harper gives me a hug before I follow Drake down the hallway and into the entrance hall. River is dressed similarly to his best friend in dark colors, and his tie — an olive green which makes his eyes seem even more luminous — is the only color on him tonight.

"This is it." He offers me a smile, pressing a kiss to my forehead. And it's then I notice the woman beside him. She's pretty, but the glare she pins me with when River's lips touch me is clear — she's jealous.

We make our way to the car waiting outside, and my nerves get the better of me. I'm shaking when I slip into the passenger seat alongside Drake, who's driving tonight.

His hand finds my knee. The heat of his touch calms me somewhat, but deep down, the fear that's been rooted in me all these years is prominent.

I attempt to focus on the houses we pass by, but nothing allows my heart to cease the violent thrumming in my chest. My throat is tight with anxiety, and by the time we're pulling into the long driveway of my childhood home, I'm blinking back tears.

It looks so different. It's nothing like I remember. Expensive cars line the driveway, and I know all the men here tonight are wealthy. They're some of the richest in the country, all here to celebrate with my father, a monster in angel's clothing.

Once the car comes to a stop, Drake exits. Rounding the front, he opens my door. His hand in mine is the only grounding I have, because my feet no longer want to carry me inside. I thought I could be strong, seeing my father again, but I'm not a warrior right now.

No.

Right now, I'm the little girl whose father ensured she'd never have a normal life.

Drake leans in, his mouth close to my ear when he

whispers, "I'm right beside you. You're the strongest woman I know, and nothing will hurt you ever again." His confident words do nothing to calm me. But I don't allow him to see my fear. I meet his gaze and nod. I can't find the words to respond, but my wordless answer is enough.

We make our way into the house, welcomed by a butler who offers a swift dip of his chin. The inner sanctum of the devil himself is furnished in only the finest. From the artwork to the furniture we are escorted toward. There are crowds of people all sipping champagne, dressed in expensive suits and gowns. It looks like a royal party from the outside, but I know once you delve deeper into it, there aren't any flawless people in this house tonight.

Each man has one girl beside him. And each girl, half the age of the man she's standing beside, wears a necklace similar to mine. As if she's branded. Collared. Owned.

"Do you see anyone you recognize?" Drake questions in a low tone so only I can hear him.

Shaking my head, I tell him, "Not yet." We grab a couple glasses of champagne and move farther into the house I grew up in. The living room is exactly like the day I walked out to go to a party. The patio, which is to our right, is filled with men and women laughing, chatting, and having a good time.

I'm about to tell Drake I see one of the men from Thanos's parties, but I can't, because my gaze lands on a man sitting at the head of the long dinner table that's been set up in the garden.

The man I called father.

On his lap is a girl who can't be more than twenty. She's wearing a thick silver collar, similar to that of a dog. Hanging from the ring in the center of her neck is a leash.

She's beautiful, but what makes my stomach turn and bile force its way into my throat is how much she looks like Harper. If I didn't know better, I would've called her sister.

"It seems your father has found a replacement for his runaway daughter," River comments from my left, while Drake on my right is silent, his hand squeezing mine. It's as if he knows I need him to be strong for me in this moment.

"I guess so." My voice is raspy when I respond to River.

I blink back the tears, seeing for myself the monster my father really is.

DRAKE

My girl turns to me. "I need the restroom. Stay here," she tells me urgently, excusing herself, and I can tell this is affecting her more than she had anticipated. I know it can't be easy seeing this. She'd been shielded from it for so long, and now, thrown in at the deep end. It was a mistake bringing her here. I realize that now. But she asked for revenge.

She wanted to kill him, and I know if I had refused her, she would've gone out and done it on her own. That would've only gotten her killed. And that is not something I could live with. Not now, not ever. I watch her race up the stairs, but I don't follow. Allowing her time to think will perhaps have her changing her mind about going through with this.

Regardless of her decision, tonight, her father will die. Whether by my hand or hers.

"Savage." Amoretto notices me and waves me over. His eyes are dark, wild, and when I near him, I wonder if he's high. Possibly. He offers a hand, which I shake, and give him a smirk. Playing to the games of these men is easy. "How are you doing?"

"Good. It's been a while," I tell him.

"It has been. I have a treat for you tonight." This time, he tugs on the chain linked to the girl in his lap. She drops to the ground on all fours like a dog. My anger is simmering when I watch him rise and lead her over to a small bench on the manicured lawn.

"What is this?" I question, the men behind me watching intently. It's as if I can feel their eyes burning through my back.

He chuckles before unzipping his slacks, pulling out his flaccid dick, and I know what he's about to do before he does it. A stream of urine hits the girl's face, her mouth wide, accepting it. She doesn't move, doesn't cower. He continues laughing, the men behind me cheer him on, and my fingers tingle for the gun holstered on my ankle.

Since the security failed to search us, we still have our weapons.

"She's so obedient. I think your future toys should be this well trained," he offers while zipping back up. Tugging the leash once more, he drags her closer to where we're standing on the patio. When she looks up at me, I notice her eyes are dilated. They're a stormy blue, but she's so strung out on something she doesn't even notice when he slaps her.

"Well, you've certainly done a job on her." My response is rigid, and River's hand finds my shoulder, squeezing in warning. I need to play along until we make sure all the men are seated. Dinner is in a few minutes, and that's when our team will enter, and we'll have a chance to take out these assholes once and for all.

"I'd like a go with her," one of the men chuckles beside me.

"Of course. That's why we're here tonight, to enjoy ourselves," Amoretto responds happily.

I can't watch any more of this, and I need to find Caia. "I need to find my toy. She went to the restroom. I'll be back shortly," I tell our host, who waves me off because he is far too interested in watching the poor girl take another mouthful from the man dressed in white.

Racing into the entrance, I take the stairs two at a time. I don't know the house very well, but I can only guess where Caia has disappeared to. The hallway is long with numerous doors, which are closed. I try each one, finding them locked.

Finally, the last door opens when I turn the handle. Shoving it open, I find Caia standing only inches over the threshold. She's staring at the room, and even though I can't see her face, I know she's crying.

I want to pull her into my arms, hold her, but I don't.

"I thought I could do this," she rasps. When she turns to me, I notice the pain in her eyes. It reflects my own, because as much as I don't tell her, or admit my feelings, all her pain is inside me. I've been there. I've lived through it.

"You can," I tell her, stepping farther into the room. Glancing around, I take in what I can only guess was her bedroom growing up. The blue and silver color scheme wasn't what I would've expected from her, but somehow, it fits the girl standing before me.

"Seeing him again," she starts, allowing me to cocoon her with my arms. "It's something I've thought about all the years I've been away, but nothing prepared me for what I saw."

"He's a monster," I concur, pressing a kiss to the top of her head. "But this is closure. It's something you need. Saying goodbye to your old life . . ." My words taper off because I can't tell her what she has to do. She needs to let herself realize it.

"You're right." Her voice is muffled by my jacket. Her tiny hands fist the material, holding onto me as if she's afraid I'm going to disappear. I couldn't ever leave her. I know it now, and I knew it back then. She's ingrained in me.

"We need to get back downstairs," I tell her.

She nods, and I lead her with my hand in hers down to the party that will soon be a massacre. When we reach the lower level, I seek out River, finding him beside his date. There are people still milling about, and I glance at the watch on my wrist. Our team was briefed to make an appearance soon. The dinner seems to be delayed, which doesn't bode well for our plan.

"What's going on?" I question my best friend when I reach him.

"Amoretto got called away. He's just left, told us he'll be back soon." *Shit.*

"This is not something we were banking on," I tell River, but he knows it already. I don't have to tell him. This is something that should've been done today. The men in this room should all be dead by the end of the night.

"I've called the team, told them to go ahead." River's voice is low so only I can hear. I snap my gaze to his. "I reckon if we only have Amoretto to take down, it's fine. We can do it ourselves. They'll be here in two minutes."

"Fine."

I tug Caia alongside me as we make our way through

the crowd. I need to get her outside before my men rush into the house and kill everyone in sight. River follows me out into the garden with the girl who seems to be glued to him.

"Mr. Savage." I halt at the words. Not because I recognize the woman immediately. Ice solidifies in my veins. Anger and revulsion churn my stomach when I turn to find the source of the voice.

"Mrs. Thornhill." I glance at her, offering her an indifferent smile. All these years, and this woman still has the power to turn me vengeful. Her eyes are bright green, almost luminous. The thick makeup she wears hides the imperfections on her wrinkled face, but I know they're there.

She's dressed in black. Her body nothing like it used to be, and I can tell she's aging badly. Even in the low light.

"I trust you'll be able to show me to the restroom?" she questions coolly, her voice attempting a seductive tone but failing miserably. She's probably in her late forties now, perhaps even early fifties. But she was one of the first clients my father had sent me to meet with. When I met her at eighteen, she was curvaceous with a penchant for my dick. And of course, father told me to always ensure the clients were happy.

"Unfortunately, I'm rather busy." I turn and lead Caia away from her. I don't want her to know this woman, or even ask me about her, but I know she will. Her big hazel eyes are already burning into me.

The glass shattering from the patio windows is a sign my men have arrived. We're at the bottom of the garden when the screams play out. Music to my ears. When I turn to find the war raging through the house, I stop. Watching the men who've been partners with my father for so long finally meet their maker is something I'll never forget.

Greta Thornhill's body is on the grass, close to where I left her, blood oozing from a bullet hole in her forehead.

"Who was she?" Caia asks.

"Someone from my past. Come. We need to get out of here," I tell her. The words come out harsher than I want them to, but there's nothing I can do about how I feel seeing that vile woman again. As much as I want to make sure Caia never leaves me again, I want her to also have a life free from this shit. From all the horrors and nightmares we've faced.

We race through the house. Every one of the men dressed in their expensive suits is dead. All except one. Caia's father isn't here, but when he returns to his home, he'll find the massacre I've left for him.

"Do you think he knew I was here?" Caia questions beside me as we reach the cars. I want to say no, but something doesn't feel right. If he did know, he never let on.

"Let's get home so we can revisit our plan." My response isn't an answer to her question, but it's something. River slides into the driver's seat after helping his date into the passenger side. I pull Caia onto my lap in the back of the car, holding her close to my chest.

My phone vibrating in my pocket startles my girl. She settles beside me, allowing me to answer the call. "Yes?"

"Sir, we've taken everyone out. The bodies . . ." The man who's led the team since I took over the Savage Organization is the only person I trust besides River and my brother. Jacob Fielding is one of the most ruthless mercenaries to come out of the army. He's killed hundreds without flinching. And that's why he is my go-to for anything.

"Leave them. It's a message to let him know we'll be back. Find out why Amoretto left. I want all the intel you can muster."

"Yes, sir. I'll get back to you early morning."

He hangs up, leaving me to ponder my own thoughts on the man who narrowly escaped his death sentence. Watching the darkness fly by the window, I try hard to see through it, to figure out what I'm missing. What happened tonight doesn't make sense. He was called away, but who would've saved him?

Caia's hand on my thigh ignites my blood. I'm burning up for her, just for her, from the inside. I glance at the rearview mirror to find green eyes staring back at me. River. His glance holds affection, love.

Then I look at my girl. *My* girl. She's sad. It's written all over her pretty face, and I know I have to do something about this. She needed tonight more than I needed it. I'll make sure she gets her revenge. Even if it's the last thing I do.

Suddenly, there are bright lights blinding through the windshield, coming right for us. They're on the wrong side of the road. River swerves from the asphalt, attempting to dodge the oncoming car. We're sliding. My arms instinctively go for Caia, pulling her closer, shielding her from the disaster that's about to strike. We're spinning. I hear the crash.

Darkness envelops us, and then, there's nothing.

CHAPTER TWENTY-SIX

DANTE

For as long as I can remember, my brother has kept me safe. He's hidden me from the filth that played out behind the walls of our mansion. But he doesn't know how much of it I've experienced myself.

Over the years, we've tried to keep each other protected, but we've both failed miserably. I wonder why he never told me the secrets he found in our father's paperwork.

Was I that volatile that I couldn't be trusted?

Perhaps.

Only, Drake never knew all the things I'd done to keep him safe. He doesn't know that if it weren't for me, he would have found Caia long before he did. I don't feel guilty for not telling him the truth, because he kept far too much from me.

I open my eyes to the woman above me. She's riding my dick like a pro, her tits bouncing, dark brown nipples peaked, making my mouth water.

The knife I have pressed against her sternum breaks skin each time she lowers herself onto my shaft. The blood that trickles from the blade drips onto my bared chest. I can't help smiling. She's high. She's fucking flying after the coke she snorted from the table beside my bed.

The best thing is, she doesn't know half the things that are about to unfold within the walls of this mansion. The secrets that are soon about to tumble free from the closet's they've been hiding in all these years.

Her big hazel eyes meet mine, the dilated pupils turning her gaze almost black. Her pouty lips remind me of her daughter's. Plump, ready to be bitten and sucked until she cries out in agony.

My dick jolts, and I'm certain she thinks it's her cunt doing it. Unfortunately, it's nothing like that. I'm only hard because I'm thinking about what I'm about to do to her husband.

He's on his way here.

When I called him and told him about Drake's plan to kill him, he thanked me. He offered up a sum of money that was laughable. I have more money than God. I don't need his bullshit payoff.

"Oh fuck," the woman cries above me, her slick walls pulsing around my dick, but I don't come. She, however, screeches like a banshee.

My phone vibrates on the nightstand with a message. I know what it says before I read it. Drake, River, and Caia were found.

"Time to play," I utter, watching the whore climb off me.

"What?" she questions breathlessly, but I don't offer a response. She doesn't need to know what my plan is. The bedroom door flies open. Two of the men who work for the

Savage Organization saunter in, and she squeals in surprise.

"Take her to the cells."

They nod at my command. Once I'm alone, I close my eyes and recall the day Caia was shot, bleeding out over my brother whom I've loved from the moment we were born. Even before I knew what love was.

They say twins have a connection like no other. I believe it's true.

There's blood. Far too much blood.

My feet are moving before I have time to think.

Drake doesn't move for a moment, and my heart thuds painfully against my chest. He can't be dead. I watch as River kneels beside him, tugging him wildly, begging him to breathe, to open his eyes. I can't pull in a breath. My lungs feel as if they're filled with lead, heavy, unyielding, and I stare at my brother's body lying on the ground.

I finally find my footing and lean down after the guard pulls the limp form of the pretty girl away from on top of Drake. She's was bleeding profusely. The metallic stench fills my nostrils My father is shouting at us, at me, but I can't look at him.

I know my brother cared for her, I saw it in the way his eyes found her in the room, how he looked at her. I pray she's alive. I don't know why, because she didn't make me feel anything, but I knew Drake wanted her.

The man who raised me is livid. His face red with rage, and I no longer recognize him as human. He's pure animal. Feral and wild. Another man in a white coat, one of the doctors, is working on the girl. I'm sure she's dead.

I turn to see Drake's eyes open.

"He's alive. He's okay," River tells me, but I don't feel happiness. Actually, I'm at war with myself. Sadness takes hold of me because he's not escaped this life, merely wounded by the evil that our family has been a part of for so long. Even though we're both alive, we're most certainly dead inside this hell.

Hours later, I hear my name.

"Dante." The deep rumble of River comes from behind me. He stalks into the library where I'm hiding in the darkness. I love sitting in here. It's the only place my father hardly enters. And there's reason enough to avoid him like the plague.

I do my job, I make sure Father is happy with me, and then I come in here to spend my evenings watching the darkening forest swallow up everything in view. Once the blackness of night cloaks the mansion, I head to my room, lock the door, and close my eyes.

You'd think at twenty-five I'd be out of here, running for the city where no one from this vile existence can find me, but I can't. There are two people I can't leave behind, and I'd never forgive myself if I did.

River, my best friend, and my brother, Drake, are the only people alive that I want in my life. But that's not the only reason I stay. My father has a hold over me, one I haven't told Drake about yet. One I've hidden from even the closest person in my life, and the guilt eats at me each day.

"I'm busy," I tell him, not needing him to interrupt my thoughts. A lifetime far too long to live with the memories I have. With the agony I've been hiding deep beneath the surface, but somehow, River finds it. He pulls and tugs like I'm a ball of twine. Soon, I'll be unraveled before him, and I'm not comfortable with that.

"There's a meeting in a few minutes. Drake said I should remind you that you have to be there," he tells me. I know about the meeting. My father is handing over the reins to Drake and me.

"I'll be there," I offer, my eyes still glued to the window where the night has consumed the light, and all I can see is the mist and fog that's appeared over the trees. Our home is nestled in the forest, with only a large silver-top lake behind it. There's nobody for miles, and that's why my father can do what he does.

The money he forks out allows him to continue the sick games. That's all they are. Vile fucking games. My brother and I have been shoved into the darkness with no way out. No fucking glimmer of hope, so that's why I've become accustomed to walking through the halls of the Savage Mansion like a soulless, mindless drone.

"I'm sorry, you know," River says then, shocking me enough to make me turn my head toward him. My eyes land on his expensive suit. It's tailored to his broad frame. The ink that adorns his skin is hidden, but I know it's there. Beneath the material lies beautiful, intricate patterns. The same artwork I've traced with my tongue while he jerked me off all over his toned stomach.

"I know." I nod, offering him a glimpse of a smile. Nothing more. That's all I can give because that's all that lies within me.

"I'll see you down there." He turns and leaves me in the library while I take a deep breath, attempting to ready myself for the words that will soon fall from my father's lips.

It's all yours, sons. Make me proud.

Or some shit like that.

Malcolm Savage is a ruthless, cold-hearted murderer. There's no doubt about what my father is. And he expects nothing less from his two boys, twins, born to a woman who died while pushing us out of her body. Not even my mother could love us enough to stick around.

. . .

SWINGING MY LEGS OVER THE EDGE OF THE BED, I RISE AND HEAD to the closet. Pulling on a pair of black slacks, I grab a white button-up and shrug it on. The cool material does nothing to calm the heat running through me.

When my phone vibrates on the wooden nightstand, I know it's time to finally finish this fucked-up game. Every moment that passes brings me closer to being free. And that's my plan. To be far away from this place.

Sauntering over to pick up the device, I unlock it with my thumbprint and smile at the words. Drake is ready. So is Caia and River.

They'll never see this coming. They'll never see me coming.

CHAPTER TWENTY-SEVEN
DRAKE

Opening my eyes, I find myself in the familiar space of my bedroom. Caia's body is draped over mine as if we'd fallen asleep last night. But when I glance at the window that overlooks the back garden, I notice the sky is black.

Something's wrong. Very fucking wrong. Lifting my girl's arm, I place it on the mattress and get up. I feel as if I've been drugged. My head is foggy, and memories from last night — or is it tonight? — are jumbled around in my mind.

The bedroom door opens, and one of our security team strolls in. He offers a nod. "Dante says that dinner will be served in an hour."

"What?" Confusion settles in my thoughts.

"There's a dinner that's been set out. You, Caia, and River are to attend."

Shaking my head, I'm about to ask him what he means, but he leaves, closing the door before I can get the words out. My body aches everywhere, but there aren't bruises on my arms when I glance down.

My phone vibrates on the nightstand, which has me moving quickly to retrieve it. It's lit up with a message from Dante.

They have Amoretto?

Why the fuck did my brother not wake me?

When my bedroom door swings open again, I glance over my shoulder to find River sauntering in. He's dressed in a pair of dark jeans. The turtleneck he's wearing is black, which only makes the green of his eyes pop from his tanned skin.

"We're apparently wanted for dinner," he offers, settling beside Caia on the bed, which causes her to open her eyes.

"Do you know what's going on?" I question, staring at my best friend who shakes his head.

"No, I'm as clueless as you."

"What happened?" My girl scoots up against the headboard, her gaze darting between River and me.

"We've been brought home. I don't remember much after we left the house," I tell her. I'm not sure what happened, but nothing feels broken, just achy, so it couldn't have been an accident. "Get up. We need to figure out what's going on."

My brother has never wanted to get involved in my revenge plan. He offered his assistance but didn't show much interest when it came to taking down the assholes I was so adamant in killing.

But then again, Dante has always been a live wire. More volatile than I ever was. I'd seen him lose control a few times, and to be honest, it scared me.

Once we're dressed, the three of us make our way down the hallway toward the sweeping staircase which will lead us into the living room, dining room, and kitchen area.

As soon as I step into our large dining room, I'm halted in my tracks by three people sitting at the fourteen-seater table. At the head farthest from me is Caia's father, bound to the chair. His mouth is covered with black tape, his eyes wide with fear.

To the left of him is a woman I would recognize anywhere. Not because I've met her before, but because the woman standing beside me is the spitting image of her. Caia's soft gasp falls from her plump lips, and I don't blame her. Coming face to face with a ghost is never easy.

To the right of Hamish Amoretto is another woman. She has her back to us, but my chest tightens when she shifts slowly. Time moves at a snail's pace when she turns her face toward us. Her familiar, wide blue eyes meet mine, and my breath is knocked from me.

I'm unsure of what to do or say, so I stand speechless at the entrance. The three people at the dinner table are all bound, their mouths covered so I can't hear their pleas.

Most importantly, I can't hear *her* voice.

The woman with the eyes that match mine and Dante's.

The woman I believed was dead.

The woman I would be calling mom if she'd stuck around to be the mother Dante and I never had.

CHAPTER TWENTY-EIGHT
CAIA

I'm not sure how I find strength to move, but I do.

Closing the distance between me and the table, I can't drag my eyes away from my mother. She's sitting on a chair, bound, muted, and helpless. I find myself wanting to save her and wanting to slap her for leaving me. For leaving Harper.

"Ah, the dinner party has arrived." Dante's voice comes from the doorway. Beside him is Harper. She's smiling as she leans into him. His arm is draped around her shoulders as if they're out on a date, not standing in a room with people who have been kidnapped.

"What's going on here, brother?" Drake hisses under his breath, but I'm close enough to hear him. The tension in the room hangs heavily, a thick cloud of anger and distrust grips us all in its feral claws.

"We're having parents evening at the Savage Mansion," Dante tells us. Tugging Harper alongside him, they settle at the opposite side of the table from where my father is sitting, with Harper on Dante's lap.

Everything feels slightly surreal when she leans into him as if he's her savior. I want to stop her, to tell her to be careful, but to be truthful, I have no idea what is actually going on.

One more person joins us. Rayne. The girl from Thanos's mansion. She slides into a chair to the right of Dante, and my sister finally takes a seat to the left.

"Please, sit down," Dante says. It's alarming how the twins can look so alike, but their personalities are so vastly different.

Drake laces his fingers through mine, pulling me closer as we settle beside each other on the chairs that have been set out. The long, dark wood table can seat a fair number of guests, but I have a feeling this party is only for us.

River is beside me, his hand on my thigh, holding me steady, and I wonder if he's keeping himself upright or me. Drake has my hand clenched so tightly in his I feel the tingle start in the tips as the circulation is cut off.

"Now," Dante starts. "I've found out a few things about our wonderful parents that may make you recoil, but then again, this is the Savage Mansion," he chuckles. "Many things that happen in here would make you cringe."

"Dante, this game—"

"Oh, I assure you brother, this is far from a game." Dante smiles, staring at me then turning his gaze on my mother. "The woman over there, *Mrs. Amoretto*." He says her name for effect, to slowly slice at my heart. "Has two daughters, who are here tonight, Harper and Caia." Blue eyes land on us both, flitting between my sister and me. "The thing about it is, you both thought dear mommy was dead," Dante continues, and I wonder briefly if he's stoned or high.

"Dante, this is ridiculous." River's voice is tight with tension and anxiety.

"Oh, but wait." Our host rises. "My own mother," he says, pointing to the other woman bound to a chair. "She walked out on Drake and me before we even knew her name. So, this brings me back to the reason for the dinner party tonight." Dante lifts a bottle of wine which was set on the table and proceeds in filling the glasses. "Harper, if you'd be so kind." He gestures to my sister who obeys him without question.

She rises, setting a glass down in front of each of us, then settles beside Dante again. She looks beautiful, poised, strong. Better than she did when I left her only hours ago.

"I was the one who informed Hamish about your plan, brother," Dante informs us all, but his gaze is pinned on his brother. "Now, before you fight me on this, I'll explain. You see, I found out our mother, along with your beautiful girlfriend's mother, were both fucking Hamish," Dante says. He lifts his wine glass as if he's about to make a toast. "I wish him luck on his ventures, because since I found this out, I figured, we should all meet him, have a meal, and get to know the man who was responsible for a variety of deaths, kidnappings, and even a few broken souls along the way."

"What?" I croak, unsure where this is going.

"Hamish Amoretto was the mind behind the Savage Organization," Dante says. "He was blackmailing Malcolm to perform certain . . . *duties*, so that he can live a life of luxury."

"That doesn't make sense," Drake says, to which Dante smirks, sliding over a folder which he'd set on the table when he joined us.

Drake flips open the manila folder with pages of information about my father's investment, or rather, startup costs which he had given Malcolm to get the enterprise up and running. My father was the mastermind behind everything that happened to me. But then he fucked up. It appears he lost money gambling, paying for whores, and also paying for the delivery of the *toys* from various operations.

When Drake gets to the last page, my vision blurs. I was payment for my father's debt to Thanos. He'd borrowed money from the man, and I was the auctioned item to clear my father's name.

"So." Dante smiles. "I brought you all here today to get your take on the events that took place as we grew up," he tells us. "For years, Drake tried to protect me. He hid the things he'd seen, the things he experienced, but I knew. Deep down, I realized my brother wasn't okay. Each smile was offset by darkness that danced in his eyes, and I figured, I'll be the big brother for once. I'll save him."

"What are you talking about, Dante?" This time, Drake sounds frustrated with his brother. His hand still clutches mine, and I'm sure if he lets go, I'll fall to my knees and weep.

The silence is thick, heavy, and daunting. I don't know if I want to know the truth. I honestly don't think I can handle any more than I already have.

"Well, it turns out, dear brother, that Mommy Dearest knows exactly where River's mother is hiding." Dante looks excited about the prospect of finding the woman who birthed the boys' best friend. He seems jovial.

"And where exactly is that?" River finally speaks beside me. I grip his hand, knowing that this could set him off. I don't know River as well as I do Drake, but something tells me that he could lose his mind over the fact that his mother could be closer than he believed.

"Well." Dante rises. He strides over to where his and Drake's mother is sitting. We watch as he rips the black tape from over her mouth. "Tell them, Mommy Dearest," Dante utters in her ear so we can all hear him. "Tell them where your sister is."

DRAKE

"What?" My voice is raspy. I growl the word through clenched teeth. This can't be happening. Shaking my head, I watch as my mother trembles and shivers as the tears stream down her face. She's begging and pleading, but all I see is red. Blood-fucking-rage red. There's nothing that can stop me from moving from my seat, not even Caia.

I'm in her face, tugging the rope until she's free, then I wrench her from the chair by her neck. She's so light I easily lift her and pin her against the wall. Her slim frame shudders with fear, but I don't give a shit.

My blood has passed simmering. It's fucking boiling. Her wide eyes that look so familiar meet mine in agony and apology, but nothing can make up for what she did.

"Please, let me explain."

"River is my fucking cousin? Your filthy whore of a sister left him to live a life of filth and depravity?" Spittle flies from my mouth, landing on her face, causing her to flinch as I pray my words burn her. But I know they don't. Sadly, they only cause her more heartache. I want to see the bitch burn. I don't care if she carried me for nine months, I don't care if she forced me from her cunt. I'm just angry she isn't really dead.

My fingers tighten around her delicate neck. Tears race down her cheeks like a salty waterfall of despair.

"She needed money. Your . . . Your father said he'd care for River." Her words make no sense.

"She needed money for what? To run a fucking organization in Thailand?"

She shakes her head, her blue gaze landing on the man behind me. Hamish Amoretto. When I glance over my shoulder, he's shaking his head. His fear is like a fucking aphrodisiac, and my cock hardens at the thought of making him watch me take his daughter, making him look into her eyes as she comes with my dick inside her. Shaking my head, I realize I'm as sick as Malcolm was.

"So, Malcolm did what?"

"Hamish promised her the money if she opened an import company for him in Asia. He offered her over ten million dollars to move there, never come back here, but leave her son with Malcolm. You have to understand, before you boys were born," she murmurs. "Money was tight."

I no longer know what to believe, but one thing is certain. Tonight I will be killing someone. And the person that will experience my wrath is behind me at the table, shaking his head.

"What a lovely story, Mom," Dante laughs. When I glance at him, I wonder if he's high. Perhaps he's been snorting shit again to numb the memories. God knows I've done it far too many times in the past.

"Tell me something." I meet my mother's worried stare.

"Did you ever love us? Was there ever an inkling of emotion for your sons?"

Her mouth falls open to respond, but no words come out, and I know what I have to do. This shit ends tonight. And it starts with the woman I don't know. The stranger who I'm slowly squeezing the life out of.

Caia's hand lands on my arm. Her wide eyes meet mine when I turn toward her. "Are you sure you want to do this?" she questions, looking out for my well-being when I should be the one caring for her. "There's no going back." Her warning is clear. Once I kill my own mother, I'll never be able to forget or take it back.

"It's because of her you're here. It's also because of her that Dante, River, and I lived through the horrific, fucked-up life we did," I tell her. My choice has been made; she can see it in my eyes.

Caia nods. Releasing me from her grip, she steps back, allowing me space to do what I need to. I turn back to my mother. Dante is beside me, watching me lose control.

"Brother," he murmurs beside me. "We can keep her in the cells." He's right. It's an option, but I plan to burn this house down when this is over. There will no longer be any cells. There'll be no Savage Mansion when I'm done.

I glance at Dante who seems to have come back down to earth from his rather flamboyant high.

"I promised you something a long time ago, brother," I tell him. "I'll get you out of this. There will no longer be a house, cells. There'll no longer be a Savage Organization. They're all dead."

My mother's hand grips my wrist, holding onto me as if I'm about to save her. But the only people I am saving are the people who've been there for me.

The grip I have on her neck tightens, and I watch as she gasps for air. Mumbled pleas of mercy are ignored as she claws at me, her body flailing, and I find myself smiling as my mother takes her last breath.

Her lips turn a shade of purple then slowly blue as I watch in awe. The colors make such a beautiful rainbow as her breaths are stolen. *Whoever said death wasn't beautiful?*

CHAPTER THIRTY
CAIA

I can't tear my gaze away from the man I love as he steals his mother's life with a single hand. The veins in his forearm thick and angry, pulsing as they trail down toward his fingers, as if they're offering more strength to finish the deed.

I should be afraid of him. He could easily kill me. He could simply turn to me and decide he's had enough. But when Drake's fingers finally unravel from his mother's delicate neck and she tumbles to the ground, he turns to me with fire and affection dancing in those piercing blue orbs, and he doesn't steal my life. Instead, he is the thief of my heart.

"Come here, sweet girl," he calls to me, reaching for me with one hand, and the other hangs at his side as if it's tired from the strain of squeezing every last heartbeat from the lifeless form on the floor.

I don't deny him the affection he so clearly seeks. When I reach him, I mold myself into the crook of his arm. His warmth calms my erratic heartbeat. Everything has happened way too fast. I still have no idea why my sister is so in love with Dante, how my mother and father are sitting here, but all I focus on is one thing. The one thing I've wanted to do for so long — to kill my father while he looks into my eyes.

"It's time for you to decide how you end this, little bird," Drake murmurs in my ear. Dante places a hand on my shoulder. When I glance up at both men, I take in their similarities up close. Dante hands me a weapon — a sleek, silver blade with a handle carved from wood. The ridges dig into my hand when I grip it.

"It's your birthday today, sweet Caia." Dante smiles. "Your gifts await you." His voice is almost ethereal, along with his handsome face. I take in his angular jaw and the dimples I'm sure have my sister in their grip, as well as his full, pink lips, the mischievous grin, and the way flames dance in his eyes. As handsome as Dante is, my heart belongs to his brother.

Turning my attention to Drake, I smile at how rugged he looks beside me. A slight dusting of stubble darkens his jaw. He only has one dimple in the right cheek when he smiles. There's a softness to him, even in this darkness. He offers affection I know Dante doesn't hold. And that makes me wonder how the brother who went through the worst of it can still care so much.

That's when my eyes land on another man. River. He's watching me intently, and I know he's worried. I can see it in his expression. The quiet one of the three, he offers solace in his silence.

With a touch, glance, or smile, he can diffuse a situation. But I know his heart holds more than that. It overflows with love. For Dante, for me, and most importantly, for Drake. And just as I figured, he gives me a smirk along with a nod.

It's time for me to say goodbye to my past and move on. It's time for my father to pay for what he's done. Harper steps up beside me. She's holding a knife similar to the one in my hand.

"It's time, sister," she whispers, and we make our way toward the table. The man who we grew up calling *Daddy* is shivering and shaking his head as if pleading for mercy. But there's none left. He made sure of that when he took our lives into his hands and toyed with us like pawns in a much larger game.

Leaning in, I whisper in his ear, "This is for all the years I've lost." Pressing the tip of the blade at his ear, I push it into the opening, watching and reveling in the way the sharp steel slices through the wrinkled flesh.

Blood spurts from the wound I inflict, staining my hand in crimson as I shove it in deeper. Cutting into the man who allowed me to lose all my innocence, I trail the object down his right cheek toward the corner of his mouth.

I can't help laughing when the tape falls away from his lips and he pleads with me. Begging for his life. For me to think about what I'm doing.

"Did you think, Daddy?" Harper mimics my action while taunting our father with her words. "Did you think when you pinned me to the bed? When I cried, and you told me it was best for me?" Her words echo the pain my chest. I wasn't there to save her, but when I see my sister now, I know she's her own heroine. She's strong. She's a warrior. She's a survivor.

CHAPTER THIRTY-ONE
DRAKE

I don't think there's anything hotter than seeing Caia drenched in blood. Her father is dead. He's bleeding out in our dining room, but I don't care. The only thing I want and need is my girl. I want to go to her, but she's with Harper, so I allow her time to be with her sister.

Dante leans in and whispers, "You know, this was one of the best dinner parties we've had in this house."

"How did you do all this?" I question, not tearing my eyes away from the woman I love. I know Dante is somewhat of a loose cannon, but this is something else. The fact that he forgives me for not telling him the truth about our mother being alive is a miracle in itself, but what he did for Caia and Harper confirms that my brother can love.

"There were many times over the years you saved me," he tells me. "But as much as you think you were the one who kept me from the shit that you had been through, I experienced some of the same, Drake."

Snapping my gaze to his, I find the hurt in his eyes.

Being the *older* brother made me believe I was meant to be stronger. And perhaps in a way I was, but I realize that by trying to save my brother, I was only hurting him more.

"I felt your pain all these years." His confession causes my chest to tighten with anxiety, with fear that he hates me. "I saw it every time you looked at me, and this time, I wanted to be the one to save you. To show you I'm all grown up now, brother," he smirks.

"You're leaving. Aren't you?" My question stills him, and I watch in awe as he drags his gaze toward the girl beside Caia. He's found someone to love more than me. More than River. And even though I've always been protective of my brother, I realize it's time to let him go.

Harper pulls Caia into a hug. Their father has taken his final breath, but there's one more person still alive. Her eyes are wide. She's watching her daughters with agony and guilt falling in watery emotion down her cheeks.

"I am," Dante finally agrees. "It's time I found my own life, brother," he tells me, but he's watching his girl. I'm about to respond when Rayne sidles up to him, wrapping her arm around his waist.

"Both of them?" My question causes him to chuckle.

When he finally turns to me, he shrugs. "If you can have two, why can't I?"

He's right. I've got Caia and River, and it seems as if my brother has two feisty females to contend with, but something tells me he'll be able to handle them.

"What are we going to do with the mother?" he questions, lowering his voice so only I can hear him.

When I look at her, I note how fearful she is. But that doesn't matter. Just like my own mother, the woman sitting at the table is as guilty as the other adults who were meant to care for us.

"The girls will decide," I tell him.

Just then, Caia turns to me, a small, relieved smile on her face. I crook my finger, calling her toward me, and when she obeys, it only serves to make my cock hard.

"You and Harper need to decide what we're doing with your mother," I tell her.

"Well, she's a filthy fuck," Dante chuckles, earning him a swat from Harper. "It had to be done." His shrug only confirms the asshole fucked their mother.

"And for what purpose?" I question.

"I figured if she escaped, I'd have a recording of her. Blackmail is the most popular way of making sure people do as you say. Also, I think my little minx over here enjoyed the show," he smirks, tugging Harper under the other arm. My glare burns into him. "What? I wrapped my dick." He rolls his eyes as if it's a joke, and I know Dante doesn't give a shit who thinks badly about him.

That's the thing about my younger brother. Unpredictable, volatile, but he will always make sure he's safe in any situation. Looking out for him, me, River, and the girls.

"Can . . .?" Caia starts, but lowers her gaze, allowing her words to trickle into nothing. The silence is deafening for a moment before she looks up at me again. "Can we keep her in the cells? Just until we decide what we're going to do?"

I'd do anything for her. I'd fucking kill everyone who's ever looked at her the wrong way. She has to know how much I love her. How much she's changed me and made me realize that my heart isn't cold and rigid. It's beating, but it only does so for her and one other person.

River steps forward, his green eyes meet mine when I flit my gaze to his. He offers a nod of understanding. He knows this is the only choice we have right now. Realization hits me. I'm in love with him, and he's no longer just my best friend.

He's more than that. He's family.

"We should clean this mess up," he suggests, placing a hand on my shoulder and one on Caia. I can't find words, so all I offer is a nod. He moves quickly, getting the team of men in.

I watch as they escort Caia and Harper's mother through the room and out the double doors. She'll be locked in one of the cells. I should kill her right here and now, but my girl has asked for time. That's what I'll give her.

"This is . . ." Her gentle voice lingers in my ears, and I want to grasp onto it for a moment longer, but I know I can't.

"It's a fuck up," I tell her. Glancing at Dante who's staring at me, I tell him, "We should never have had this happen."

"It was my idea." Harper steps forward. "My father spent years making my life hell. And when I found out what he did to my sister, to you and your brother, and to River, I knew he had to pay."

"I get that—"

"No, Drake, you don't. What you're trying to do is protect my sister, and that's admirable. I'm glad she's found someone who is here for her, but Dante is here for me. We see things differently, and that's okay."

That we certainly do. As much as I wanted to kill

Hamish, I also wanted more information from him. Perhaps his wife can offer that.

"What is your plan for your mother?" My question is aimed at both girls. I look over at Harper, then meet Caia's beautiful, teary eyes.

"We need to know who else was working for my father." Harper's suggestion is spot-on. But I know her mother would never rat on the man she loves. There's always been an unspoken rule about loving someone in this house.

My father was adamant that as soon as the affection grew, you'd be severed from the real world. Stolen and forced to support the person you love. I realize the moment my mother supposedly died, she took my father's heart with her. But now I know she was alive and breathing, and I wonder if there was any love between them.

Many times over the years, I've looked at Malcolm Savage and wondered just how much it had taken to break him. Life. My mother. The fact that he had to put on a show for every client and customer that walked through the door.

He wasn't real. He'd hidden his feelings behind a mask, just like he taught Dante and me to do. Only, we never could get it right.

"Drake." Caia's gentle voice breaks through the darkness that clouds my mind. "Let's go to bed. You need to rest." She's everything I've always wanted. Someone who knew about my family but still loved me anyway.

CHAPTER THIRTY-TWO
CAIA

Drake leads me back to his bedroom. I'm still in a daze after everything that's happened, and having the man I love beside me only makes things seem more surreal. When I first met him, he was nothing more than a stranger who hurt me. He was someone I feared, but as time passed and I learned about the man in question, he became so much more. He became the love of my life.

Perhaps that makes me sick. Fucked up. I fell in love with my captor. But I know I'm stronger for it. Knowing Drake has offered me strength I never had before. He isn't a knight in shining armor. He definitely is not the most romantic person in the world, but he makes my heart soar. He offers me something I never thought I'd ever have again.

Drake gives me hope.

For years, I was hidden away in the dark. I was merely a toy for people to use, by men and women, and they made sure I was nothing more than a device for their sick needs.

When we reach Drake's room, he ushers me inside, shutting the door behind River who joins us. We're all in shock. The silence is thick and heavy, hanging over the three of us, and I don't know what to say.

I perch myself on the mattress, my eyes watchful of the two men in the room with me. My body is still trembling when I settle on the bed. My hands are drenched in my father's blood.

Staring at my fingers, I note how they shake. It's a slight movement, but it's there. I've always wanted to kill him. After being tortured, knowing that he sent me here, seeing what he did to Harper, I knew I had to do something. My need for revenge was fierce. And now that it's over, I'm not sure what the next step is.

I replay in my mind the look in his eyes as I did it. When I watched the life drain from him. He didn't deserve to live. That was always clear to me. And I knew I would never spare his life. If I didn't do it, I know Drake would've.

But the truths that tumbled free tonight only confirm he needed to die. My father was always a smart man. When I was growing up, I admired his ideas for business. I'd watch him sit behind his large mahogany desk as he told me what he was planning. The software he wanted to develop. The partners he would bring in to help with marketing, with actually creating the apps.

He made money, and perhaps that was his downfall. Too much money made him bored. It made him believe he was God and he could play with lives. But it also made him sick.

The things I watched on the videos of him and Harper made me sick. Violent. Shaking my head to clear the thoughts, I glance up to find both men staring at me. River is leaning against the door, his arms folded in front of his chest. Drake is sitting on his desk, blue eyes searing me as he watches my reaction.

I know Drake has killed before. It's no secret, so he knows how I'm feeling. There's no doubt I did the right thing, but taking someone's life is not something you can just walk away from. It's life-altering. It's scary how easily I could do it without a second thought.

"You look beautiful," Drake offers, breaking the silence.

I can't help smiling. In all this destruction, he still sees me as beautiful.

"I've never seen anything hotter than you taking his life. Watching a monster die for what he did, I feel relieved. And it's because you were strong enough. Since the first moment I laid my eyes on you, I knew," he smirks.

"You knew what?"

"I knew you were stronger than any of the girls that were brought in here."

River chuckles, making his way toward me. "He's right. He was besotted with you the moment you pissed on him."

His comment makes me laugh, and I can't stop. My shoulders shake, and the tension that held me captive for so long finally abates.

River settles beside me, his hand finding my thigh, stroking me slowly. My body trembles when he reaches the apex between my thighs. He taunts me gently, as if waiting for me to refuse him, but I can't. There's no way I can ever refuse River or Drake.

I open my eyes to meet the deep green pools of River's. Smiling up at him, I lean in and plant a kiss on his cheek. The soft stubble that darkens his jaw makes him look older than I know he is.

His golden blond hair is tousled, messy, and sexy. His smirk is filthy. His eyes shine with desire.

"Drake is right. You've never looked more beautiful," he tells me. He takes my bloody hand, pressing it to his crotch, and I feel how much he wants me in that moment. "Take out my dick," he orders gruffly.

My fingers move of their own accord. Gripping his shaft, I pull it from his slacks. The thick, hard cock throbs in my hand, and I stroke it slowly.

A groan comes from Drake as he nears us. He seats himself on the other side of me. And I follow his hands as they shove his slacks down, and he allows me to fist his cock.

Both men are entranced at me stroking them with the blood of my father on my hands. The sounds of feral grunting surround me, and I find myself whimpering with want. The need to forget what I've just done takes hold of me, and I keep my eyes locked on either man, flitting between the two.

River teases my legs wider, draping one leg over his, and my other over Drake's. I'm spread for them, and all I want to do is feel them open me, stretch me, make me cry in pained pleasure.

Once they're both solid steel in my hands, Drake lies down, his head positioned on the pillows. His cock jutting from his hips. I take my cue and rise, pulling my dress up and over my head. I'm not wearing a bra, and I allow my panties to pool at my feet. He crooks his finger, pulling me onto him. I straddle his hips, sliding down on him, taking him into my already drenched center.

"Fuck, little bird, you're so tight," Drake grits out as if

the restraint he's holding onto is pulled taut and about to snap.

River reaches for the nightstand, grabbing a bottle of lube, then moves behind me. With a snap, he opens it and drizzles the cool liquid over the crack of my ass. The way he massages me, teasing my hole, scissoring me open makes me whimper loudly.

Drake doesn't move. River eases his cock into me. Inch by torturous inch, he opens me wide. Painfully so. I cry out when he finally bottoms out and I'm filled like never before. I can't breathe for a moment, but two sets of hands on my body ground me. They hold me close, and we start to move.

CHAPTER THIRTY-THREE
DRAKE

With River inside Caia, I'm lost in pleasure watching her take us both. Her face is euphoric as we both move, sliding back and forth. Her delicate hands hold onto me, her tits are at my mouth, and I can't stop myself from capturing her nipple, grazing my teeth over the taut bud, which only makes her clench around us tighter, milking us for the seed I'm dying to empty inside her.

I've had women between River and me before, but this is something else. This is no longer just a moment to get myself off, to find release I need. There is emotion in this moment.

"I love you, both," I utter, causing River to still. Both sets of eyes — River's and Caia's — bore into me. "I love you both. I never want to be without either of you."

The corner of my best friend's mouth kicks up into a full blow grin. He always knew I loved him, but I could never say the words. I could never admit my feelings because we still had monsters to slay.

"I love you, Drake," River tells me.

Caia leans in, her mouth close to mine, and her breaths fan the words over my lips. "I love you more than anything," she informs me. Then, she turns her head to meet the eyes of the other man who's owning her. "I love you too. More than you can ever imagine."

"I love you, sweetheart." River winks, then slowly slides from her body and drives back in harder and faster than she expects, making her cry out a *yes* as pleasure rockets through her.

We move in earnest then.

We fuck.

We make love.

Writhing, trembling, clawing at each other with a need only animals would ever feel. It's basal. Feral. I'm tempted to bite into her, to suck the life force that pumps through her veins and taste her essence as I watch her ride us both. Taking us inside her beautifully tight body.

We're nothing but grunts and sweat, slick and slippery. Passion ignites us, and we're burning from the love, the desire, and the lust driving us forward to find euphoria.

Then I feel River's cock throbbing as he empties himself into her, marking her. I grip her hips, holding her against me, and bury my cock deep inside her, wishing with all my heart that I'm filling her womb with potent seed.

My girl doesn't disappoint with the whimpers of pleasure as she calls out mine and River's names. Her nails dig into my flesh as she shudders above me, between our bodies.

STALKING THROUGH THE HALLWAY, I MAKE MY WAY DOWN TO THE cells. If there's any more information I can get out of Caia's mother, I'll ensure I get it. I've just left both River and my girl sleeping in my bed, and the need to go back up to them, to curl myself between them is ever-present, but there's work to be done.

A screech comes from the dungeon, and my feet move faster toward the sound. When I shove open the thick metal door, I find Dante and Harper inside. The girl's mother is chained to the wall where my father used to bind us while he ensured our training went as planned.

Turning to the sound of the screech, I realize it's not the woman who's cuffed to the wall. Instead, I find the screen playing out the video of Harper's abuse. They're forcing this woman to watch what her daughter had to go through.

Tears stream from her eyes, and I wonder if she feels any guilt. When she attempts to turn her face away, her daughter forces it forward, making sure she watches every gruesome detail.

"Drake." My brother sidles up beside me. "We wanted to get more information from Holly before the girls sat down with her."

"I was coming down here to do the same, only I don't think I would've tortured her like this," I tell Dante, gesturing to the television screen which has the horrific scenes playing out.

"This was Harper's idea."

I nod at this information. Caia has a streak of fire in her, it burns brightly when she's making a kill and it seems her sister is as vicious as she is. I don't blame her in the slightest. In fact, I'm proud of her.

"So, you're with both girls?" I question, realizing last

night flew by. Everything that had happened was so fast I didn't get a chance to talk to Dante.

"I am," he tells me. "They're both beautiful, they both want me, and since you're delving into a lifetime threesome, I figured I'd try it out. And," he says, leaning in closer. "Watching them lick my sticky seed from each other's pretty little cunts is hot as hell."

Shaking my head, I glance over at Dante. He's always been more open about things than I have. And I can tell he'll have his hands full with the two little spitfires.

"And how did you find out about Dad?"

"Hamish was more than happy to share the information when I threatened to slice off his balls."

I watch my brother for a moment before telling him, "And you had us . . . what? Drugged? Brought back here?"

"The girl's needed retribution. We needed the truth, and I think I did well."

I nod. He's right. This was a better idea than racing into the man's home to kill him, but I only did that because I wanted to give Caia the one thing she needed.

Revenge.

"I will never forgive him." My words are cold, harsh, but I don't care. "He did things to us I can never forget, things that will always leave me broken."

"Aren't we all, brother?" Dante offers when he glances over at Harper who's smiling at her mother's tears. When the video clicks off, she takes one of the metal implements similar to a pair of pliers and knocks her mother out.

"I'm done." She smiles at my brother as if he's her savior.

"Get your girl down here, brother," Dante informs me.

"Because I can't keep Harper from killing her all day. Make it quick."

He reaches for Harper's hand and tugs her past me toward the door. She offers an innocent smile when she looks over at me, and I wonder just how broken this girl truly is, and if my brother can save her.

CHAPTER THIRTY-FOUR
CAIA

The knife presses against his flesh. I can feel their eyes on me, burning into me as they watch me take his life. His eyes are wide with shock, but I feel no remorse, no guilt at what I'm doing. He deserves what is happening, and I find my mouth kicking up into a smile. A happy grin as the blood drains from him.

Harper's soft giggle is the only other sound besides my father whimpering and pleading with me to stop. He's finally the one in agony, and it makes me happy. I can see how people get addicted to murder, how they bask in the power they hold from taking someone's life in their hands.

He's shuddering as I watch the vital fluid drenching my hand. It's sticky, the scent metallic and strong as it invades my nostrils. It's the only thing I can smell.

"This is for all those young lives you stole," I tell him. "And this," I press the blade against the vein pumping wildly, severing the flesh as the silver edge drags across the wrinkles. "Is for me and Harper, your daughters."

. . .

"Caia." Drake's voice steals me from the memory, and I glance up to find him standing behind me. I'm seated at the dressing table in his bedroom, staring at myself in the mirror. "We need to decide what to do with your mother."

"And we need to find out why my father did what he did," I tell him. I need to know how a man who is meant to love his daughters can do something so vile.

I rise, turning to face the man who holds my heart. He pulls me closer. Leaning in, he presses his lips to mine. For a moment, I feel him. I feel his emotions — guilt, fear, love, anger, rage — whirling through him, and they tumble into me.

I'm the one to break the kiss before I offer him a whispered response. "She doesn't deserve to live, but I need to say goodbye," I tell him.

He laces his fingers through mine, and we make our way down to the dungeon that brings back memories I had long-since buried. I always knew this place was here, but since I'd been back in Drake's life, I never ventured down here. I didn't want to see it. But once you've purged yourself of the past, it's remarkable how differently you feel about things.

"Hello, Mother," I offer as soon as we step into the familiar room. She's bound, but her mouth is no longer covered with tape.

"Baby girl," she utters, and her voice sends me right back to being ten years old and listening to her read me fairytales before bed. The same woman who taught me about dragons and princes was the same woman who let me be stolen.

"I'm no longer anyone's *baby girl*," I tell her. "*You* made sure of that."

Shaking her head, she meets my angry glare with a sad gaze of her own. "I didn't mean to hurt you," she whimpers. "Your father . . . He's always had . . . He's been a bad person for a long time." Her words tumble freely as she confesses. "His own childhood was filled with darkness."

"So you decided to leave your daughters with a fucked-up monster?"

"No, I . . . I didn't have a way of taking you with me, and he would've found me. I allowed him to rule my life."

"Why Malcolm?" I question, needing to know for me, for Drake, and for Dante. "What did Malcolm do to Hamish that he could blackmail him into starting this horror show?"

The door clicks behind us. Dante and Harper stroll inside, and I know we're nearing the end of my mother's life. My sister is raging, her eyes wide, darkness swirling in them, and I'm certain she's as ready as I am to move on.

But I want answers. I need them.

"Tell me," I hiss, stepping closer to her. My face right in hers, and I see it. I see Harper and me in her features. We're her daughters, there's no doubt about it. "What did my father have over Malcolm Savage?"

"When Malcolm was at college, he and your father were best of friends. Until one night, they had gone to a frat party." She finally sighs, and my heartrate only spikes at the revelations. "Malcolm had a girlfriend who was . . . She wanted to do drugs with him while partying with boys who were far too old for her." My mother lowers her gaze for a moment, and I wonder if she's stalling. Then she looks up at me again as tears trickle down her cheeks. "Malcolm gave her some pills she swallowed without knowing what they were. Hamish found her on Malcolm's bed. She died."

"That still doesn't—"

"The girl was your father's sister."

Silence hangs heavily in the air. The truth grips my chest with a painful ferocity I didn't expect. Drake and Dante's father killed my aunt.

"The problem is that she wanted to die. I found her diary months later; your father had been with her since she was too young to fight back. She fell in love with Malcolm and confessed everything. Hamish knew, and he told Malcolm if the truth ever came out they'd both be put in prison. As time went on, your father's *needs* only intensified." She spits the word *needs,* and I don't blame her.

"And you still left us with him?"

"I made a mistake. I wasn't there when you—"

I can't listen to her anymore. My body is vibrating with rage as I rear back, and my fist connects with her jaw.

"You're dead to me," I tell her. Turning to face Drake, I shake my head. "I don't want anything more to do with her. Kill her if you want to. I'm done."

Without a backward glance, I head back to Drake's room. Throwing my body on the bed, I allow my tears to fall free. I allow my pain and sadness to overtake me, and I finally cry. It feels like I'm purging the pain from my body. I grip the pillow, holding it close to me as I sob so hard my whole body is wracked, shaking and trembling.

It's finally over.

EPILOGUE

Caia

S*ix months later*

MONTHS HAVE GONE BY SINCE WE WERE FREED FROM THE PAST.
My stomach is slowly swelling with every day that passes. I
never thought I'd be pregnant after the horrors I faced, but
either Drake's or River's baby is growing inside me. We
didn't need to find out who the father is because we're in
this together.

The sun is shining through the large bay windows. I
glance out to the garden to find River and Drake sparring in
the heat. They're both shirtless because of the hot summer
weather. River's wearing gray sweatpants as he punches
the mitts Drake has bound to his hands. Both bodies glisten
with sweat, and I find myself intoxicated at the sight.

The house is quiet. I enjoy time alone inside. After

Dante, Harper, and Rayne decided they were going to travel to Europe for a few months, we threw a goodbye party and burned down the Savage Mansion.

Drake suggested we move into the cabin for a few months, which seems to be doing us all some good. I recall the time I spent here when they'd saved me from Thanos. It was the first time I'd seen Drake after four long years.

He was everything I remembered. Cold, savage, and still as handsome as the moment I'd realized I was in love with him. For years, I prayed for him to find me, and when he finally did, my life took a turn once more. He offered me strength in his own way.

I think if River wasn't there, he'd still be locked up in the guilt he lived with for so long. He may not have shown it, but it certainly danced in his eyes, like a flame. I watched in awe as each day passed and he allowed me in. He opened his life to me, but it was only when he finally let me into his heart did I really get to know Drake Savage.

He may have killed and maimed in the past — some of it I still don't know — but I choose not to. I told him it wasn't important. If he wanted to go back there, to relive it while he confessed, I'd listen, but the man I love is not a monster.

River glances at me through the window, offering a wink as he and his best friend swap mitts. This time, Drake is punching, and I watch with a grin as the two most handsome men I've ever laid eyes on workout while I sip my apple juice.

It took some time for me to come to terms with killing my father, but I knew I'd finally set myself, along with my sister, free. She's finally allowing herself to be happy. Her love for Dante is strong, and he gives her what she needs.

I never knew my sister was into both men and women, but watching her with Rayne and Dante, it's clear she's finally found a family she can love. We'll always love each other, but she needs to be happy on her own now.

I always promised myself I'd free her. And I did. And in the process, I freed us all from the monsters that didn't just hide under our beds, they lurked within the homes we grew up in, within the lives we thought we were safe in.

My hand gently lands on my stomach, circling the small bump just visible through the tank top I'm wearing. At least I know our baby will grow up in a safe, loving home.

And all I can do is pray the past will stay buried.

Do you like it Sinful, steamy, and downright filthy? Check out the Sins of Seven, starting with Kneel, book one.

Sign up for my newsletter and receive a free novella from me.

Keep reading for an excerpt of Kneel

SNEAK PEEK - KNEEL

PROLOGUE
NATE

Greed is my vice. A sin that leads to my addictions. One of the seven deadly sins to be exact. Perhaps greed didn't lead to my demise, but it did, in many ways, change me. My tastes differ from most men. I enjoy the tears on a beautiful rosy hued cheek. I revel in degrading women in sexual ways for my gratification and theirs.

Don't get me wrong, I'm not saying my tastes are right. All I'm saying is that there are women out there who come to me to be degraded. At thirty-six, I've had many slaves in my dungeon. A Sir to beautiful, intelligent, and submissive women who enjoy being called names while I'm fucking them.

In their humiliation, I command them what to do, while spitting out taunts at them. You'd be surprised how many get off on it. As if being called beautiful was wrong. In this world etched with darkness, that's where I find comfort. It's where I'm most myself. Where I'm allowed to let go of life's stresses, to see things in a completely different way.

Where I revel and play with my demons, other's shy away from their true, animalistic needs.

I've currently got a raven-haired beauty on her knees before me. She's being watched by three other dominant men while she kisses my shoes in exchange for an orgasm. I can tell she's needy because her breaths are ragged and I can smell her arousal. It drenches the room in a scent so intoxicating, the men watching have their dicks out, stroking themselves to the slave on her knees.

Like darkness feeds and preys on my soul, I do the same with curvaceous beauties. "Up, on your back. Open your legs as far as they will go," I command, my voice raspy with lust.

Her real name is Kristine, but in this dungeon, where devils come to play, she's called Fuck Toy. It's written on her stomach, just above her belly button.

Her smooth-shaven cunt is bared to me, the soft pink flesh glistening. Picking up the champagne glass I brought into the dungeon only moments ago, I drizzle the contents over her mound, watching the clear, bubbly liquid drip down her folds.

"Please, Sir Nate," she begs.

They all plead at one time or another. Her thighs are trembling. Her big green eyes peek at me with unabashed need. I pick up the scrap of material she was wearing, a thong, pink and girly, yet there's nothing innocent about her. Kneeling at her cunt, I push the silk into her hole, fucking it into her like I would my cock. Her moans skyrocket through the room. The desire, lust, and darkness is palpable. A living breathing entity joining us in our depravity's.

I glance at the men. They're edging, bringing themselves to edge of orgasm to make their lust last. They're in awe of the woman who's allowing me to degrade her. "Come on your panties. Soak them," I grunt before clamping her clit with the metal teeth attached to a slinky chain, which is connected to the clamps on her nipples. She screeches in pleasure, pain, I don't fucking care. All I know is that I need to be inside her. "You love being a slut, don't you?" I ask, but all I hear are her moans and whimpers. The sounds vibrate through her and she shudders.

The three men to my left grunt as they find their own releases. I move to her mouth, gripping my thick cock in my fist and slamming it down her throat, gagging her.

"That's a good whore," I growl as my own release shoots through me. And like any good slave, she swallows every damn drop.

Keep reading about Nate by clicking here!

Already been to Seven Sins? Why not check out Fragile Innocence, a dark ménage romance.

Keep reading for an excerpt of Fragile Innocence

SNEAK PEEK - FRAGILE INNOCENCE

PROLOGUE - ELLA

Experiences define us. Memories taunt us. Dreams remind us.

Mine are dark, vicious, and demanding.

They've pulled and tugged at me, dragging me into crippling sadness.

Dreams, nightmares, images of what happened, of who I became.

The reality of my past has shaped me, molded me with its vicious claws.

When you're a child you're taught about the boogie man. The monster beneath your bed, the one hiding in the dark corner of your closet. But they're all just stories. They're tales made up to scare us.

Aren't they?

Not for me because I've met the monster. I came face-to-face with evil.

He, however, didn't lurk under my bed. Or in the recesses of my imagination.

And it was in the shroud of darkness that my soul was ripped from me. When all I knew was taken and I was left a shell of a girl.

I no longer believed in fairy tales.

The day I turned sixteen I learned the devil lurked in plain sight. And for two years, I had no way of escaping the clutches of the man I once trusted.

The scars are not external, but internal, and they haunt me when I close my eyes, leaving me crippled and damaged, and there's nothing I can do about it.

The memories of those years plague me on a daily basis. Like a horror movie playing out on a film reel. He violated me, stole my mind, and tainted every cell in my body. Wicked, vile images of when innocence was wretched from me violently, leaving me what he always called me—a broken girl.

I GLANCE OUT THE WINDOW AND GAZE AT THE STARS TWINKLING IN the night sky. As it always does when I'm lying in bed, the memory comes to me unbidden, unwanted, and it pains me as if I've cut myself and I'm bleeding out onto the pristine sheets.

Two weeks ago my life changed forever. When the girl I was became a stranger. The birthday party my mother held for me was beautiful. She went all out with a cake, decorations, and all the kids from my grade were invited.

What made me happiest was the fact my stepfather was home late from work. I didn't want him there, but I could tell Mom was angry—even though she put on a smile for me.

I noticed the ongoing fights, the bruises, and marks on her arms and legs.

They got married two years after my father passed away and even though most kids would think their mother was replacing their dad, I didn't. She looked happy again, so I accepted him. Our new family.

He was amazing, friendly, and polite. When he took us on trips it felt like we were a real family, but something changed and it was only after the night of my birthday I realized what it was.

I was the problem.

It was my fault.

At least, that's what he tells me.

I had noticed the change in him in those weeks leading up to my birthday. He stopped hiding the way he looked at me. Or the way his hand would brush against me and I could feel his disgusting drunken glare on me, especially when I wore my gym shorts.

When he's been at the bar and comes home late, those are the days he hurts her. I don't know why she doesn't take me and leave. Even though I've mentioned it when he wasn't around, she laughed it off and told me to go do my homework, or that I didn't understand.

I did, though.

I hate when they have those arguments that turn into bruises and cuts. I hide in my room, curled up, trying to drown out the noise. After the first night, I made the promise to myself to get out.

Once I'm eighteen, I'll be free.

Rolling over, I glance out of my bedroom window. It's almost midnight. The full moon bathes me in its blue light and the stars twinkle in the inky sky. I used to love the dark, when everything is calm and quiet, but now it brings my nightmares. The sound of the lock has my ears pricking and I glance at the bedroom door, realizing too late that he's used his own key.

The door cracks and the large, formidable bulk watches me from the entrance of my bedroom. I want to scream, but no one will hear me. Mom passed out again. She told me she had a migraine, but I knew she was drunk.

I'm not stupid. The foul smelling liquor wafted from her like a sickly perfume.

I watch him walk into the room and shut the door behind him. Only when the lock clicks does my body start trembling with fear. I want to be stronger, to fight back, but then he only hurts me more.

I used to hear stories about men like him, sick monsters who lurk in the dark waiting, watching.

My heart thunders in my chest and there's a lump in my throat threatening to choke me. My mouth opens, but no words come.

"Hello, little snowflake," he slurs, and I know why he didn't come home for dinner. The bar down the road must have been more inviting. He trudges toward me with a sway in his step. He's drunk again.

The man I used to trust, who used to care for me, is now the monster in my nightmares. He's the one who makes me cry.

"Answer me!" His gruff tone is enough to make me puke, but I swallow down the acidic bile and close my eyes.

"Please, don't do this again." My whimper annoys me because I want to sound stronger. I want to make sure he knows I hate him, but I'm afraid and the fear makes me weak.

"I'll fucking do what I want since your frigid bitch of a mother is passed out again. She doesn't let me touch her

anymore, but you can make me happy." My stepfather turns to my window, tugging the blinds closed.

They say the strongest people are the ones who cry behind closed doors. Maybe that's me. Maybe I'm strong. The cotton sheet that was covering me gets ripped away and the cool breeze that sweeps over my body sends a shiver through me.

"My sweet girl, a fragile snowflake. I won't hurt you. I know you like to feel how much I love you. You're my temptation."

The sinister smirk that curls his cracked lips has revulsion crawling over my skin.

"Our little secret. You won't tell your mother because you know what you are. You're a whore. And you know she'll see you that way. She'll throw you out of this house so fast your head will spin. You'll never find someone to love you and you know why? Because you're broken and tainted. By me."

The demented chuckle echoes through my room and that's when the tears spill.

I'm strong. I'm strong. I'm strong. *I chant in my head, hoping the words will one day ring true.*

"Don't do this, please." Begging does nothing to stop him, but I ask anyway, hoping he'll see the error of his ways.

Rough, calloused hands stroke my legs and I want to crawl inside myself. I want to hide from him, from my mother, from the world. "Open your fucking legs." Without waiting for me to move, he forces my thighs apart. His heavy bulk now presses my body into the mattress. My eyes are shut so tight I can see white behind my lids. "That's it, you feel that? Feel how happy you make me." His erection painfully presses against my core.

The pain is coming. The pain is coming. The pain is coming.

I get a small reprieve when he sits up to pull my shorts down along with my panties. Then suddenly I'm pinned down and he's driving into my body. His big, rough hand over my mouth muffles my scream at the searing pain that shoots through me as he takes my body. The same way he did the first night when he took the one thing I held onto—my innocence.

I am strong. I am strong. I am strong.

There are memories that bind us, memories that free us, and memories that destroy us.

I've been destroyed for too long.

I severed myself from friends, family, and even love because I couldn't be near anyone. I couldn't bring myself to smile and act like life was perfect when it so clearly wasn't. When my soul was carved out, held in the hand of a man I grew to love.

A man I grew to trust.

Can Ella heal from the past? Click here to grab Fragile Innocence!

Have you already met Ella and her Princes? Need something just as steamy? Why not try my Forbidden Series! But be warned, this one is HOT!

Keep reading for an excerpt of From the Ashes...

SNEAK PEEK - FROM THE ASHES

PROLOGUE - SKYLA

The lights are focused on us as we finish up our routine. The stages are in the center of a large lounge area and every man's eyes are glued to the two of us. We've become somewhat of a team. Men love my red hair and her chestnut locks. Her hazel eyes and my emerald pools seem to hypnotize them.

There are two platforms, mine which is off to the left has one sleek, silver pole, and to the right Dakota's has a chair, which she's currently leaning on as the song ends. Her long, slender legs shimmer with the glitter she brushed on earlier.

Inferno.

The nightclub that's given me a sanctuary from my past. An elite club with only the richest of clientele. They pay an exorbitant fee to see me wrap my legs around a metal pole. They watch me and the girls, sway and gyrate, wearing slinky outfits. They beg us to taunt them.

For the more exclusive clients, there's a menu if they'd like more than just a dance. When they request something from that sleek silver card, we're at their beck and call.

From where I'm positioned backstage, I notice Dax, my boss, and Axel, the head of security—the only two men I trust since leaving the hell I came from—stalking toward the bar. They've been good to me and the other girls who work for them.

"Skyla,"—Dakota's melodic voice drags me from my daydreams of another life—"orders up!" she quips, with a smile so bright it lights up her face. I know what she means, two clients requested us. The VIP package in this place means men can ask for any girl to join them in a private room, and if they pay the premium, they get to fuck us, and it seems tonight Kota—which is her stage name—and I will be entertaining someone.

I follow my best friend down the hallway. "Which room are we in?"

She glances at the card that Theia gave her and responds over her shoulder. "The Raven Room, looks like we have two men to dance for tonight." This room is mine—well, it's my favorite. With muted colors and a beautiful pole in the center, I feel as if they made it for me.

Upon entering we find the clients already seated in the onyx wingback chairs. They're both older, possibly mid-forties. One of them has a thick gold band on his ring finger, glimmering under the low lights coming from the ceiling.

"What can we do for you gentlemen today?" I stop only a few feet from them, my red panties and bra leave little to the imagination. Dakota heads to the pole, twirling around it hypnotically. I've been teaching her some moves and she's picking them up quickly.

"I'm Travis. This is Rich. He wants to watch, doesn't want to

cheat on his wife," the one with salt-and-pepper hair says, gesturing to his friend. I almost laugh at that. Of course he doesn't. "I, on the other hand, would love to control you and your little friend," he quips, and I nod in understanding.

"You want a dirty show?" I question, meeting the steel gray eyes of Rich. His dark brown hair is just graying at the sides. He nods. No fucking shame. "Fine, make yourselves comfortable."

Since I've been at Inferno, Dakota's one of the girls I've grown close to, the other is our hostess, Theia. They've both been an incredible support after the horrors I faced. They're both honest to a fault, and love me even in my self-loathing moments.

I think we do that for each other.

After my escape from Caged with the help of Dax, I've gotten attached to my makeshift family. Now, here in the Big Apple, a year into our friendship, we're like sisters.

Dakota's dressed in a skimpy, blue baby doll negligee, which is so short and see through, it's pretty pointless. She might as well be naked. She gives me that sexy little pout that drives her clients crazy. Raising my finger, I crook it to call her over. When I turn back to the men, I find both clients are now shirtless, and for older men, they're toned in all the right places.

Without a word, Dakota heads toward me. Her tits bounce with every step and their eyes are glued to her. "This here is Kota, boys, and I'm Skyla." Two sets of eyes flit between us with eagerness. "Kitten, why don't you show these gentlemen how sweet you can be."

I reach for her arm and tug her against me. My chest against her back. We're standing in front of Travis as I reach for her tits, groping them, tugging and tweaking her pebbled buds.

"Isn't she pretty boys?" Rich is fixated on our display. My one hand travels down her flat stomach to find her bare little pussy.

"Open your legs, K," she does and my fingers slip in easily. She's already wet and we've only just begun. I plunge two fingers into her, pumping them in and out. Her soft moans are the only sound in the room, until I hear the hiss of one zipper, then a second.

When I look at our audience, they've both got their dicks in their fists. Rich is smaller and not as thick, but the one who gets to play must easily be ten inches. That's going to hurt like a motherfucker. Pulling my fingers from her, I reach out to Travis. "Taste her," I murmur. He moves quickly, taking my fingers in his mouth and licking the sticky sweet juice from them.

"Fuck, that's delicious." He growls, then rises from the chair with his hungry gaze trained on us and shoves off the rest of his clothes. "I'm taking charge now. You're both going to lie down and obey." We don't argue because he doesn't look like he's joking.

His expression is something akin to someone who just hit the fucking jackpot. With two incredibly beautiful women doing as you wish, no man in his right mind could resist.

"Go sit on her face, pet. I think she needs to get a taste," he orders Dakota in a deep and rough tone. "Toys?" He turns to me, and I gesture to the chest of drawers. I know what he wants and he'll find them all in there. He pulls out the four thick leather cuffs and turns to the bed.

I lie back, watching him gawk as Kota's pert ass wiggles as she climbs on the bed. Rich is in awe staring at us as he strokes himself. She straddles my face and I immediately grip her hips, holding her against my mouth.

My tongue darts out, licking her smooth lips, tasting the sweetness of her honey. The moans that escape her are feral and sexy. The sound of sex is in the air and the scent of K's sweet little cunt has me salivating.

"Enough." The word rumbles between us. Her eyes are glazed as she glares at Travis. I know she was close, wet and primed. "Lie down, sweetheart. We'll make you feel better." We swap positions, and he goes to work using the cuffs to bind her to the bed. Her legs are spread wide and her arms are locked in place. No escaping now, little one.

She watches me and I offer a wink.

"I need to come, please?" she begs, but he ignores her.

"Soon," I whisper. Her plump lips part with a moan when he tugs on her nipple. Grabbing the ten-inch dildo, he joins us on the bed, and in my peripheral, I notice Rich has moved closer.

"First we're going to devour you." Travis's tone is filled with need. He hands me the clamps and I nod. He doesn't need any motivation. Leaning in, he licks and sucks her sweet flesh.

Her nipples are peaks and I set to work laving and teasing them. Once I've got them both wet, I use the metal clamps—which are attached to a thin metal chain—securing them to each taut bud.

Her soft mewls are evidence that she's aching for her orgasm. I've learned over the year that she's very much a little masochist. She thrives on pain and this has put her in her element. "Oh, please, please?" she pleads, and I almost feel sorry for her, but he's in charge. He reaches for the third clamp from my hand—the one I haven't yet used—and stares at her pretty eyes.

"Now," he orders, and pinches her clit with the metal teeth. Her body convulses and Travis's face is soaked in her release. "Good girl, so fucking sweet." He murmurs and licks every drop she's given him. His cock is rigid between his legs. With a quick glance at me, he commands in a deep tone, "I want you on her face while I fuck her." He grips his cock and I watch him rip the foil packet. "Sit on her face," he growls as he sheaths himself. I shift myself and straddle Dakota's pretty face. "Eat her cunt *while I fuck you, little toy." I'm hovering over her mouth, and when her tongue darts out, it sends me spiraling. I grip the headboard and hold myself steady when I feel her sucking my hardened clit into her mouth. The pleasure shoots through my body, igniting my blood with a fire that races through my veins and I'm overcome with lust.*

Her body is shoved up every time he thrusts into her, which in turn has my body convulsing without thought and my release detonates, bursting through me as I cry out.

"What a beautiful fucking sight," he murmurs, in awe of me and my best friend. "Get off her face. We're both going to fuck her." On wobbly legs, I move off Kota, her face glistening with my arousal. He slips out of her and I help untie her. "I want you on your back." He points at me, then turns to her. "You, little doll, will ride that plastic cock while I own your tight ass." Rich is now standing at the bed. His body is tense as his hand moves slowly over his erection.

I lie back, donning the strap-on with Dakota on all fours over me. Her gasp as she sinks down on the dildo is a loud one. It's thick and I know it's filling her almost painfully. Pulling her over me, I watch her face contort as her puckered entrance is invaded by another solid intrusion. "Oh fuck, it's too much." Her whimper is soft and her eyes roll back in her head.

I latch on to her nipple, tugging the clamp with my teeth. I know the chain in turn tugs her clit and her body is now sandwiched between Travis and me. Suddenly, I feel the strap between my legs shifting and a dildo being teased into my pussy. Rich pushes it deeper. It's too much, too soon, when he starts fucking me with it.

We move in a rhythm that has fireworks shooting off behind my eyelids. My body convulses and spasms with the plastic cock inside me. When Travis hisses and spanks Dakota, her cries, his growl, and my own moans send me over and my orgasm grips me, sending me into outer-fucking-space.

CLICK HERE TO KEEP READING!

ALSO BY DANI RENÉ

Click here for a full list of Dani René's incredible titles

ABOUT THE AUTHOR

Dani is a *USA Today* Bestselling Author of seductive and deviant romance.

Her books range from the dark to emotional, but every hero is alpha, and each heroine is strong-willed, bringing the men down to their knees.

She now lives in the UK, after moving from Cape Town, with her better half who does all the cooking while she writes all the words.

When she's not writing, she can be found binge-watching the latest TV series, or working on graphic design. She has a healthy addiction to reading, tattoos, coffee, and ice cream.

www.danirene.com | info@danirene.com | *Spotify*

My exclusive reader group gets news on all up and coming releases, sales, and a chance at early ARC copy giveaways! Join us, we don't bite... hard ;)

Dani's Deviants

Printed in Great Britain
by Amazon